It would have been the easiest thing to simply put a bullet in Matt Slaughter's back. P. D. would have preferred to do it that way, but Mathis had offered an extra two hundred and fifty dollars if Slaughter was brought back to stand trial.

"Slaughter!" P. D. called out. "If you leave that rifle . . . and come out peaceful-like, we won't kill you."

"Where's Molly?"

"I got her safe and sound, waitin' for you."

"Who the hell are you?" Matt asked.

"I'm the one come to take you back to Virginia. I always get who I go after. The only choice you have to make is whether you go back sittin' in the saddle or belly-down across it."

"If you show me the girl, I'll come out."

"Dammit, I told you she ain't here," P. D. replied heatedly. *I shoulda just shot him in the leg while I had the chance.* "I ain't got all day. You come on outta there now, or I'm gonna hafta burn you out."

"I reckon you're gonna have to come and get me."

VENGEANCE MOON

Charles G. West

BERKLEY
New York

BERKLEY
An imprint of Penguin Random House LLC
penguinrandomhouse.com

Copyright © 2007 by Charles G. West
Penguin Random House supports copyright. Copyright fuels creativity, encourages
diverse voices, promotes free speech, and creates a vibrant culture. Thank you for buying
an authorized edition of this book and for complying with copyright laws by not
reproducing, scanning, or distributing any part of it in any form without permission.
You are supporting writers and allowing Penguin Random House to continue to
publish books for every reader.

BERKLEY and the BERKLEY & B colophon are registered
trademarks of Penguin Random House LLC.

ISBN: 9780593441480

Signet mass-market edition / January 2007
Berkley mass-market edition / October 2022

Printed in the United States of America
1 3 5 7 9 10 8 6 4 2

For Ronda

Chapter I

All he had was a name, P. D. Wildmoon, and a post office box where this person might be reached in Cheyenne, Dakota Territory. Jonathan Mathis was aware that the person he traveled to meet recognized no line between lawful and lawless activity. This fact did not overly concern him, for as a successful criminal attorney in Springfield, Missouri, he had dealt with any number of men of the most evil convictions. Two years of frustrating dealings with regional provost marshals in Virginia and the Dakota Territory had hammered home one cold, hard fact that Jonathan Mathis could not accept. As far as the army was concerned, Matthew Scott Slaughter was going to get away with the murder of Jonathan's brother.

The thought of his brother's murder brought the bitter taste of bile to his throat. He had been duly proud of his younger brother's successful rise to the rank of captain in the Union Army. His death had been hard to accept. Harvey had survived two years in the war only to lose his life after the fighting was over—murdered by a wild young Rebel over a land dispute. Especially galling was the army's seeming disinterest after this man, Slaughter, fled to the West.

To add to his frustration with the army's incompetence, Mathis had learned that the fugitive had actually been in custody in the post hospital at Fort Laramie, and was allowed to escape. Nothing more had been seen or heard of Slaughter for over a year, but Mathis refused to abandon his quest for justice for the murder of his only brother.

Riding now on the train as it pulled into the newly built station in Cheyenne, he took out a piece of paper, unfolded it, and stared again at the name at the bottom. P. D. Wildmoon it was signed, at the end of a short, childish scrawl that informed him that the sender of the letter would be in *Shianne* on the fifteenth of the month and could be reached at Cassidy's Saloon. Mathis could only imagine the manner of man he was on his way to meet. He knew nothing about him other than the fact that Wildmoon was a name well-known in the murky shadows outside the law, in the dark world of bushwhackers and bounty hunters. The name had been given to him by a sympathetic lieutenant in the regional provost marshal's office in Omaha, along with a word of caution. "Don't say I gave you the name," he had said. "There's not much difference between Wildmoon and an outlaw. But if you've got any chance of finding Slaughter in that country out there, Wildmoon's your best bet."

Mathis remained seated until the train rolled to a complete stop. He gazed out the window at the sprawling town created by the arrival of the Union Pacific Railroad. He was a day early for his appointment with P. D. Wildmoon and, from his first impression of the wild frontier town, he already regretted the necessity of having to stay there for two nights before being able to take a train back to civilization. Resigned to his self-imposed task, he pulled his suitcase from under the seat and stepped down onto the station platform.

"Cassidy's?" the operator in the telegraph office responded. He took a moment to eye the rather distinguished-looking gentleman asking for directions. Dressed in a business suit of obvious eastern fashion, he didn't look the part of one of Cassidy's patrons. Finally the telegrapher replied, "Cassidy's Saloon is down at the far end of Front Street, next to the stables." He felt compelled to warn the stranger, "None of my business, sir, but if you're wanting a drink, there's another saloon in Cheyenne that might suit you better. If you're looking for a place to stay, Cassidy has a few rooms upstairs, but I'd recommend you try the hotel instead."

"I appreciate the information," Mathis said. "Where is the hotel?"

The operator walked outside with him and pointed out the Railroad Hotel. Mathis thanked him and departed the train station.

The following morning found Mathis taking his time over breakfast in the hotel dining room. There had been no time of day specified for his meeting with Wildmoon, but he felt pretty confident that it would be a waste of his time to look for him in the saloon this early in the morning. So the rest of the morning, until noon, was spent killing time, talking to the desk clerk, reading a legal brief he had brought to work on, and taking a short walk down the main street to locate Cassidy's. After a noon meal at the hotel, he walked down to the saloon again.

Though still early in the day, the saloon was already half filled with patrons. Mathis could see right away why the telegraph operator had seen fit to advise him against Cassidy's. It was obviously a gathering place for the less genteel folk of Cheyenne. Mathis felt a slight shiver race down his spine as he stepped inside the door. Feeling as out of place as if he had entered hell's waiting room, he walked straight to the bar under the gaze of a sea of curious eyes.

"I'm looking for P. D. Wildmoon," he said to the bartender.

The bartender, a stubby-bearded man wearing a filthy apron, took a moment to study the stranger before answering in a bored tone. "That's P. D. and the boys yonder," he said, nodding toward a table in the back corner of the room.

Mathis turned his head to follow the direction indicated. At the very back of the saloon, a group of four dusty individuals sat around a table. By the collection of empty beer mugs corralled in the center of the table, he reasoned that he could have come earlier after all. He thanked the bartender and walked to the table. Focusing his gaze on the obviously eldest member of the group, and the only one clean-shaven, he inquired, "Mr. Wildmoon?"

All went quiet at the table. The person addressed looked up, fixing Mathis with a dull stare for a long moment before shifting her gaze to look him up and down. "Missus Wildmoon," she then replied evenly. "You'd be Mr. Mathis?"

Taken aback, he could not disguise his surprise. After the initial shock, he recovered briefly, only to feel a slight tinge of irritation in discovering that he might have traveled halfway across the country to find that P. D. Wildmoon was in fact a woman. Surely this was not the case. Taking a closer look, he could understand why he had taken her for a man, and a hard-looking one at that. Thinking that, surely, one of the other three must be the man he was there to meet, he answered, "I'm Mathis. Where is *Mister* Wildmoon?"

His question brought grins to the faces of the three younger men. "There ain't no Mr. Wildmoon," the woman replied. "I'm P. D. Wildmoon, the one you come to see. These here is my boys: Arlo, Bo, and Wiley." She nodded toward the young man seated on her left. "Wiley, pull up another chair so's the gentleman can set down."

Mathis was perplexed at that moment, undecided as to whether he should bother wasting time with the woman and her sons, or just do an about-face and leave. He wondered if the lieutenant back in Omaha knew P. D. Wildmoon was a woman, and if he did, why he hadn't told him so. He hesitated long enough

for his decision to be made for him when Wiley
dragged a chair from the next table and shoved it
against the back of the lawyer's knees, leaving him
no choice but to sit. "Charley," P. D. yelled, "bring the
gent some beer." Turning her attention back to Mathis
then, she said, "Let's talk business."

In his law practice, Jonathan Mathis had defended
some despicable individuals, but he could not recall
having confronted a more vile collection of degener-
ates than the three men grinning at him at this table.
The one introduced as Arlo was a rough-edged brute
of a man. His brothers, though not as imposing phys-
ically, appeared to be cut from the same rough stock.
The younger one, Wiley, seemed to be permanently
fixed with an openmouthed, vacant stare. Mathis
would have taken him for a moron.

Glancing around at the general clientele in the saloon, he began to worry that he had stumbled into a
den of rattlesnakes. He also worried that to suddenly
withdraw might cause him some discomfort. There
was a slight distraction when the bartender set a mug
of beer down before him, hard enough to cause a
good portion of it to spill on the table. As one, the
three sons looked in their mother's direction expec-
tantly. She dismissed their inquiry with a simple
shake of her head. Obviously disappointed, they sat
back to ponder their empty mugs.

Resigning himself to the task, he finally voiced
what was troubling him. "Uh, Mrs. Wildmoon," he
began.

"P. D.," she corrected.

"P. D.," he amended. She smiled patiently then and nodded, exposing a wide gap where her two front teeth had once been. He continued, "When I wrote you, I just naturally assumed I was contracting with a man—a bounty hunter, I was told. I'm not sure you understand the nature of the job I have in mind."

If she was offended, she did not show it. Rather, she nodded as if understanding his confusion, doubtless having faced the situation before. "I understand what you want," she said. "You want a man tracked down. That's what I do. I catch them what can't be caught by your prissy soldiers and lawmen." She nodded toward her three sons. "These boys is like a pack of hounds. I raised 'em that way. When we get on a scent, cold trail or no trail, we run 'em to ground, sure as bears shit and briars don't. All I need to know is whether to catch 'em or kill 'em. If the money's all the same, I'd just as soon kill 'em—less trouble. I guarantee proof of the job—anything you want, the head or any other parts." She leaned back in her chair then, waiting for his response.

He was too dumbfounded to reply at once, continuing to sit there staring at the committee of self-proclaimed scavengers, totally aghast when confronting such callous disregard for human life. His gaze darted from one villainous face to the next, settling upon that of the matriarch. Looking into the cruel eyes of the pudgy-faced woman with stray wisps of graying hair protruding from under a Montana Peak hat that framed deep ruts across a weathered forehead, he was struck with the realization that she was fully capable of doing everything she claimed. At that moment, he almost wished he had never undertaken his mission. But then he reminded himself of the shocking death of his only brother, shot down while performing his duty in a small Virginia town, and he made his decision. "How much are we talking about?"

"Depends," P. D. shot back. "*Who* we talkin' about? And where do me and the boys have to go to get him?"

Mathis laid out the history of events, as he had learned them, starting from young Matt Slaughter's flight from Virginia. Then came his appearance at Fort Laramie, his time as a scout for the army before they learned he was a fugitive, and finally his escape from the authorities at Fort Laramie. "He's supposed to have spent a good deal of time living in the Powder River country. The people I've talked to at Fort Laramie seem to think he could be anywhere between there and Virginia City."

"Powder River country," P. D. repeated. "That's pretty hot country right now. There's a damn war goin' on with the Sioux and Cheyenne. I expect that's the main reason the army ain't interested in findin' your man. They ain't got the time. There's fightin' all along the Bozeman Trail."

"Are you saying it's too dangerous to go after Slaughter now?"

"Oh, it's dangerous all right. But it ain't enough to stop me and my boys. I reckon we've kilt our share of Injuns. Bo, there, has a scalp string he's right fond of." The son named Bo, who was at that moment absentmindedly occupied with the excavation of his nose with a grimy forefinger, was distracted long enough to smile at Mathis. "No, we ain't a'feared to track him in that country," P. D. continued, raising one eyebrow as she summed it up. "It'll just cost a little more, that's all."

"How much?"

"If this varmint is hidin' out in the mountains," she answered, continuing to justify her price, "we might be trackin' him for three or four months." She grimaced as if thinking hard. "We're gonna need a lot of supplies."

"How much?" Mathis repeated.

She shook her head, still concentrating, reluctant to throw the figure out, trying to judge what her client might bear. Finally, she responded, "Two thousand dollars."

"Fifteen hundred," he countered.

"Done," she immediately responded. "Half now, and half when we get the job done."

"Five hundred now," he shot back, realizing that he could have gotten her cheaper.

She sat back again and shook her head in mock exasperation. "Damn, mister, I hope your underdrawers ain't as tight as your purse strings." She waited a second while her sons laughed at her comment. "All right, then, five hundred now." She got back to business then. "Tell me ever'thin' you can about this polecat."

Mathis shrugged. "I've told you pretty much all I

know." He remembered one more thing. "When he escaped from Fort Laramie, he was traveling with a woman and an old trapper."

P. D. cocked her head up at that. "Wait a minute! You didn't say nothin' about him havin' two people with him."

Mathis was quick to counter any notions she might have for an added fee. "A young girl who can't speak and an old man," he insisted. "No need for concern."

She thought about that for a moment before dismissing it. Then her curiosity prompted her. "Whaddaya mean, a young girl who can't speak?"

Mathis shrugged then. "Can't speak. She's a mute. That's what I was told. She shouldn't be any worry for you." He thought about it a moment before suggesting, "She might make it easier to find Slaughter."

"Might at that," P. D. agreed, nodding her head. "All right, then, this feller Slaughter's a dead man." She extended her hand, and Mathis took it.

He thought about the deal he had just made, and changed his mind. "I'd like to try Slaughter in a court of law, and then see him hang." P. D. shrugged, frowning. Obviously it was not her preference. "I'll pay you two hundred and fifty extra if you bring him in alive."

This changed things. "Does it matter what kinda shape he's in," P. D. asked, "long as he's breathin'?"

"Just as long as he can understand what's happening to him," Mathis replied. "When can you get started?"

"As soon as I get that five hundred," she replied.

Mathis got up from his chair. "The money is in the hotel safe. If you could go with me . . ." The picture of the swarthy-looking woman accompanying him back to the hotel came to his mind then. "Or I could just go and get the money, and bring it back here."

"Arlo can go with you, and you can give it to him," P. D. said, much to his relief.

"Fine, we'll do that," Mathis said. "I'll also give him a card with instructions on how to telegraph me." He stood back while she got to her feet. "I hope I'll be hearing from you soon."

"We'll be headin' out in the mornin' for Fort Laramie," she said. "I figure that's the best place to start."

He took one last look at her before departing, wondering if he was about to throw five hundred dollars away. As if she could read his thoughts, she gave him a broad, gap-toothed smile as reassurance. Dressed in men's clothing and knee-high boots, she presented a solid picture that would remain vivid in his mind. With a .44 revolver strapped around her ample girth and a rawhide horse whip in her hand, she stood watching confidently as he and Arlo walked out the door. Behind her, her other two sons remained seated, watching them depart, like two young vultures waiting in the nest for mama to return with food.

Heading due north out of Cheyenne, P. D. led her three sons toward Fort Laramie. It figured to take two full days' ride, so she departed the town at sunup. Arlo, her eldest, rode directly behind his mother, with

Wiley directly behind him. Bo lagged farther behind, still grousing to himself about having to arise so early. Of the three Wildmoon men, Bo was the maverick, a role he seemed to enjoy.

Hoping to gain information on the whereabouts of Matt Slaughter, P. D. was disappointed upon reaching Fort Laramie. Figuring that the post trader's store was the most likely place to get information on her prey, the sutler's was the first stop.

Seth Ward glanced up when the four entered his store. He paused to take a longer look before greeting them. "Well, P. D. Wildmoon," he finally acknowledged, with no hint of cordiality. "I ain't seen you and your boys around here for a spell."

"Reckon not," P. D. responded.

"What poor soul is unlucky enough to have you on his trail?"

P. D. smiled, pleased to have a reputation precede her, and indifferent to the fact that it was one without respect. She ignored Seth's sarcastic tone. "I'm lookin' for a feller name of Matt Slaughter," she replied. "Know him?"

Seth paused for a long moment before answering. He knew Matt Slaughter, counted him as a friend, and even if he didn't, he would be reluctant to give the likes of P. D. Wildmoon any information that would help her find him. After a few more moments of silence, he answered, "I know him. A lot of folks around here know him, but he's long gone from these parts."

"I expect I know that," P. D. replied, "but I figured

you might know where he headed when he left Fort Laramie."

"Hell, who knows? He didn't exactly leave no for-wardin' address," Seth snorted. "Why don't you go ask at the post adjutant's office? They're the folks who let him get away."

P. D. didn't reply at once, responding only with a sarcastic smile. He knew the army had no liking for P. D. and her kind. She was well aware of the fact. "I don't expect I'd get much help from them soldier boys," she said. "I figured you might tell me more about him." She waited for a few seconds for his reply. When he merely shrugged his shoulders, she added, "We're just doin' a job. The man's wanted in Virginia for murder."

"Yeah, that's what they say," Seth replied, "but I ain't so sure." He shrugged again. "Anyway, it was a while ago he left here. I don't expect he's anywhere in this part of the country." Seth had known Matt Slaughter for a brief time, but in that time he had come to believe that the Matt Slaughter he knew could not have shot someone down in cold blood un-less the shooting was justified.

P. D. was not willing to accept it at that. She had a suspicion that the post trader knew more than he was willing to share. She glanced behind her at her three sons, standing idly by like so many dumb cows in a pasture. "We're gonna find him. It's just a matter of when." Seeing that she was wasting her time with Seth, she tilted her head toward the door. "Let's go, boys. Can't ever'body on this post be a friend of that murderin' son of a bitch."

P. D. lingered in the store only long enough to let her boys have a glass of beer. Leaving the sutler's, she next went to the post stables to inquire about the possibility of leaving the horses there overnight. Informed at the stables that they had no arrangements for boarding civilian horses, she asked if there was a stable that did. A young private on stable duty walked outside with her to point out the direction to a stable in the nearby settlement.

"You fellers just passin' through?" Private Adams asked, making conversation and, like most everyone else, not realizing P. D. was a woman.

"That's a fact," P. D. answered. "We're tryin' to find a cousin of mine from back east. All we know is he passed this way."

"Is that so?" Adams replied. "What was his name?"

"Slaughter," P. D. answered. "Matt Slaughter. He was my sister's oldest boy, and we'd dearly love to find him." There was a noticeable widening of the soldier's eyes, so she asked, "Did you know him?"

"I didn't rightly know him, but I heard about him. Hell, ever'body did." Adams hesitated then, uncertain if he should say more, since these folks claimed to be kin of Slaughter's. He glanced up at the three men sitting their saddles, all looking back at him with identical blank stares.

Sensing his hesitation, P. D. sought to encourage him to go on. "Ever'body in the family knows about

Cousin Matt's wild ways. Why, I believe I heard that he was under guard here, but busted out." She shook her head, seeming to laugh at the picture forming in her mind. "He always was a wild one, that Matt." She glanced up in time to catch Wiley about to say something. She cut him off with a frown and a shake of her head.

Private Adams grinned then. "I reckon so," he said. "They had a guard on him in the hospital, but he broke out. Lieutenant O'Connor caught him right here at the stables. He thought he had him cornered. Slaughter and Zeb Benson rode off and left O'Connor hangin' in a tree back of the stables." Adams had a good chuckle as he thought about the lieutenant dangling from a tree limb.

"That sounds like somethin' ol' Slaughter would do, all right," P. D. said, joining in the laughter. "Reckon where he headed when he left here?"

"Virginia City, most likely," Adams said. "Folks that knew him said him and Zeb talked about them mountains beyond the Big Horns all the time."

P. D. and her sons rode out of Fort Laramie early the next morning, heading for Virginia City. Several attempts to gain additional information regarding the whereabouts of Matt Slaughter had been met with little success the night before. Private Adams had been the only one who even speculated where the fugitive might have gone. After giving it some thought, P. D. decided that it was a fifty-fifty shot that Adams might have guessed correctly. Virginia City was a reasonable place to look for an outlaw on the run. She would have preferred odds better than fifty-fifty, but she figured she had to start searching somewhere. Why not Virginia City? Her decision made, the main concern to be dealt with was the Sioux Indians. The recent government parlay with Red Cloud and his allies, the Cheyenne, had met with failure, and the Sioux leader had stormed out of the peace talks vowing to kill any white men trying to travel the Bozeman Trail across Sioux hunting grounds. While P. D. was confident she and her boys, all with repeating rifles, could handle a small hunting party, she was not willing to risk an encounter with a sizable war party. With that in mind, the Wildmoon family took a trail leading northwest along the North Platte, figuring to strike the Sweetwater and South Pass. It promised to be a hard ride to Virginia City, and the long way around, but there was a sizable payday at the other end.

Chapter 2

Hoping to make the trip to Virginia City in little more than two weeks' time, the bounty hunters rode free of trouble until skirting the southern end of the Big Horn Mountains. Crossing over wide-open prairies with rolling hills for most of that day, they were glad to see a small stream in the distance. After fifteen minutes or more, they entered the trees that lined the stream and let the horses drink. After horses and riders had their fill of the cool water, they were in the saddle again with Arlo taking the lead. He had not cleared the line of cottonwoods on the west side of the little stream when he suddenly pulled his horse to a stop. "Ma!" he called out, and pointed toward a long ridge on the northern slope of the valley.

P. D. pulled her horse up beside Arlo's. "Damn!" she uttered as she looked toward the ridge. "I wonder how long they've been watchin' us." Sitting impassively on the brow of the ridge, a line of thirty or more Sioux warriors watched the progress of the four white riders as they followed the valley west.

"What do you reckon they want?" Wiley asked.

Bo, never hesitating to remind his younger brother that he was the simpleminded member of the family, answered him, "Now what the hell do you think they want, dummy? They want that pretty head of hair you're wearin'."

"What they want is these rifles we're carryin'," P. D. said as she quickly surveyed the terrain around them. Looking directly ahead, she picked her spot. "I expect they're waitin' for us to come out in the open after we cross the stream." She pointed toward a pocket of trees near the base of the western slope. "If we can get to that bunch of pines on the other side of the clearin', we oughta be able to hold 'em off—maybe run 'em off for good if we can cut down a few of 'em." She pushed her horse up ahead of Arlo's. "You boys follow me. We'll take it nice and easy till we get clear of these trees. Then ride like hell for that pocket over yonder."

High on the ridge that formed the northern side of the valley, the Sioux war party waited, watching the trees for sign of the white men. Spotting a rider about to emerge into the open, then stop, Iron Claw, leader of the war party, signaled his warriors to wait. When the four white riders suddenly charged out of the trees at full gallop, he knew his warriors had been spotted. "After them," he shouted. Sweeping down the slope, the war party drove its ponies hard to cut off the white trespassers' escape.

It was a race, but P. D. and her sons managed to gain the angle on their pursuers and capture a sizable lead. Whipping her horse, calling for all the stallion could give her, P. D. rode low on his neck, calling out encouragement to her sons behind her. Seeing that they had lost their advantage, Iron Claw's warriors began shooting at the fleeing four, but to no avail. P. D. and her boys reached the safety of the pocket with lead flying harmlessly in the trees around them. While Bo and Wiley led the horses back into the trees where they would be safe, P. D. and Arlo took cover in a gully at the edge and began to return fire.

"By God, that slowed 'em down," P. D. exclaimed as she laid her front sight on a warrior riding a white pony and knocked him off the horse. Equally adept with a rifle, Arlo accounted for another warrior down. Wiley and Bo scrambled up beside them, their rifles searching for targets.

With two warriors killed, Iron Claw called his war party back out of range. Furious at having let the white men gain the cover of the wooded pocket, he drew back to decide on another plan. Two dead was already a higher price than he had intended to pay. With the rifle fire now coming from the gully, it was confirmed that all four had repeating rifles, and he was determined to have the weapons. "They have closed themselves up in a trap," Iron Claw said to one of his warriors, a man called Yellow Horn. "I'll take half the warriors and cross over the ridge, then circle above them on the slope. The rest of you can use the cover of the stream bank to work your way down in close to that gully."

Yellow Horn agreed. He could see that Iron Claw

would be able to shoot down from above the white men and drive them out in the open, where they would be picked off by him and the others.

Back in the shallow depression that served as their protection, P. D. had much the same thought. "Bo," she called out, "get on back there and see what kinda hole we landed in. Them devils might be able to get up behind us."

Bo did as he was told, crawling away from the gully and disappearing in the trees where the horses were tied. After a quarter of an hour, he returned to report. "We ain't in too good a spot. If they're smart enough to get up on that slope above us, they can make it pretty damn hot for us."

"Damn," P. D. swore. "I was afraid of that. Maybe they won't think of that."

"Ma," Wiley called out, "they're sneakin' down the crick, tryin' to get closer."

P. D. turned back to take a look for herself. Then she fired a couple of shots at a glimpse of buckskin, her bullets kicking up dirt on the stream bank. As near as she could tell, the war party didn't seem as big as before. "They've already split up," she decided. "Arlo, you and Bo drop back and find you a place to watch that slope behind us."

There was nothing they could do but wait until the Sioux made some move toward their position. Using the stream bank as cover, the warriors offered no opportunity for P. D. and Wiley to pick a target. "You boys keep your eyes peeled back there," P. D. yelled over her shoulder. More than a little angry at her poor choice of defensive positions, she was determined to make the assault costly for the Indians. In her own defense, she had to admit that there had been few choices in the short amount of time she was allotted to choose. "Make every shot count," she said to Wiley.

"If they ever give me somethin' to shoot at," Wiley complained in reply.

"They will," P. D. said. "They're just waitin' for the rest of their crowd to get above us."

To confirm P. D.'s prediction, several minutes later the short period of silence was blasted by a sudden barrage of rifle fire from the slope behind them. "Here they come!" P. D. exclaimed as Arlo and Bo opened up with their weapons. But Yellow Horn and his warriors remained concealed behind the banks of the stream. Behind her, the sound of a heavy exchange of shots told her that Arlo and Bo had their hands full. Worried that they might be overrun, and puzzled by the lack of fire from the Sioux at the stream, she sent Wiley back to help his brothers. "I can cut anybody down that shows his ass over that bank," she assured him.

It soon became apparent to P. D. why the warriors in the stream had remained quiet, as she spotted the appearance of a rifle barrel here and there. The Indians had been busy digging out firing pits. Within a few minutes after Wiley had retreated to help his brothers, the warriors before her began to deliver fire in her direction, kicking up dirt and gravel on either side of her. It was apparent that they did not have her position pinpointed, and she knew that as soon as she returned fire, they would have. "Well, this ol' gal is smarter'n that," she mumbled. Raising up slightly, she cranked out four quick shots, spraying the bank, then ducked down and scrambled several yards to her left. As she expected, the spot she had fired from was immediately peppered with rifle balls. She soon realized that the best she could expect to do was to hold them at bay, for it appeared they were not going to risk an all-out charge across the clearing.

On the slope behind her, the battle continued with no sign of letup from the attacking warriors. However, the momentum was gradually being gained by Iron Claw's warriors. "Gawdam!" Bo exclaimed when a rifle ball tore the bark off the tree trunk a scant few inches above his head. Lying as flat as he could manage, he pushed himself backward, looking for a better spot. Glancing to his right, he tried to see where Arlo was, realizing then that both Arlo and Wiley had already been forced back to find safer positions. "Arlo!" he called out.

"Over here!" his brother called back, some ten yards below him in the trees.

"You bastard," Bo yelled. "Why didn't you tell me you was droppin' back? Leavin' me here to hold 'em off by myself." Without further comment, he rolled over and, half crawling, half running, scrambled down the slope to join his brother. "Where's Wiley?" he blurted upon settling behind a pine trunk beside Arlo.

"Over here," Wiley answered, lying behind a small boulder a dozen yards to Arlo's right.

"You hit anythin'?" Arlo asked anxiously.

"Shit no," Bo came back. "The son of a bitches don't never show theirselves."

The three brothers tried to hold where they were but, as before, the hostile fire soon became too hot around them, forcing them back down to the bottom of the slope, almost backing up to P. D. Still trying to get a clear shot at one of the warriors in the stream, P. D. was alarmed to discover her sons had been pushed back from the slope. For the first time, she realized that there might not be a way out of the trap she had ridden into. It was obvious that the Sioux plan was to push the four of them out in the open where they would be easily cut down by the warriors by the stream. Fighting off a rage that was building up inside her, she was forced to concede defeat, furious that she was to cash in this way—cut down by a bunch of wild Indians. There was no choice but to take as many with her as possible. "Boys," she called back, her voice solemn as a preacher's, "you've got to hunker down and don't let 'em push you any further back down the mountain. If we let 'em drive us out in the open we're goners, sure as hell." The three young men took what cover they could, but were still trying to shoot at targets they could not see.

High up the mountain on a ledge below the tree line, a lone figure sat astride a paint pony, a silent observer of the skirmish taking place three hundred feet below him. Following an old game trail on the far side of the mountain, Matt Slaughter had heard the gunfire and decided to take a look for himself. From the sound of it, someone was in real trouble. High above the thick ring of lodgepole pines, he had taken cover in the boulders of a broad rock formation when he saw the party of Indians filing up from below him. As he watched, they spread out and disappeared into the trees. It became obvious to him right away that they were intent upon attacking someone at the foot of the mountain.

Leaving his horse in the rocks, he drew his Henry rifle from the saddle sling and made his way down the slope on foot. Working his way carefully from one patch of trees to the next, he descended to a spot directly above the stalking warriors. He could see them clearly now, since they were not expecting anyone above them on the mountain. They were Sioux, as he had expected. As he watched, one man stood up and, with hand signals, gestured toward a group of trees below him. Matt followed the direction of his signal. A glimpse of a man crawling up behind a tree was all he got, but it was enough to identify him as a white man. Matt scanned the trees below the warriors. A slight movement several yards past the white man caught his eye, telling him that there was at least one more hiding in the forest.

His attention was brought back to the line of Sioux warriors when the war chief signaled again, and a barrage of gunfire burst out, rattling the pine boughs below them. About to lend a hand to the entrapped white men, he suddenly hesitated. Taking another look at the Sioux war chief, he realized that he had seen that savage face before. At first he could not believe his eyes, and he paused to focus his gaze to be certain. *Iron Claw*—it was him all right. There could be no mistaking the cruel, hawklike face of the Sioux war chief, and thoughts came rushing back to his brain—thoughts of the savage murder of his friend Ike Brister. Ike's death at the hand of Iron Claw had been a slow and torturous one, judging by the battered body Matt had found suspended between two trees. He had made a promise over Ike's grave that he would avenge his death, but it had never come to pass. He had searched for the notorious Lakota war chief for most of a year before giving up hope of ever finding him. Zeb and Molly had finally persuaded him to leave thoughts of Iron Claw in the past. Now, on this day when he no longer searched for Iron Claw, providence, the Great Spirit, or whomever, had caused their two paths to cross. *Iron Claw*, he thought, *and up to his favorite trick—killing innocent white men.*

With grim determination, he cranked a cartridge into the chamber of his rifle and started working his way farther down the slope. When he arrived at a position on a small hump some forty yards above the line of advancing warriors, he dropped to one knee and prepared to go to work. From this vantage point, he could now see the shape of things as they were planned to happen. There were more than two white men. Of that he was certain. How many more, he could not yet tell, but there were evidently more in a gully at the base of the slope. In his descent from the slope above, he had lost sight of Iron Claw momentarily, but he was determined that the bloodthirsty war chief would not escape again. In the meantime, he began to reduce the odds against the white men. In rapid succession, he fired three times, each shot claiming a Lakota warrior. Then, before the Sioux could determine where the killing rain had come from, he moved quickly off the hump and down into a pine thicket where he prepared to shoot again.

Confused by the sudden attack from behind, the warriors were uncertain from which direction they should take cover. Several scattered to find safer protection, only to expose themselves to the deadly fire of their unseen antagonist. Two more warriors fell.

Halfway to the bottom of the slope, Iron Claw was stopped in his tracks by the solid barking of the rifle fire behind him. He heard cries of alarm from his warriors and screams of pain from one of the casualties. But it was the sound of the rifle that triggered the emotion in his brain. He had heard that sound on more than one occasion, and it brought back agony and frustration that had dwelt in his mind to this day. *Slaughter!* It could be no other—the devil the Sioux called Igmutaka, the *mountain lion*.

His mind ablaze with deep, burning fury, Iron Claw forgot the four white men trapped between him and the stream. The Great Spirit had seen fit to grant him one more chance to rid his tormented soul of the hated Igmutaka. "Back!" he commanded the warriors on either side of him as he turned to charge up the slope, following the sound of the repeating rifle known to the Sioux as the *Spirit Gun*. Confused by the sudden order to retreat and the blistering rifle fire above them, his warriors were left to thrash about, uncertain as to which direction they should take. Most of them, however, followed Iron Claw as he pushed himself feverishly up the slope.

They spotted each other at almost the same instant. "Slaughter!" Iron Claw roared in uncontrollable rage. Impassioned to carve the very heart out of the white man he hated above all others, he cast his rifle aside and charged his enemy with war ax raised to strike.

Equally eager to rid the world of the man responsible for the death of his old friend, but with the patience of the lion he was named for, Matt remained in control of his passion. He stood unmoving, patiently waiting for the charging warrior to clear the screen of pine boughs. When Iron Claw was clear of the trees, Slaughter dropped to one knee again, and took careful aim. When the enraged warrior had closed to within ten yards of him, he calmly squeezed the trigger and the Henry spoke once more. An ugly black hole immediately appeared in Iron Claw's forehead. The momentum of his charge carried him forward to crash at the feet of his adversary.

It was done; Matt's promise to Ike Brister's soul was fulfilled. He dwelt upon the thought for only a moment before realizing that the danger was not over. Spinning around to level his rifle at the warriors who had followed Iron Claw up the mountain, he started to cut the closest one down, but hesitated. The forest had suddenly become silent. The warriors, stunned by the death of their chief, one they had thought to be invincible, were certain that there was big medicine at work, and Iron Claw's medicine was obviously not strong enough to fight it. Without a signal, the remaining warriors turned and left the battle, knowing the spirits were not on their side. Content to let them leave unharmed, Matt stood aside, rifle cradled in his arms, and watched in amazement.

Distracted by the conflict above her, P. D. turned to see her three sons retreating from the slope above. "We couldn't hold 'em," Arlo shouted as he and his brothers scrambled back to join P. D. in the gully. "There's too many of 'em."

"Damn!" P. D. swore, disgusted by her sons' failure. "Well, we're in a helluva pickle now." She looked around her frantically to see if there was any way they could improve their fortifications and prepare for an all-out assault from front and rear. "How many did you kill?" she asked, hoping the odds were trimmed down some.

Arlo looked at Bo, then at Wiley. They both shook their heads. "We didn't kill any of 'em," he said.

"Not a one?" P. D. asked in angry astonishment. "I heard a helluva lot of shootin' goin' on up there. And nobody hit a damn thing?"

"Most of that happened after we left," Bo said. "I don't know what they was shootin' at, 'cause we was done gone."

"Well, ever'thin's quiet now," P. D. warned. "They're most likely sneakin' down through the trees. Get ready, 'cause hell's gonna break loose any minute." Fearing she had been distracted too long, she turned her attention back to the stream bank. Everything was quiet there as well. "That's mighty peculiar," she muttered when she realized she could no longer see rifle barrels protruding from the firing pits dug into the bank. She turned once again to look behind her. "See any sign of 'em yet?" All three replied that they had not. They waited through a full quarter of an hour of eerie silence before P. D. announced in utter amazement, "They're gone." A few seconds later they heard the sound of the Sioux ponies departing on the other side of the ridge.

Still finding it hard to believe, P. D. crawled up out of the gully and stood there for a moment, halfway expecting a shot to ring out. There was nothing. "Well, if that don't beat all," she murmured. "They had us squeezed in like rats in a corncrib." She was about to walk over to the stream to see for herself when a voice called out.

"You fellows all right down there?"

It had come from the trees behind them. P. D.'s immediate reaction was to dive back for the cover of the gully. Looking desperately back and forth, she searched for the source of the question. It occurred to her that the voice had spoken in English, but she still considered the possibility of a trick.

"The Indians have pulled out." This time the voice came from a closer point, some thirty yards above them.

The whole picture became obvious to P. D. then. Whomever their benefactor, he was the source of all the shooting on the mountainside after her boys had fled, and the cause of the Sioux's sudden departure. She propped her rifle against the side of the gully and climbed out again. Her sons followed her, and all four stood on the edge of the gully to meet their rescuer. "Come on down, mister," P. D. said. "You sure enough saved our bacon, and that's a fact."

He suddenly appeared then, emerging from the trees, a tall broad-shouldered man dressed from head to foot in animal skins, cradling a Henry rifle in his arms. "Yessir," he replied. "It looked like you were in a bind."

P. D. strode forward to meet him. "I'm P. D. Wildmoon, and these are my boys."

Matt looked from one face to the next, then back again at P. D. They were a rough-looking bunch, he decided, but so was everybody who rode through this part of the territory with no wagons, womenfolk, or children. They were definitely not settlers. "Where you fellows headin'?" he asked.

"Virginia City," P. D. answered.

Matt nodded. That made sense. They looked the kind to follow the scent of gold. "Well, I reckon you'd best stay south of the Big Horns, and maybe you won't run into any more Sioux war parties till you make the other side of the Absarokas." That said, he turned to leave.

P. D. stopped him. "Hell, mister, we owe you some thanks for runnin' off them Injuns. What's your name?"

Matt thought about it for a brief second before answering. "Johnson," he replied. "No need for thanks—you'da probably done the same for me." He saw no need to give his real name to someone he didn't expect to see again. There was no point in taking the risk they might pass it along to someone looking for him.

"Well, Mr. Johnson, if you're headin' toward Virginia City yourself, you might as well ride along with us. We'd be glad to have you—as handy as you are with that rifle."

"Thanks just the same," Matt replied, "but I'm headin' straight north." In the next instant, he was gone, disappearing into the forest without so much as one small tremor of a pine needle.

"Well, ain't he the odd one," Bo remarked as he stood staring at the empty pines where the stranger had disappeared.

"He saved our bacon," P. D. said. Then, remembering, she added, "After you boys hightailed it down that mountain."

"Hell, Ma, there was bullets flying everywhere, and we couldn't see where they was coming from."

P. D. shook her head in disgust. "Let's get the hell outta here before them Injuns change their minds."

They wasted no time fetching the horses and leaving the gully behind them. P. D. always believed she was lucky, and the sudden appearance of the lone mountain man confirmed it yet again in her mind. He had appeared, almost ghostlike, out of nowhere, and then he was gone. *Mighty peculiar,* she thought with a shake of her head and a smile.

Chapter 3

Stepping gracefully from one rock to another, Molly tracked the movements of the unsuspecting fish working its way through the channels of the narrow creek. It was getting on in the summer, but there were still some beds along the banks, out of the current. Glancing briefly at the sun overhead to make sure she would not cast her shadow upon it, she moved to a large rock closer to the bed, and squatted upon her heels to watch the miniature drama taking place.

Distressed to find a short stick forced into the creek bottom next to its bed, the fish paused a moment to sort things out. The stick was one thing, but the crude hook resting among the unhatched eggs was of immediate concern. Moving then to remove the offensive object from the nest, it tried to fan the hook away with its tail, only to find that it was anchored by a small rock tied several inches above it on the short line. After moving around the bed to fan its tail from several different angles, the fish abandoned that unsuccessful effort and took a bolder approach. Darting in quickly, it took the hook in its mouth to carry it away from the eggs. Watching from her position on the rock, Molly smiled sadly as the unsuspecting fish set the hook when it reached the limit of the short line. She always felt sorry for each fish she caught this way. Zeb liked to tease her about her tender feelings. The old scout would say, "Maybe we could hold a little funeral service for the poor fish. It ain't nothin' but the ol' papa fish, anyway. The mama's probably glad to be rid of him."

Sure that the fish was caught, she stepped over next to the bank and pulled the stick out of the sandy bottom. Holding her catch up to admire it, she smiled in satisfaction. Adding it to the three others she had caught, she tiptoed back across the rocks to the opposite bank. Matt would be pleased.

Thoughts of the tall, broad-shouldered young man brought an instant smile to her face. Though hard in her younger years, life for Molly was now as good as she could have ever dreamed. She supposed that some might think life in this rugged part of the world was difficult for a woman, but it never seemed that way to her. The past year and a half had presented some rough months when the mountain passes had been piled high with snow, and the frigid winds had swept down from the lofty peaks, making it dangerous for man or beast to be away from the fireside. Those were the times when Matt and Zeb spent almost all their time and effort in pursuit of food for them and the horses. The mountains were unyielding in their demands, but they were also protective, for no soldiers ventured into the valleys of these mountains. Zeb called them the Upper Yellowstone Mountains. Matt called them the Absarokas because they had long been home to the Crow Indians. They were also home to all manner of game—deer, elk, moose, sheep, grizzly bear—and Zeb and Matt could always find food, no matter the weather or the season.

No matter how cold the winter nights, Molly was always warm in the snug cabin the men had built during that first summer. Constructed of lodgepole and white bark pine, and chinked with clay from the banks of the stream, it served them well on the coldest of nights. Under a bearskin robe, snuggled close to Matt, she knew complete contentment. And on some of those nights, when Zeb's snoring threatened to shake the snow from the roof, she knew total fulfillment in Matt's arms. She could not want for more.

As harsh as the winters were in the mountains, the spring and summer were equally brilliant. The valley meadows were transformed into blankets of wildflowers throughout the summer and into the fall. The mountains wore dark green cloaks of spruce, fir, and pine draped about their massive shoulders below the rugged, rocky peaks that pierced the deep blue sky above. To some, it might seem to be a hostile and unforgiving land, but to those who accepted her terms, like Matt Slaughter and Zeb Benson, it was a land of plenty and peace.

Molly led her horse over beside a rock so she could climb on the mousy dun's back. She very seldom saddled the horse for her short rides down to the creek, and without the stirrups she needed a platform to give her a boost. Up through the meadow she rode, heading for the trail that wound its way through the spruce trees and over the eastern ridge to the little valley beyond and the cabin by the rushing brook.

When she approached the cabin, she could see that Matt had not returned from hunting. Zeb's horse was not in the small corral next to the cabin, either. *Probably visiting the Crow village,* she thought, smiling. Zeb spent quite a bit of time at the Crow village in the Boulder Valley, sometimes staying as long as three or four days before returning to the cabin. He always denied it, but Matt said it was because of Broken Hand's sister. Her husband had been killed in a raid against the Blackfeet five years before, and she had never remarried. She always gave Zeb a lot of attention whenever he visited Broken Hand. Molly was happy that Zeb had found someone to shine up to. He was not a young man, and he needed a good woman to keep him warm at night. She halfway expected Zeb to one day announce that he was moving in with her. He would still be close. The Crow village was only a half day's ride from the cabin.

She had just finished cleaning her fish when she heard her horse nicker in the corral—a friendly greeting. She could tell by the sound that the dun had recognized either Matt's or Zeb's horse returning. She picked up the fish, and walked back up to the cabin in time to see Matt ride into the clearing. With a proud smile, she held the fish up for him to see as she went to meet him.

"Well, aren't they pretty?" Matt commented, smiling broadly. "You're gettin' to be so good at catchin' fish, I don't know why I even bother with huntin'. I might just start layin' around the cabin all day, and let you go after the meat."

She beamed silently, delighted by his teasing, and stepped back while he dismounted. As soon as he was on the ground, she laid her fish down and threw her arms around his neck, almost causing him to lose his balance. "Whoa!" he exclaimed as he steadied himself to catch her. Then he picked her up in his arms. "You keep gettin' bigger, and soon I won't be able to pick you up." He was about to say more, but was silenced by her lips upon his. He placed her carefully back on her feet then, and gently patted her stomach, which was swollen with the child inside— four months by her reckoning.

She walked with him to the corral, and stood watching him in her silent way as he pulled the saddle off his horse and stowed it under the rough lean-to that served as a barn. While he pulled the bridle off the paint Indian pony, she took the lead rope in hand and led his packhorse to a large pine near the stream. This was where he always butchered and dressed the meat he brought home.

"She's a pretty doe," he said when he came after her. "I almost let her go, but she was close enough to use my bow, so I figured I'd best not waste the opportunity to save cartridges." She nodded in response. He took the loose end of a rope and tied it to a limb of the tree. Then, after tying it securely around the doe's neck, hoisted the carcass up off the packhorse. "I expect Zeb and I better go find that tradin' post we heard about. We've got a fair amount of skins piled up, and I'm runnin' low on .44 cartridges."

She frowned at that, for it probably meant she would be alone for a couple of days. He didn't miss her reaction. "Don't go poutin' now. Maybe I'll take you with me," he said. Her expression immediately brightened. He was not sure it was a good idea to take her. From what he had heard of it from the Crows, it sounded like a rough place for a woman. A Frenchman named Bordeaux had set up a trading post on the site of an old temporary fort, and called it LaFrance's, although it was more commonly known as *the Frenchman's.* It might be no place for Molly, but he knew how she hated to be alone, so he decided he would take her along. "You'd best go along and cook those fish before they start to get rank," he said. "Don't wait for Zeb to show up. I expect he's sniffin' around Singing Woman."

She nodded and smiled. He watched her as she walked back toward the cabin. Every once in a while he found himself stalled in a moment, marveling at the situation he had fallen into. Such a moment was upon him now as he gazed after the slight young woman stepping lightly over the rocks by the stream. She turned once more and smiled at him before disappearing around the corner of the cabin. He sometimes wondered how he had come to be so taken with the young woman. He had never meant for it to happen. There had been no place for a woman in his life as it now was, as an outlaw, hiding out in the remote wilderness of the Rocky Mountains. But she had given him no choice. Determined to be with him, and knowing him to be innocent of the crime he was accused of, she had been instrumental in his escape from military custody. With her involvement, he had little choice but to take her with him.

The first summer in the mountains was awkward at best, for he had thought of her as little more than a child at that time. But at nineteen, she was more than enough woman for any man, and that fact gradually became clear to him. When he finally began to look at her with open eyes, she was ready to take his hand and lead him where he had not been before. Life was not the same after that. Did he love her? He wasn't sure. He only knew that he didn't like being away from her for any length of time, and that when he was around her, he felt a warm glow inside that had never been there before her. He couldn't help but wonder what kind of future the two of them could hope for. There was now a child to consider. He supposed that if it were a boy, he could teach him to live off the land just as he did. But what if it were a girl? Maybe he could send her back to Virginia to live with his brother Owen, so she could be raised proper. The thought troubled him. "I'll worry about it when the time comes," he announced. "Right now I've got a deer to skin."

It was almost dark when he finished his butchering, and Molly had already signaled for him to come eat the fish she had cooked. Zeb had still not come home. Matt thought it unusual because Zeb generally returned when he said he would, but he was not overly concerned. "Most likely Singing Woman invited the old fool into her tipi," he said, laughing. "He might as well go ahead and move in with her." Molly put her fork down, and signed, *Good for him*. Matt nodded. "You're probably right," he agreed.

Suppertime came and went, still with no sign of the old scout, and Matt began to wonder if maybe he should go in search of him. His better sense told him that Zeb Benson could take care of himself, and most likely he was resting in the arms of his Crow lover. Of the same opinion, Molly saw it as an opportunity for the two of them to be alone for the evening. "I figured he'd wanna go find that tradin' post the Indians were talkin' about," Matt said. "I told him I was thinkin' about headin' up that way in the mornin'. I reckon we can stop by Broken Hand's village on the way, and pick him up."

Chapter 4

Winding down through the mountains, following an old game trail that led down to the Boulder River valley, Matt and Molly emerged from the dense forest to arrive on a long ridge that overlooked the river. Born high in the Absaroka-Beartooth Mountains, the Boulder surged north, tumbling down over a bed of small rocks and around large boulders where grizzlies waited for unwary fish, and deer and elk came to drink. Through mountainous canyons its crystal-clear waters flowed, angry at times, forming silver waterfalls and treacherous rapids. Leaving the mountains, it became peaceful and forgiving as it flowed into the Yellowstone near the site of the Frenchman's trading post.

From the ridge, they could see the Crow village where the valley broadened to accommodate the juncture of the west fork of the river. The Crow camp lay between the forks of the river in a lush meadow among a scattering of spruce trees. Consisting of some seventy-five lodges, the village had remained in this one spot for most of the summer, having moved only once to find new grass. The abundance of game in this valley, as well as in neighboring valleys, further contributed to the attraction of this camping spot, making it unnecessary to move constantly.

As Matt and Molly rode into the gathering of tipis, they were greeted warmly by the people they passed. Thanks to Zeb's ambassadorship, the Crows were openly friendly with the three white people who had built a cabin in one of the high valleys. Zeb was already like one of their own, and the Crows were highly amused by his obvious affection for Broken Hand's sister, Singing Woman. Matt was held in somewhat different regard. Quiet and reserved, Zeb's young friend, although friendly, was still of a cautious nature, seeming to be always alert. He had been immediately accepted by the Crows when they learned that he had been a friend of Spotted Horse and Red Hawk, two brothers from the village who had ridden with the soldiers as scouts at Fort Laramie. It was said that the tall, fair-haired young man had killed many of their enemies, the Sioux, and that the Lakotas had given him the name of Igmu-taka, mountain lion.

They found Broken Hand sitting before his lodge, dozing in the afternoon sun. After a few minutes' conversation, it became apparent to Matt that the Indian had been trying to sleep off a drunk. This could explain why Zeb had failed to come home. Zeb and alcohol usually made an unpredictable combination.

Upon further questioning, Matt learned that some of the younger men of the village had returned the night before with whiskey from the Frenchman's. Zeb had evidently decided to go get more that morning. Broken Hand made an attempt to be hospitable, even though it was quite obvious that his head was aching severely. Matt declined his invitation to stay and have something to eat, explaining that he had best go looking for Zeb, and that he would have to leave right away if he was to reach the trading post before dark.

"Zeb is not here," Broken Hand said, forgetting that he had already told Matt that. "He was here last night, but left here to go to the trading post this morning."

"I understand," Matt said, not sure his Crow was good enough to catch everything Broken Hand had said. "Zeb went to the Frenchman's."

"Yes," Broken Hand replied, nodding. Then he rolled his eyes sorrowfully, registering his regret. "I drank the white man's firewater. No good—it makes my head crazy—no more."

Matt looked at Molly and shook his head. Zeb had obviously made the same mistake. It seemed to him that the older Zeb got, the more childlike he became. When he left the cabin, the old scout had not taken any of his hides, so Matt wondered what he planned to trade for his whiskey. "We'd best go find him," Matt said.

*   *   *

It was late afternoon when Matt and Molly arrived at the mouth of the Boulder, where it emptied into the Yellowstone. Just as he had been told, he found the trading post near the confluence of the two rivers on the bank of the Yellowstone. The Frenchman, Bordeaux, had evidently used some of the old timbers of the abandoned fort to erect a small stockade big enough to afford protection for him and his four men in the event of hostile activity.

Matt pulled his horse to a stop while he sized up the rough structure before crossing over to the other side. Other timbers had been used to build a sizable cabin, which from all appearances served as a store as well as a dwelling. Behind the cabin, Matt saw a corral with eight or ten horses within. There were no horses tied to a hitching post out front, and Matt wondered if he had gotten there too late to catch Zeb. The whole establishment didn't look like much of a trading post, and if he hadn't needed ammunition for his rifle, he might have decided to forgo the visit. "It don't look like much, does it?" he said to Molly before guiding his horse down the bank to cross at the ford below the camp.

Their arrival was announced by a barking dog that rushed down to the river to yap and snarl around the paint's hooves until the horse aimed a kick that almost caught the ill-tempered mongrel in the head. The near miss served to teach some respect for the paint's hooves, and the dog retreated to redirect his attack to Molly's horse. Matt, concerned that the dog might cause her horse to buck, quickly untied the bow that rode beneath his right leg and, using it as a whip, promptly dispatched the bothersome mongrel.

"One of these days somebody's liable to shoot that damn dog." The comment came from the doorway of the cabin. Matt looked up to find Bordeaux standing on the step. "Good evenin' to you, stranger, and welcome." He stood watching as they rode up to the hitching post, looking Matt over thoroughly before turning his gaze upon the slight young woman on the dun. "Don't believe I've seen you around here before."

"Howdy," Matt replied. Under Bordeaux's watchful eye, he dismounted and helped Molly down.

"Evenin', ma'am," the Frenchman said. "We don't get to see many white women around here, and that's a fact, 'specially one as pretty as you."

Molly nodded shyly and favored him with a faint smile. She stepped over close to Matt. "She don't talk," Matt explained when Bordeaux seemed to be waiting for her response. He reached over the saddle and drew his Henry rifle from the sling.

Still watching the stranger's movements carefully, Bordeaux suddenly exclaimed, "You're Slaughter, ain't you? The feller the Injuns talk about." When Matt failed to answer, Bordeaux went on, "You folks come on inside. Looks like you've got a right smart passel of skins to trade." He stood aside to permit them to enter. "I bet you'd like a drink of likker. I've got some as smooth as anythin' you'd find in St. Louie."

Matt had little doubt that whiskey was the main thing Bordeaux sold the Indians. "No, thanks," he replied. "Have you got any .44 cartridges?" He glanced at Molly. "Maybe some coffee and sugar?"

"I sure have," Bordeaux replied. "Why don't you and the little lady go on inside, and I'll take a quick gander at them skins there."

Inside, there were five men seated around a table playing cards. They were a rough enough bunch, and all five turned to stare brazenly at the man and woman in the doorway. One of them, a heavyset man with a bushy black beard, grinned blatantly as he looked Molly up and down. Molly stepped even closer to Matt. Glancing from one dirty, unshaven face to the next, Matt noticed a badly bruised eye on one, and a swollen and cut lip on another. They had obviously been in a recent fight. *Little wonder,* he thought, noticing the whiskey bottle in the middle of the table. He decided to do his trading as quickly as possible, and depart. In the meantime, he cautioned himself to make sure he didn't present his back to the five at the table.

Bordeaux came inside then. Turning to keep an eye on him as well, Matt said, "I expected to see my partner here. Zeb Benson's his name."

"Zeb Benson," Bordeaux repeated. "There was a feller here this mornin'." He looked quickly toward the table. "Luther, was that the feller's name was in here this mornin'?" He turned back to Matt. "Older feller. He didn't stay long. He was wantin' some whiskey."

"Hell, I don't know." The surly answer came back from the table.

"Well, like I said, he warn't here long," Bordeaux said.

"I won't be either," Matt said. "Let's count up those hides." Taking Molly by the elbow, he turned and went back outside to the packhorse.

"These look mighty prime," Bordeaux said as they took the hides off one by one. "Too bad hides ain't bringin' as much as they used to." He sorted them into two piles, then added up the amount of credit he would offer.

Matt was surprised. It could not be considered generous, but he had expected much less. A voice inside his head warned him that Bordeaux might be planning to cheat him on the trade. "All right, then," he said when he was told the final figure. "We'll go back in and get what we need." He was about to follow the Frenchman inside when Molly tugged impatiently at his sleeve. He turned to look at her, and she nodded toward the corral. He at once saw what she was trying to tell him. "Hold on, mister," he said softly. "That's Zeb Benson's sorrel."

Bordeaux stopped at once. There was only a hesitation of five or six seconds before he smiled and said, "Why, right you are." He walked over and propped one foot up on the bottom rail as if looking the sorrel over. "Your friend wanted to buy some whiskey pretty bad, but he didn't have much to trade for it, so I traded him a little mare I had, and a gallon of good whiskey to boot." His smile still in place, he turned back to face Matt. "He seemed pretty happy with the trade. He took his jug and headed back up the river, yonder."

"Is that a fact?" Matt said, not at all satisfied with the story. *I'll have to see about that, myself,* he thought. Maybe that's the way it had happened, and maybe it wasn't. If what Bordeaux said was true, he would have most likely met Zeb coming back up the river. One thing for sure: he wouldn't trust Bordeaux or the five saddle trash he saw inside any farther than he could spit. "Well, I'll take my goods and be on my way," he announced abruptly. Seeing the frown of concern on Molly's face, he said to her, "Climb on your pony, girl. We'd best be goin'."

"You oughta stay a while and play some cards."

Matt looked back to see the man with the black, bushy beard standing in the doorway. Although the words were aimed at him, the man's gaze was settled directly upon Molly, watching her every move as she climbed up on her horse. "Reckon not," Matt replied with little emotion as he finished tying off the supplies he had just traded for. The thought ran across his mind that he might have gotten a fair price for his hides because the Frenchman planned to get it all back. Black Beard stepped outside the door. Matt's hand immediately dropped to settle on his rifle propped against the hitching post.

"Whoa, mister!" the bearded man quickly blurted. "You're a mite touchy, ain't you?" When Matt declined to answer, he stared at him a while longer until he had stepped up in the saddle. "I've heared some stories 'bout you and that there Henry rifle. That is, if you're that Slaughter feller the Injuns talk about."

Matt didn't take the trouble to respond. Speaking softly to Molly, he said, "Go along, now. I'll be right behind you." He waited for a few moments while she led the packhorse down toward the river. Facing the two men outside the cabin, he sat calmly, his rifle cradled across his arms, until Molly disappeared below the high bank. Then he backed the paint slowly away. When a safe distance away, he wheeled the horse and followed after her, chased several yards by the same snarling mongrel that had greeted him on the way in.

"Come back when you ain't in such a hurry," Bordeaux called after him.

"And don't forget to bring the missus," the man with the bushy beard added, laughing.

When Matt caught up with Molly at the ford, she began signing frantically, too fast for him to interpret, in fact. He held up his hand to quiet her. "I know what you're tryin' to tell me," he said. "And you're right. Zeb ain't never got so out-of-his-mind drunk that he'd trade that sorrel. That fellow's story stunk to high heaven. I'm takin' you back to Broken Hand's camp. If Zeb ain't there, I'm coming back to find him."

Fingers flying, she immediately protested. "You'll be all right, honey," he said. "You can stay with Singing Woman. You'll be safe there. I'd take you back to our cabin, but I'm afraid I've already lost too much time." He didn't express it, but he was also afraid that he could guess how the cuts and bruises on two of the five back at the table had happened. It had been all he could do to maintain his calm back at the Frenchman's, but his first concern was to remove Molly from danger. Thoughts of the old scout, lying in a ravine somewhere with his head bashed in, made him almost sick with anger. *The old fool,* he thought. *Why didn't he wait for me to go with him?* Then he told himself to quit fretting about it. Zeb did what he did, but there was no question about it. Matt would find him, or tear that trading post apart if he didn't.

As he had feared, Zeb had not returned to the Crow village. It was past dark when Matt and Molly rode into the meadow by the river. As expected, Singing Woman was more than willing to have Molly stay in her tipi. Broken Hand offered to send several warriors back with Matt, but he declined, preferring to go alone.

"It is dark in the river canyons," the Crow chief cautioned. "Maybe you better wait till morning."

"I wanna be there before sunup," Matt replied. "Besides, I've been there and back already. I reckon I can find my way in the dark. All I have to do is follow the river."

I can help you, Molly signed.

Matt shook his head. "No. I need to know you're safe." She rushed to him then, throwing her arms around his neck. He held her close for a long moment before gently pushing her away. "I'll be back soon," he said. "You can give Singing Woman some of that coffee and sugar."

Singing Woman hurried from her lodge with some dried deer meat wrapped in a hide pouch, and pressed it in his hand. "Thank you," he said, "and thank you for lookin' after Molly." With one last reassuring smile for Molly, he mounted and wheeled the paint to retrace his trail.

Chapter 5

He moved with the surefooted grace of a man endowed with the skills necessary to survive in a world of wolves and grizzlies, where strength and cunning were mandatory traits. Scouting a wide circle around the sleeping trading post, he searched for any sign that might give him a clue to Zeb's departure from that place. Morning approached with a thin gray light that filtered through the leaves of the cottonwoods by the riverbank. Soon the sun would show itself above the rolling prairie to the east. His horse had been left to feed on the green shoots beside the river, tethered safely out of harm's way. His rifle in his hand and his bow on his back, he moved quickly toward a thick clump of bushes at the back of the log compound.

Seeing what he thought was a hoofprint in the gray light, he knelt down for a closer look. It would have been easy to miss it in this early morning light, but it was what he had searched for. He was directly behind the trading post at this point, and there was certainly no trail, not even a game trail through the thick patch of brush. So there had to be definite purpose for a horse to have pushed through there, and he feared he knew what that purpose might be. He examined the ground carefully, looking for another print. When he found it, he could then confirm the general direction in which the horse had been moving. Looking ahead through the tangle of vines and scrubby trees, he spotted what appeared to be a drop-off of some kind, probably a ravine. He could feel his blood beginning to heat up as a picture formed in his mind of his partner's fate.

With a renewed feeling of urgency, he hurried straight for the ravine. Behind him, he heard Bordeaux's mongrel dog bark. Knowing he was downwind of the store, he was sure the dog had not caught his scent. Still cautious, however, he knelt down on one knee and waited, listening. After a few minutes, the ill-tempered mongrel stopped barking. He rose and continued on toward the ravine. As he approached the edge, he could see clear evidence left by a horse pushing through a thicket of low brush bordering the rim. He followed the trail until he came upon a sudden drop-off into a deep gulch with steep sides that appeared to converge into a narrow chasm. In the gray light of morning, it was too deep to see the bottom from where he stood on the brim. Without hesitation, he scrambled over the side, descending as fast as he could manage while still trying to keep from tumbling head over heels down the steep precipice. Alternately finding handholds on rocks and scrubby pines, while holding onto his rifle with one hand, he slid most of the way down before finally reaching the narrow bottom.

It was still dark in the bottom of the gulch, so he paused to look around him until his eyes adjusted to the poor light. As his eyes became accustomed to the darkness, he was able to see the confines of the pit he had descended into. No more than ten feet wide where he stood, the ravine extended to his right and left with no end in sight in either direction. There was no sign of the body he had been certain he would find, but the light was so poor that he could not really tell what might lie twenty feet away.

He decided to search to his right first, and had started to take a step when his foot snagged something that almost tripped him. Looking down at his feet, he discovered the skeletal remains of a human body. Stunned for a moment, his common sense told him that it couldn't be Zeb. These bones had been there for a long time, long enough for some predator to have devoured the flesh. It told him something else—Zeb, if he was down here, was not the first body to be discarded over the side of the gulch.

Moving carefully now, Matt followed the narrow defile as it wound around the base of the ridge above. It was just a guess, but he figured there was a good chance the ravine might have started in the bluffs by the river. There would not be decent light in the steep-sided gulch until the sun shone directly overhead, but the deep darkness faded a little as daylight descended upon the river, allowing him to at least see the rocky bottom. He could not be certain, but he thought it appeared that something or somebody had been dragged along the loose gravel of the ravine floor. Coming to a sharp bend in the gulch, the question was answered for him just as he made the turn.

The body lay facedown against the side of the ravine. Matt knew in an instant that it was Zeb. Like a bolt of lightning, a sudden burst of anger surged through his brain when he saw the pitiful body. They had stripped him clean, leaving nothing but shirt and pants. Unable to act for a long moment while the shock of finding his friend seemed to halt the flow of his blood, Matt finally moved to kneel by Zeb's side.

Very gently, he rolled the body over. It was obvious why they had not taken the deerskin shirt. It was crusted solid with the blood that had flowed from two bullet holes in the chest. "Damn, partner," he uttered softly, "why didn't you wait for me?"

Zeb's eyes fluttered weakly. His lips barely moving, he whispered, "I was drunk."

Matt sat back, astonished, not knowing whether to laugh or cry, wondering if he had actually heard what he had just heard, or if it was his imagination. "Zeb? And you came back here for more?" Matt asked, hardly believing.

"I wasn't after more," Zeb protested weakly. "I come back 'cause that whiskey they sold the Injuns was watered down so bad I had to drink damn near a gallon to get drunk. That's why they jumped me."

Zeb's eyes fluttered again before remaining open. "I figured you'd come lookin' for me." His words were weak, with barely enough strength to be heard.

"Damn! I thought you were dead," Matt said, still finding it hard to believe he wasn't.

"Me, too," Zeb said. "I still ain't sure I ain't. I'm hurtin' pretty bad inside, and I think I broke my leg when they throwed me down here."

Matt looked down at Zeb's leg. From the angle of his foot, it was apparent that the bone below the knee had snapped. "I expect you're right," he agreed. "I've gotta get you outta here, back to Broken Hand's village."

"I don't know, Matt," Zeb forced between clenched teeth. "I think somethin's busted up inside me." He paused to allow the pain of talking to subside a moment before continuing. "Damned old fool—I let 'em get the jump on me." He paused again to groan. "I was holdin' my own with 'em until that Bordeaux feller shot me." His voice trailed off then. After a moment, he mumbled, "I was tryin' to drag myself outta here, but I don't know . . ."

"I'll get you outta here," Matt insisted. "You're too damn ornery to die from two puny little bullet holes. You were already headin' in the right direction—if I'm guessin' right. I figure this damn gully has to lead to the river. I expect you were thinkin' the same." He paused a moment while he looked at Zeb's chest. "I ain't much of a doctor, but it doesn't look like you're bleedin' right now. There ain't much I could do to help those wounds, anyway. Your shirt's stuck to 'em, but it's probably best to leave it alone right now. Maybe it's what's keepin' 'em from bleedin'." He turned his attention to the leg. "Maybe I can set the bone in that leg, though."

With his skinning knife, Matt cut a split down Zeb's trouser leg so he could see the leg. It was already bruised and swelling, the location of the break obvious. He had never set a leg before, but he had seen it done during the war. "Think you can stand it?" he asked. Zeb nodded briefly and closed his eyes. "All right," Matt said. "Here we go." With one hand on Zeb's knee, and the other on his ankle, he pulled with all the strength he could muster. Zeb's eyes, closed tightly moments before, opened wide as he clenched his teeth. Unable to remain silent, he grunted one loud protest before his eyes rolled toward the top of his head and he fainted away.

Seeing that his patient had passed out, Matt strained to exert more pressure until the leg became straight. Then he let the broken ends of the bone draw back together. There was no way he could be sure they had settled back in perfect alignment, but the leg looked to be straight. "Best I can do," he mumbled apologetically.

Using his knife, he hacked away at a couple of little pines growing on the side of the ravine until he had fashioned a splint. The problem then was to find something to tie the splint with. Looking around him, he could see no vines or anything that might serve the purpose, until his eye lit on the decorative fringe on Zeb's shirt. He promptly cut off a dozen of the deerskin strings. Knotting them together, he was able to make a cord long enough to bind the pine stakes to form Zeb's splint.

It was going to be a sizable task to carry Zeb out of

the ravine. He decided he'd better explore a little farther along to make sure he would come out near the
river before loading Zeb on his shoulder. He considered the fact that he might even find that he could
lead his horse down into the dark chasm. After following the narrow gulch for about two hundred
yards, he found what he was hoping for, but not entirely. The ravine did, in fact, start out as a deep gully,
cut into the high bluffs along the river, not too distant
from where he had left his horse. It began as a fifteen-
foot sheer drop into a narrow slit of a crevice, however—too severe for a horse to negotiate. He studied
the problem for a few moments longer. *Well, at least
there's a way out of this hole*, he thought, and retraced
his steps to fetch the wounded man.

He returned to find his friend alert again, but in severe pain. "This ain't gonna be pleasant, but there
ain't no other way to get you outta here."

"Reckon not," Zeb replied weakly, not certain at
that point if he could even stand up.

After considerable effort, and a great deal of pain,
Matt got the old scout standing on his one good leg,
leaning against the wall of the gulch for support. He
first thought he would heft Zeb across his shoulder,
but Zeb was sure that he would be unable to tolerate
the pain it might cause his bullet wounds. They finally decided that piggyback was the only way he
could make it. So with Zeb's legs locked around his
hips, and his arms around his neck, Matt started toward the river carrying his partner on his back.

Zeb was not a small man, and Matt was beginning

to wonder if he was going to have to stop and rest before reaching the river. The floor of the ravine was rough and uneven, causing him to stagger several times in the semidarkness, each misstep resulting in a painful grunt from his passenger. As he labored toward the end, he could feel a growing patch of wetness on the back of his shirt; perspiration or blood, he was not sure which. Finally a splash of bright sunlight illuminated his path, and he knew he had made it to the river. A few yards farther, and he staggered up to the head of the gully. As gently as he could manage, he sat Zeb down against the side. Zeb groaned and released a long, painful sigh before lying back.

Breathing heavily from the effort just expended, Matt stood over him for a long moment, watching him intently. As he had feared, the rough passage had started Zeb bleeding again. "Dammit, you'd damn-sure better not die after I carried you all the way here."

"I ain't makin' no promises," Zeb groaned painfully.

"Rest here while I go get my horse. Then we'll pull you up outta this hole." He turned his head from side to side, still looking the wounded man over carefully. "If you're thinkin' about givin' up before I get back with my horse, I'm warnin' you, I'll kick your ass until you come back to life." He crawled up out of the gully then and paused to listen for sounds from the trading post, some two hundred yards downstream.

Satisfied that there was no one coming his way, he went to retrieve his horse.

Although it took less than a quarter of an hour to fetch his horse, he was more than a little apprehensive by the time he returned to the gully. Zeb hadn't looked too good when he left. He had lost a little more blood, a good bit of it on the back of Matt's shirt, and Matt was concerned that the ordeal of raising him out of the gully might be the final straw for the suffering man. There was, however, no alternative.

Taking a coil of rope from his saddle, Matt dropped down into the gully. Zeb was slumped over against the clay side, his chin almost resting on his chest, with his eyes closed. Matt stood over him for a few moments, watching intently, thinking that he was too late. Sorrow, mixed with an intense anger toward the men who had done this to his friend, overcame him.

"I ain't dead yet," Zeb mumbled softly, his eyes still closed.

The announcement startled Matt for a moment, but he recovered quickly enough to fire back, "Are you sure? 'Cause I've seen men dead for two weeks that looked better than you." He went to work then— looped the rope under Zeb's armpits and knotted it. "Keep your back toward the side of the gully, and I'll pull you up outta here. All right?" Zeb nodded weakly, and Matt climbed up out of the gully again.

On top of the bluff, he led his horse into position and looped the loose end of the rope a couple of turns around the saddle horn. Holding the paint by the bridal, he led the horse slowly away, gradually lifting Zeb up out of the pit. Once Zeb was safely on top, Matt untied him and boosted him up in the saddle. He climbed up behind him and they departed the banks of the Yellowstone, cutting a wide circle around the trading post.

When she heard cries of recognition from some of the women down by the river, Molly hurried from Singing Woman's lodge, anxious to meet the approaching riders. Giving silent thanks for Matt's safe return, she ran gleefully until stopped in her tracks by the sight of Zeb Benson. Sagging weakly, held upright only by Matt's arm around him, Zeb looked little more than barely alive.

Matt pulled the paint up to a stop before her. Seeing the distress in her face, he shook his head solemnly. "He's hurt bad," he confirmed. "They left him for dead." Within seconds he was surrounded by a multitude of helping hands as the people of Broken Hand's village came to assist him. Devastated by the sight of their friend's blood-encrusted garments, Molly bit her lip in an effort to keep from crying. She looked at Matt helplessly. "He's got two bullets in him and a broken leg," Matt answered in response. "I set the leg as best I could. I reckon we'd best see if we can get the bullets out."

Several of Broken Hand's warriors carried Zeb inside Singing Woman's tipi, and laid him on a buffalo robe that the Crow woman had prepared for him. The medicine man, Burning Sky, was sent for, and when he arrived, he sent all but Singing Woman away. Matt was reluctant to leave the old scout's side, but Broken Hand assured him that Burning Sky had treated many bullet wounds. Matt was not totally convinced, but he knew of no better alternative. "He's lost a helluva lot of blood," he insisted. "It's gonna take a lot more than a medicine man wavin' some eagle feathers over him."

Broken Hand smiled patiently, although he could have taken offense. "Burning Sky took the bullet from my side when we fought the Blackfeet," he said. "He will remove the bullets from your friend, and Singing Woman will make some strong potion to give his blood strength."

Knowing he could offer Zeb nothing better, Matt nodded, and immediately turned his mind to another matter that required his attention. Molly read his eyes, and immediately knew what he was thinking. She grabbed his arm, pleading with her eyes. Fearfully concerned, she signed, *No!* with her trembling fingers, wishing with all her heart that she could cry out to him.

He looked down at her, feeling her concern, but unable to quell the flame of fury that had been rapidly building every mile of the way back from the Yellowstone. "I'm gonna clean that nest of rattlesnakes outta there," he said in a soft, even voice. It was as final a judgment as if God Himself had uttered it.

Molly locked her arms around his waist, holding him as tight as she could in a desperate effort to keep him from going back. He made no move to escape her embrace, but reached down to stroke her hair. "It'll be all right, little one," he whispered.

"That is an evil place," Broken Hand said. He had been silently watching the drama taking place between the man and woman. "The Frenchman sells my people firewater that steals away their ability to reason. Others have gone to trade there, never to return. We will mount a war party to go with you."

Matt thought the suggestion over for a moment or two. It was tempting to accept the offer, but he felt the need to personally avenge the wrong done his partner. Furthermore, he envisioned a wild Indian attack on the palisades of the trading post. He could imagine a stout defense by the white men, resulting in the sacrifice of innocent Crow lives. It would be easier for him to get inside if he were alone. Besides, he figured he had war party enough in the form of his Henry rifle. "No," he decided. "This is for me to do alone, but I thank you for your offer. If you'll take care of Molly for me, that'll be enough."

It was more than an hour before Burning Sky emerged from the tipi, followed by Singing Woman carrying a clay basin that she took to the edge of the camp and emptied. While she went down to the river to wash the basin, Burning Sky came to talk to Matt and Molly. "The bullets are deep," he said. "I could not remove but one of them. I cleaned the wounds and wrapped them. If he is strong enough, he will be well again. Another day will tell us."

It was not the report that Matt had hoped for, but

at least Zeb's chances seemed to be fifty-fifty. *He is a tough ol' bird,* he thought. *Maybe his chances are better than that.* While Zeb slept, Singing Woman prepared food with Molly's help. After eating, Matt declined an invitation to stay in the tipi, preferring to spread his bedroll under the trees by the river. He remained there for the rest of that day to let his horse rest. After the camp was settled for the night, Molly picked up her blanket and stole quietly from the tipi to join Matt by the river. While a veil of stars looked down through the branches of the trees, he made love to her. Then she fell asleep in his arms. When she awoke in the morning, he was gone, having left hours before sunup.

"Rider's comin'," Ed Varner called out. He was standing in the open gate of the stockade built around the Frenchman's trading post. Only mildly interested, he pulled absentmindedly at the full, bushy, black beard that covered his face from ear to ear while he watched the rider approach. "Looks like that Slaughter feller that was in here a couple of days ago," Varner said. "Looks like that paint pony he was ridin'."

Behind him, near the door of his store, Bordeaux was examining a buffalo robe brought in by two Blackfoot men. He paused then to look toward the gate. He had not responded when Varner had first announced a visitor. When Ed identified the rider as Slaughter, however, he became interested. Leaving the two Indians to wait for their whiskey, he moved unhurriedly to stand by Varner at the gate.

"By hisself this time," Bordeaux said. "I wonder what the hell he wants." There had been something in the steady eye of the young mountain man that hinted he was not to be underestimated. He cocked an eye in Varner's direction. "You didn't leave that old man's body layin' around where somebody could find it, did you?"

"Nah," Varner replied, still unconcerned. "We threw it down that gulch with the rest of 'em. He ain't found nuthin'—probably just wants a drink of likker. You gave him too good a deal on them hides he brung in." He paused to spit a stream of tobacco juice at a beetle scurrying across the open gate. "Wish he'da brung that pretty little wife with him."

"We'd best keep an eye on him," Bordeaux said. "I don't like the way he kept askin' questions about that old trapper. He might wanna cause some trouble."

"I hope to hell he does," Varner blurted. "We'll throw his ass down that hole with his partner if he wants to find him that bad." He grunted and spat again. "I fancy that paint he's ridin'. I might wanna ride it back to find his camp and that little honey-haired woman."

Bordeaux grunted in return. "I expect we might have to draw lots to see who got the horse and who got the girl if it comes down to that. The others might have a say in it."

"To hell with 'em," Varner snorted.

They continued to stand in the gate, watching the

rider approach. As before, the ill-tempered mongrel dog ran out, snarling a warning, but when it approached the visitor, it remembered the paint pony and stopped well short of its hooves. When Matt was within a dozen yards, Bordeaux called out, "Welcome back. Slaughter, ain't it?" Matt did not reply, but continued walking the paint up to them, then reined the horse to a stop a few yards before them. "Still lookin' for that partner of yours?" Bordeaux asked.

His face deadly calm, without expression, Matt stared at the two men standing before him. Shifting his gaze from Bordeaux's attempted innocence to the confident smirk of the bearded man, he replied softly, "That's right."

"Well, you missed him," Bordeaux said. "He came back lookin' for you, not long after you was here—didn't he, Ed? He was pretty drunk when he left—mighta rode off a cliff or somethin'."

"Mighta," Matt replied stoically. "I expect it more likely he got thrown into that pit behind your place."

Both men blanched. Realizing that Matt had discovered his dark game, Bordeaux's hand dropped to his pistol. Matt, the Henry rifle already cradled in his arms, whipped the weapon around and pumped two shots into the Frenchman's chest. Varner, his face twisted with anguish, managed to get his .44 halfway out of the holster before meeting the same fate as his partner. As the two men crumpled into the dust of the stockade, Matt cocked the Henry again with an eye on the two Indians, who wisely departed the compound. When they had disappeared, he calmly prodded the paint with his heels. Stepping around the bodies, the horse walked toward the trading post. Matt did not look down at them as the horse walked past; he knew they were dead.

Alerted by the rifle shots, two more of the Frenchman's gang of cutthroats appeared in the doorway of the store. They were executed where they stood. Calm and seeming as impersonal as the rifle he carried, Slaughter continued toward the door. The burning anger that had fired the blood in his veins was past him now, having been replaced by a dull, single-minded mission. There was no thought of the taking of human life. It was no less moral than the methodical extermination of a rat's nest. He owed it to Zeb, and to the other poor soul whose bones he had tripped over at the bottom of the gulch. The job was not finished, however. There were two more rats inside.

Intent upon cheating a Blackfoot hunter out of a half-dozen prime fox pelts in exchange for a small jug of watered-down whiskey only moments before, Bordeaux's two remaining thugs were suddenly jolted by the second barrage of gunfire. Since there was no one in the compound except a couple of the Blackfoot's friends, the two white men, Luther Rainey and Bill Cotton, had assumed that the initial round of rifle fire had come from Bordeaux or Varner. The cause was of no particular interest to them. They were always shooting at something, Cotton had commented in an attempt to calm the alarmed Blackfoot hunter, who didn't know if he was in danger or not. "They're maybe trying out a new rifle or somethin'," Cotton had said. But in the next instant after these last shots, they were stunned to see their two partners crumple in the doorway, both stone dead.

"Jesus!" Rainey blurted, dumbfounded. His sudden paralysis lasted for no more than a second, however, and he set his feet into motion. Straight for the back window he ran, grabbing his rifle on the way. The Blackfoot ducked behind the counter.

Equally confused, but of a stouter fiber than his partner, Cotton yelled after the fleeing man, "Rainey!" But all he saw was Rainey's rear end as the frightened man went out the window. Angry at having been left alone to face whatever threat awaited, he pulled his pistol and wasted two shots at the now empty window. He then moved quickly to take cover behind the bar. Not wishing to be part of it, the Indian moved to the other end of the short counter. Cotton took a moment to snarl at the Blackfoot before concentrating his attention on the doorway.

Consumed by panic, which was intensified by the two pistol shots that whined through the window over his head, Rainey landed headfirst on the ground, clambering to get to his feet. He only managed to get to his knees before he discovered the moccasined feet standing before him. He immediately shrank back in terror, fumbling with his rifle as he fell back against the log wall of the store. The bullet that split his forehead sent him on his dark journey wearing the frozen expression of cold fear that gripped his face.

Inside the store, Cotton heard the fatal shot and

swung his revolver around to aim at the window. A moment later, a head appeared in the open window. He emptied his pistol, firing until the firing pin clicked on an empty chamber. Only then did he realize that it was Rainey's head. He had pumped his last three shots into a corpse. Panic-stricken then, he scrambled out from behind the counter and ran for the door. Outside the window, Slaughter let the bullet-riddled body of Luther Rainey drop to the ground. There was no time to get off a certain shot, as Cotton reached the door faster than Slaughter anticipated. He managed only one shot before the fleeing man cleared the doorway, catching Cotton in his right shoulder.

His work not yet done, the solemn angel of death walked around the cabin to the door, expecting to find Cotton's body just outside. It was not there. A sudden pounding of hooves behind him caused him to spin around and drop to one knee, ready to fire again. Too late, he got only a glimpse of Cotton as the wounded man rode out of the gate at a full gallop. Matt lowered his rifle. While the venom of vengeance was still in his veins, he gave no thought to chasing the remaining bushwhacker. There had been enough killing for one day, and the nest of vermin had been destroyed.

He paused then to look around the stockade while he reloaded the magazine of his rifle. There was no one else inside the log walls of the compound, the Indians who were there having fled when he started shooting. Shoving the two bodies blocking the door-

way aside, he entered the store and walked over behind the counter where Bordeaux had kept ammunition. A slight movement at the other end of the
counter triggered an instant reaction. In the blink of
an eye, he turned, the Henry leveled at the figure
crouched there.

Huddled against the back of the counter, the Blackfoot hunter awaited a fate that seemed certain. A
knife, the only weapon he had, was in his hand. Only
a split second before firing, Matt relaxed his grip on
the Henry. Then, waving the rifle barrel, he motioned
for the Indian to get up. The man hesitated for a moment before doing as he was bade, sensing that he
was not about to meet death, after all. "You talk white
man?" Matt asked. The Indian nodded. "Go find your
friends. Take anything you can use. I'm gonna burn
this place to the ground. You understand?" The
Blackfoot nodded again.

While the Indian hurried out the door to summon
his friends, Matt took all the .44 cartridges on the
shelf. There was not much in the way of other inventory on the shelves. It was apparent that the Frenchman's main merchandise consisted of watered-down
whiskey. He took a bag of green coffee beans, and left
the rest for the Indians. Outside, he opened the corral
and walked Zeb's sorrel out. He led the horse, along
with his paint, to the stockade gate. There he waited
while the Blackfoot hunter returned with his friends.
They paused when they saw him standing at the gate
until he motioned for them to continue.

In a matter of minutes, the small party of Indians

had cleaned out the store of anything remotely useful. Carrying firearms and ammunition, they wasted no time in clearing the structure. Outside, Matt waited stoically while the Indians collected the weapons from the bodies of Bordeaux and Varner. Pausing at the corral, the Indians hesitated to take the horses, looking instead at the menacing figure with the deadly rifle. With another wave of his Henry, Matt signaled his permission. They were quick to comply. He watched until they had disappeared beyond the bluffs, hurrying to return to their village to relate this strange turn of events and show off their recent bounty. Matt figured they were probably owed that much if they had been trading with the Frenchman for very long. He wondered then how many more remains he might have found if he had searched in the direction away from the river when he was at the bottom of the gulch.

Alone now in what had been a den of thieves and murderers, he went back inside the store. There was a small iron stove in the middle of the room with a coffeepot sitting on one corner. Opening the grate, he discovered that the coals were still hot. There was a box of kindling over against the wall, along with some split firewood. He dragged it over to the stove. Then he stood back and kicked the stove over, spilling most of the glowing coals out on the plank floor. Using the kindling and firewood, he fed the coals until he had a strong blaze going. Then he piled on everything he could find in the building that would burn. Soon he had a roaring fire going in the center of the store. Satisfied that would do the job, he then went outside to his horses, and waited there until the flames began lapping the outside walls of the log structure.

Feeling drained and tired, he stepped up in the saddle and turned the paint toward the Crow village, burdened with the heavy dread of finding his partner dead when he got there. As he rode out, the ill-tempered mongrel ran out from where it had been waiting behind the gate. Yapping and snarling, it attacked the paint's hooves, this time forgetting its earlier lesson. This time the dog came too close, and paid for its indiscretion with a kick of the paint's hind legs that sent the belligerent mutt flying. "I reckon that about does it for this place," Matt commented wryly.

It was late afternoon when Matt arrived at the Crow village. Leading Zeb's sorrel, he walked the paint slowly across the rocky shore of the river past the pony herd, where some young boys watching the horses waved to him in greeting. Hearing shouts of greeting from several of the people in the village, Molly walked outside, hoping it was the visitor she waited for. She could feel her heart beat fast in anticipation, and her face blossomed with a huge smile of relief when she saw that it was, indeed, Matt. He saw her running to meet him, so he dismounted and caught her when she jumped up into his arms.

"I told you I'd be back," he said, unable to keep from laughing when she clung to him so tightly. His expression quickly turned serious when he asked, "How is Zeb? Is he gonna make it?"

Her face was still firmly pressed against his chest, but he could feel her nodding, *yes*. She pulled away from him then to give herself room to sign, *Bad, hurt bad*. He winced as if feeling the pain himself. They walked to Singing Woman's lodge, leading the horses, Molly holding onto Matt's arm with her free hand.

Molly was right; Zeb looked bad. Lying on the bearskin pallet Singing Woman had prepared for him, the old scout looked for all the world like a man glimpsing death. Matt nodded to the Crow woman when he entered the tipi. She returned his greeting, then backed away from her patient to give Matt room.

"You old buzzard," Matt said softly. "I thought you'd be dead by now."

Zeb's eyes flickered open and a faint smile formed beneath the grizzled beard. "I ain't sure I ain't," he replied weakly.

"I believe you're gonna make it. I brought your horse back. As soon as you get strong enough to ride, I'll take you home." He looked up at Singing Woman and smiled. "That is, if Singing Woman will let me." Standing beside the Crow woman, Molly frowned and slowly shook her head. Matt understood. "Might be a better idea to let you lay up here a while longer," he said. "Looks like Singing Woman's pampering you pretty much. You might wanna play sick for a long spell."

"Did you get them bastards?" Zeb asked, with obvious effort in his voice.

Matt nodded. "I got 'em. They won't be throwin' any more poor souls down that ravine."

"Bordeaux?"

"The whole bunch," Matt answered, "except for one of 'em, and I'm pretty sure I winged him, but he hightailed it outta there. I don't expect he'll be back."

"I'm obliged, Matt." Zeb rolled weary eyes up at his young partner. "I reckon I cooked up a stew too big for me to eat. But I never meant to drag you into it."

"Hell, we're partners, ain't we?" Matt shrugged. "You'da done the same for me."

Chapter 6

Bill Cotton, although a bit unsteady on his feet, still found the strength to stagger up to the bar of the Lucky Strike Saloon. At first glance, Cotton might easily have been mistaken for any one of the many drunks who frequented the saloons of Virginia City. But Bill Cotton was stone-cold sober, and needed a drink bad. Three long and grueling days in the saddle had taken a terrible toll on a man with a rifle ball lodged in his right shoulder. The wound, festering and swollen, had rendered his right arm almost useless, and he needed to see a doctor, but not as badly as he needed a drink.

"Damn, mister," the bartender commented. "You look like you was left out in the rain."

"Whiskey," Cotton demanded.

The bartender eyed the desperate-looking man suspiciously. "Can you pay for it?"

Cotton fumbled in his pocket with his left hand, and slammed his money down on the counter. "Just pour the damn drink," he snarled.

"All right, no need to get sideways about it." While he poured a shot glass full, the bartender continued to study his customer. "Ain't I seen you here before?" he finally asked. Cotton didn't bother to answer, but the bartender's memory was already working on it. "You was hooked up with that feller, Bordeaux, that come in here for a while. Right? Hell, I remember you now." He paused to take another look at the surly Cotton. "I wondered what happened to you fellers. You have a fallin'-out with Bordeaux?" He nodded toward the wad of makeshift bandage protruding from the blood-encrusted shirt.

His tongue loosened a bit by the strong whiskey, Cotton shook his head slowly. "No, me and Bordeaux never got crossways with each other. We built a tradin' post up on the Yellowstone—was doin' all right until about a week ago. That's when I got this bullet in me. Bordeaux and the other boys are all dead. I'm the only one got away, and I damn near didn't."

"Damn!" the bartender exhaled. "Injuns?"

"Hell, no, it warn't Injuns. It was a white man."

"A white man?" the bartender asked in amazement. "Bushwhackers?"

Cotton tossed the remainder of his drink down. "Hell, no, it was one man. A crazy son of a bitch, jumped us without so much as a 'howdy-do,' and us just tryin' to make an honest livin'."

"Bless me," the bartender exclaimed. "Shot you and Bordeaux both?"

"And Luther Rainey, and Ed Varner, and Johnny

Littleton, and Grady Chapman," Cotton snorted. "He come in there blazin' away with that rifle. We never had a chance. I emptied my pistol at him, but then I got the hell outta there."

"Who was he?" the bartender asked.

"Hell, I don't know. A wild man is all I can tell you, gone loco livin' up in the mountains. I only saw him one time before that. He come into the store with a woman what couldn't talk."

"Mister, I'd admire buyin' you another drink." The offer came from a table next to the bar. Cotton turned to see a party of four listening to the exchange between him and the bartender. Cotton's story had sparked an interest at the table, especially when he mentioned a woman who couldn't talk.

Cotton cast an inquisitive eye at his benefactors, a rough-enough-looking bunch. "Why, that's mighty neighborly of you," he said, and shoved his empty shot glass toward the bartender.

"Come on over and set down. Arlo, pull up a chair for the man." Cotton picked up his drink and walked over to the table. He sat down heavily in the chair, his right arm hanging stiff and swollen. "I'm P. D. Wildmoon," his hostess introduced herself. "These here is my boys—Arlo, Bo, and Wiley."

"Bill Cotton," Cotton replied.

P. D. watched him toss his drink down, then got right to the point. "I couldn't help overhearin' you tellin' about that piece of bad luck you had. The feller that bushwhacked you—what was his name?"

Cotton shrugged. "I don't remember. I heard it

once or twice, but I don't remember what it was. I didn't pay much attention to it, I reckon."

"Was it Slaughter?" P. D. asked, watching intently as she waited for Cotton's response.

"Mighta been. Come to think of it, I believe it was Slaughter. Yeah, that was it."

P. D.'s eyes took on a definite gleam. She turned to smile at her three sons. She almost thought she detected a small spark of excitement in their otherwise blank faces. It was a welcome sight. During the past weeks, she and her sons had covered a lot of ground, all to no avail, and she was a little worried that they might be losing some of their original enthusiasm for the hunt. Without specific information of Slaughter's whereabouts, she would never find him in the lofty, rugged mountains. She had counted on the woman with him to lead them to their man. A man alone might be content living in the mountains like an animal. But it was unusual for a woman not to yearn for some semblance of civilization. The two obscure trading posts she and the boys had encountered had not seen any white women. The only women they had seen were Shoshoni or Crow. Now, with the chance encounter with Cotton, she could feel her luck changing and the trail getting warmer.

"Looks like we mighta struck gold here, boys," she said, grinning at Cotton. "I expect we'd best do a little doctorin' on that shoulder of your'n, Bill Cotton, and then I might have a little proposition for ya."

Cotton cocked an eye, suspicious of anyone offering a deal to someone they had just met in a saloon.

Blinking hard to clear his eyes of the alcohol he'd just tossed down, he studied the faces of the three younger men seated with P. D. Trying to size them up, he looked first at the big one, the one referred to as Arlo. He looked to be the eldest of the three, but seated next to Arlo was the one Bill judged most dangerous. He had a surly look about him. The youngest seemed a minor threat. The four seemed to be the caliber of ruffians Bill had ridden with for most of his life.

Up to that point the three had sat quietly, their faces as blank as a freshly washed blackboard, with identical inane grins their only expression. He switched his gaze back to take a hard look at P. D.—a short, squarely built person with rolls and bulges un-usual for a man. It struck him only then that P. D. was a woman. *About the ugliest woman I ever saw, at that,* he thought.

"I expect I'd best see if I can find a doctor," Cotton said.

"Nah, you don't need no doctor," P. D. insisted. "Have another drink. Another shot of that whiskey, and you won't even feel that shoulder. I'll dig that bullet outta there, and you won't have to waste no money on a doctor."

"Ma's dug 'em out before," Arlo spoke up in sup-port of his mother. "Good as any doctor."

Bo laughed at that. "She patched up Wiley's pa, and then got mad at him and shot him herself."

P. D. aimed a sideways glance at her second son. "That was Arlo's pa, son, as mean a snake as ever drew breath. Anyway, Mr. Cotton, here, don't wanna hear nothin' about that."

"I don't know . . ." Cotton stammered. His head was beginning to spin just a little—the effect of the strong drink on an empty stomach. Knowing he had already had too much to drink, but unable to refuse free whiskey as long as it was offered, he continued to toss down shot after shot until he eventually went facedown on the table.

"Get him up on his feet, boys," P. D. instructed her sons. She walked over to the bar then to talk to the bartender, who seemed only mildly interested in Cotton's welfare. "Poor feller," P. D. said to the bartender, "set upon by a murderin' devil. Me and my boys will tend to that shoulder for him."

The bartender shrugged indifferently. It was all the same to him. He was well accustomed to seeing drunks carried out of the Lucky Strike. Most of the time they woke up back of the building with their pockets empty. "That sounds like bad business," he commented, "if that feller that shot him is doin' all that killin'."

"I reckon that's somethin' that needs fixin', all right," P. D. said with a faint smile on her face, knowing who was going to do the fixing.

With a considerable amount of the up-front money paid her by Jonathan Mathis still in pocket, P. D. had rented a couple of rooms in the hotel, one for her, and one for her three boys. But Cotton was not taken directly to the hotel for his doctoring. Instead, he was taken to the stables where their horses were boarded.

There was a reason. As her sons had boasted, P. D. knew a thing or two about cutting lead out of a body, and she was interested in seeing Cotton recover. There were no stoves in the hotel rooms, and the stable offered a blacksmith's forge for cauterizing the wound.

Arlo and Bo laid the still-drunken Cotton in the hay and held him steady while P. D. went to work with a twelve-inch skinning knife. Wiley, the youngest, held a lantern and watched in gleeful excitement as his mother split the pus-filled lump that had formed over the entry wound. After letting it drain for a moment, she probed none too gently in the wound until the blade ticked on the lead ball. The stable filled with the putrid odor of the festered wound as it blended with the dank aroma of horse manure. Lolling in drunken oblivion to the butchering of his shoulder, Bill Cotton uttered only an occasional grunt in response to P. D.'s less-than-gentle touch. He became totally sober, however, after the bullet was removed, when P. D. laid the white-hot iron on the bloody wound. Emitting one ear-piercing scream, he sat bolt upright before falling back in the hay unconscious.

After the bullet was removed, Cotton's recovery was rapid. Following a full night's sleep, he awoke early the next morning, not quite sure where he was. Turning to look beside him, he could see that he had shared a bed with someone. He didn't know who, and whoever it was, was already up. He threw his legs over the side and sat up. The room spun around for a few moments, but then settled down. From the looks of it, he guessed he was in the hotel. A few minutes later, his hunch was confirmed.

"Well, looks like you done woke up." Cotton looked toward the door to see a man standing there grinning; one of P. D.'s sons, he didn't remember which one. The door was pushed open then and Arlo, P. D.'s eldest, walked into the room.

Cotton started to get up, but then realized that he had nothing on but his socks. He immediately became alarmed. "Where the hell's my clothes?"

Arlo laughed and pointed toward a chair in the corner of the room. "Right yonder," he replied.

Cotton started for the chair, staggered slightly, stopped to steady himself, then made his way over to the corner. His first thought was to see if the little bit of money he had was still there. It was, so he relaxed a bit. "How the hell did I get here?" he asked as he climbed back into his pants.

"We toted you up here," Arlo answered. "Me and my brothers."

Cotton had awakened on many mornings before, after a night of drinking, not sure where he was. Usually he found himself in the back alley of a saloon with his pockets empty, or, if he wasn't in a town, sprawled under a tree somewhere. But he'd never woken up in a hotel room, in a bed. Something fishy was going on. "I can't pay for no hotel room," he complained as he hitched up his belt.

"You ain't gotta pay for it," Arlo informed him, still amused by Cotton's confusion. "Ma's payin' for it."

"Ma?"

Arlo nodded. "Yep, Ma," he said. Then seeing that Cotton was even more confused, he said, "P. D."

Events of the night before came back to him then— the woman, P. D., and her three sons. Still it escaped him why they would go to the trouble to take him in. He looked back at the bed. "Which one of you slept in the bed with me?" For it was obvious that someone had.

"Ma," Arlo answered again. "Me and my brothers slept in the room next to this'un."

"Damn!" Cotton uttered, clearly astonished. Then another thought occurred to him. "Who took my clothes off?"

"Ma" was the answer again, this time with a chuckle.

"Damn!" Cotton repeated, and squinted his eyes tightly closed, trying to remember, but he could not. The entire evening before, after the saloon, was lost in a confusion of dreams and half dreams. The tenderness of his right shoulder was the only thing he was certain of at that moment.

Seeing him flinch as he examined the wound, Arlo cautioned him. "Ma said that there arm's gonna be a mite touchy for a day or two."

"I reckon," Cotton agreed, wincing with the effort of pulling his shirt on. "I best be gettin' outta here. Where's my boots?"

"Ma's got 'em. She said you might wanna cut and run, so she's got 'em downstairs with her. Her and my brothers is still eatin' breakfast. They'll be up directly. Ma sent me up here to look in on you. I always eat faster'n they do. Ma says I eat just like a dog—don't hardly take time to chew, just choke it on down." He laughed, amused by the mental picture of himself.

Cotton just stared at the simple oaf of a man. *Damn*, he thought, *he's dumber'n Rainey.* His patience wearing thin then, he started to get a little irritated at the thought of a woman virtually holding him prisoner. "Well, I've had about enough of this horseshit," he announced, and reached for his gun belt, hanging on the back of the chair.

Arlo watched in dumb silence, fascinated by Cotton's painful efforts to strap the gun belt around his waist. After considerable difficulty, he settled the belt on his hips. Then, reaching across with his left hand, he drew his revolver from the holster. "Now, you damn moron, let's go get my boots."

Arlo simply smiled at the cocked pistol pointed at his gut. Then, with nothing approaching a quick draw, he pulled his pistol and leveled it at Cotton. Cotton was amazed at the man's apparent stupidity, but his reaction was automatic. He pulled the trigger only to hear the dull metallic click of the hammer as it fell on an empty chamber. Arlo's smile told him it was useless to try again.

"Ma took them bullets outta your gun. She said you might try somethin' like that." He stood there, his pistol still leveled at Cotton's belly. "Ma'll be up here directly," he said. "She said I could shoot you if you tried to go, as long as I didn't kill ya."

Frustrated and angry to the point of seething, Cotton was at a loss as to what he could do. If he had had two good arms, he would have considered making a move for the gun, even though Arlo was twice his size. It didn't help that he felt foolish for standing there in his stocking feet, faced down by a halfwit wearing a huge grin, an unusually large halfwit at that. His desperate thoughts were interrupted in the next minute, however, by the arrival of P. D. and her other two sons.

"Well, now, I see our patient's on his feet again," P. D. said as she preceded Bo and Wiley into the room. "Wiley, go get Bill's boots from your room. I expect he's gonna wanna go downstairs and get somethin' to eat." She paused to watch her youngest leave, then turned back to Cotton. "First, I've got a little business proposition for you. Arlo, put that gun away. Bill ain't goin' nowhere."

Cotton was still lost in a quandary of confusion. He gazed at the square, solidly built figure of P. D. Wildmoon, dressed in men's clothing from boots to Montana Peak, totally at a loss as to the woman's interest in him. "What the hell do you want with me?" he finally asked. "You ain't took me in just 'cause of my good looks."

She smiled, wide and friendly. "Well, now, Bill, that mighta had somethin' to do with it." She fixed him with an amused twinkle in her eye, then said, "You know where Slaughter is, and I wanna find him."

Astonished, Cotton gaped at the homely woman,

her three dull-witted sons standing stoically behind her, like so many yard dogs. Finally, he shook his head in disbelief. "Hell, I told you where the tradin' post was. I don't know where the hell he is now."

P. D. continued to smile, but now the grin was forced. "From what you was babblin' about last night, it sounds like Slaughter is mighty friendly with the Injuns in them mountains, and you know where that Crow village is." She cocked her head for emphasis. "You could save me a lotta time if you led me to that village." He was already shaking his head before she finished the sentence. " 'Course, I ain't expectin' you to go along outta the kindness of your heart. Nossir, there'd be a sizable cut of the reward money for you."

This sparked Cotton's interest. "Reward money?" he responded.

"I thought that might send a spark up your ass," P. D. said. She turned to glance at her boys. All three responded with knowing grins. They had a fair notion what Bill Cotton's reward would be. P. D. went on to paint a mental picture for Cotton. "We're being paid to hunt Slaughter down by a man back in Virginia. Already got half of it. When we take him back, we get the rest. If you help me find him, your share will be about five hundred dollars."

Cotton didn't say anything at once, not sure he had heard P. D. correctly. "How much?" he stammered after a moment.

"Five hundred," P. D. repeated. She glanced at Arlo and winked. "That is, if you can lead us to him."

"Hell, yes," he eagerly agreed, "I can lead you to him. He ain't gonna be easy to take, though. I can tell you that. But, hell, for five hundred dollars, I'd even shoot him for you." The thought of having that much money in his hand at one time was enough to erase the fear he had felt when running for his life.

"All right, then, partner," P. D. said, her grin genuine now. "I reckon we'll let you rest that shoulder up today, and head out first thing in the mornin'."

"Hell," Cotton replied as he shook P. D.'s hand. "I'm feelin' good enough to ride now. We can start back today if you want to."

"Nah," P. D. insisted. "We'll stay over one more night and let you get good and rested." She cut a sharp eye at Bo when he started to snicker. "You boys go along now, but don't be gettin' in no trouble. Arlo, go down to the stable and make sure that son of a bitch feeds them horses some oats. And see that Bo and Wiley don't wander off nowhere I can't find 'em if I need 'em." She turned back to Cotton. "Our new partner is most likely wantin' some breakfast. Me and him'll go downstairs. I could use another cup of coffee myself."

Arlo did as he was told. After he herded his two younger brothers out in the hallway, Wiley complained, "I want some more coffee, too. I wanna go with Ma."

Bo giggled again. "Wiley, you dumb turd, Ma don't want you around. She's got the itch again, and I reckon she's thinkin' ol' Bill Cotton can scratch it for her. Ain't that right, Arlo?"

"I reckon," Arlo replied. "He don't know it yet, but I expect he's about to get rode harder'n he's ever been rode before."

Wiley was close to eighteen years old, but his mental capacity had been filled by the time he saw his twelfth birthday. It had made little difference in his life to that point, having never been called upon to make any decisions that called for serious thought. Very few things seemed to bother him, but he was somewhat troubled by his mother's tendency toward itches. It only happened about once a year, but he didn't understand her need to spend time alone with some strange man in order to get relief from this strange itch. He and his brothers were all for any opportunity for a roll in the hay with some young female. That was only natural, but he couldn't understand that his mother might be interested in the same sport. After all, she was an older woman, and his mother. Furthermore, he didn't see why he couldn't go have more coffee with the two of them. "She said she was gonna give him five hundred dollars," he blurted, still pouting.

Bo shook his head in mock amazement. "I swear, Wiley, you're dumber'n a stump. What ol' Bill Cotton is gonna get is a bullet in the back of the head once Ma's through with him. Ain't that right, Arlo?"

"I expect," Arlo said. "Forget about coffee, Wiley. We'll go get us some beer. You'd druther have that, wouldn't you?" Wiley nodded excitedly, his simple mind already blissful again.

* * *

While her three boys were entertaining themselves by taking in the many sights of Virginia City, P. D. was well into the preliminary stages of a planned sexual assault upon one Bill Cotton. She sat at the table with him as he finished off a sizable breakfast of flapjacks and bacon, totally unsuspecting of the demands about to be placed upon his body. There was never a thought of anything remotely connected to a romantic adventure with a woman who looked every bit the man he was. In fact, he didn't even give it a thought when the waitress greeted them with the words, "What can I get for you gents?" If it bothered P. D., she gave no indication.

For a fact, P. D. was more man than woman by her own choosing, but deep inside her private mind she knew that she was female, and, as such, she experienced certain urges from time to time. Though not as often as in earlier years, when she had given birth to each of her three sons, when the urge hit her it was just as strong as in decades before. Like land that had been untended for years, time had been harsh on P. D. Rugged and woolly, the soil had dried out over the decades, but the land was still plowable, although it had long since lost its fertility.

She was in no way attracted to the scruffy-looking bushwhacker, Bill Cotton. It was just that he had arrived on the scene at a strategic time. She was in heat. Before he showed up, she had already made up her mind that it was her time of year, and she had planned to satisfy her urges with some unsuspecting male before she left town. While not the least bit religious, she recognized the fact that Bill Cotton was the answer to two prayers, seeing as how he could also help her find Slaughter. For these reasons, P. D. was feeling exceptionally frisky as she watched Cotton wipe the grease from his two-week-old beard.

His hunger satisfied, Cotton again suggested that they might as well start out for the Yellowstone then, instead of waiting for morning. He was anxious to get that five-hundred-dollar payday, although he was a little concerned about his chances of collecting. She didn't say how or when he was to get the money. He didn't figure he could trust P. D. to keep her end of the bargain unless he was careful to keep an eye on her and her sons. On the other hand, she had said that this man in Virginia had already paid her money up front. And, he wondered, if she could afford to give him five hundred, how much was she carrying on her? Maybe, he thought, there was the possibility of a bigger payday if he just took what she had on her for himself, and left her in a gully somewhere. Her three idiot sons were a problem, however. He would just have to wait for an opportunity.

"I think it's best to rest you up another night before we start out," she said in response to his suggestion to get under way. "Let's go back up to the room now, where we can talk."

"About what?" Cotton asked.

"There's parts about this deal that I ain't showed you yet. Come on, get up."

He shrugged indifferently, drained the last swallow of coffee from his cup, and got up from the table.

Without hesitation, she reached into her pocket, pulled out a sizable roll of bills, and paid for his breakfast. The wad of money was enough to capture Cotton's interest, so he made no objection to following her upstairs.

She led him into the room, then locked the door behind them. He gave it a moment's thought, but no more than that. "I don't want nobody botherin' us," she said by way of explanation. Cotton was still clueless until she removed her hat, and unpinned her hair, letting it fall almost to her broad behind. A germ of suspicion sprouted in his mind then, but he told himself what he suspected was highly unlikely. She made it unquestionably clear in the next few moments, however, when she started unbuttoning her shirt.

"What the hell's goin' on?" Cotton blurted, still finding it hard to believe she was intent upon what her actions indicated.

"I'm just makin' myself comfortable," she said, gazing at him much as a bear might gaze at a salmon. "I'm gettin' ready to give you a bonus, for joinin' up with us. You'd best come outta them clothes if you wanna take a ride."

Fully aware of what the game was at that point, Cotton was not at all sure he wanted to play. He was never one to turn down any opportunity to enjoy a woman's favors, but this seemed more like a tussle with another man. "I don't know," he stammered, taking a backward step. "I've got this shoulder . . ."

"That shoulder ain't the part of you I'm fixin' to

use," she said as she removed the shirt, revealing two almost flat sacks that rested comfortably upon an ample belly.

Cotton wavered, still uncertain that when she removed her trousers, he might discover the same equipment down there that he saw when he looked down at himself. He slowly unbuckled his gun belt, but went no farther, his eyes riveted to the woman undressing before him. Down came the trousers, and he released a tiny sigh of relief. It occurred to him then that he had, on more than one occasion, paid women who didn't look much more attractive. *Of course, I was a helluva lot drunker than I am now,* he thought. *What the hell—ride a horse, ride a mule; they're both going to the same place.* She had the necessary equipment; it was just poorly arranged and not in the best condition. Rising to the occasion then, he started peeling off his clothes.

She paused to watch. "When's the last time you took a bath?" she asked.

"I don't know. When's the last time it rained?"

She grunted in response. At this stage in the game, it was going to matter little, anyway. The sap was rising in both parties. She couldn't help but comment, however, "Damn, when you take your pants off, there ain't a helluva lot to look at, is there?"

"There's enough to take care of you," he replied indignantly. But he was about to find that it almost wasn't. As Arlo had predicted, it was a hard ride for Bill Cotton. Unable to operate according to her timetable, he finished far in advance of her fulfillment, causing her to exhort his extra effort, playing on his pride at first, until soundly cursing his feeble attempts to stay with her to the end. When she finally arrived, she began hooting like an owl, over and over. It was a reaction that Cotton had never heard before, and, at that moment fearing he was near death, cared less about.

In a minute or two, P. D. calmed down. She lay there in relaxed satisfaction for a brief period before shoving her exhausted lover off the edge of the bed. Her sense of relief could be compared to the feeling of finally ridding herself of a splinter that had irritated her for a spell. She got up from the bed then, and went to the pitcher and basin on a stand next to the wall. "Get your clothes on and get on outta here," she ordered. "I've got to clean up."

He did as he was told, feeling spent, used, discarded, and totally dismayed. "I reckon I'll sleep in here again tonight," he said, heading for the door.

"Like hell," P. D. retorted. "I'm gonna need to get some sleep tonight. You can bunk in with the boys, or sleep in the stable with the horses. I don't care which." Then, remembering that she still needed him to find Slaughter, she softened her tone. "Maybe you and me will have us another go at it in a day or two. Be ready to ride out in the mornin', though."

When the door closed behind Bill Cotton, P. D. walked up close to the small mirror over the basin. She examined the rough, lined face in the glass as if searching for some remnants of her femininity. She often felt it a curse that she had not been born a man.

It was a man's world. When she was younger, she had halfway accepted that truth. But life had gotten harder with every year after her father ran off, abandoning twelve-year-old Priscilla Delores and her mother.

The two had taken up with a mule skinner after that, a man named Barnhill, who had two sons from a former marriage. It was a rough existence for Priscilla. After two years of abuse from Barnhill, the fourteen-year-old girl decided she was going to strike out on her own, feeling anything would be preferable to living under Barnhill's oppressive yoke. She did not leave without baggage, however, for the night before her departure she was impregnated with her first child, the result of a rape by one of Barnhill's sons.

Having not been endowed with the beauty of some of her species, Priscilla nevertheless tried her hand at whoring to feed her infant son and herself. She was able to survive due to the indisputable fact that the drunker a man got, the prettier she became. She moved from town to town and camp to camp over the next few years. The inevitable side effects of her occupation resulted in the birth of another son, and a growing contempt for men in general. Only one man penetrated the hard shell of distrust and loathing, Buck Wildmoon, the father of her third son, Wiley. That germ of affection was destroyed when she found Buck with another prostitute astride him. It was at that time in her life that she found her real satisfaction could only be realized with a gun in her hand.

Looking in the mirror now, she could find peace in the knowledge that she would probably not have feminine urges for another year. Bill Cotton had served that function, even if he never fulfilled his job as a guide. She gazed at her image for a few moments longer. Then she walked over to her gun belt hanging on the bedpost and drew the long skinning knife from its scabbard. Without another moment's hesitation, she began to hack away at her long hair, knowing that she would most likely have the urge only once more by the time it grew down to her fanny again.

Downstairs, Arlo looked at Bo and laughed. As they walked in the front door of the hotel, they had heard the loud hooting sounds from upstairs. "Ma's cured the itch," Bo said. A few minutes later, they met Bill Cotton coming down the stairs. All three brothers grinned knowingly at the disheveled man as he passed by them with nothing more than a brief nod of recognition.

Chapter 7

Bill Cotton's wound was healing nicely, a testimony to P. D. Wildmoon's surgical skills. It still pained him some after a full day in the saddle, and with P. D. giving the orders a full day meant from sunup to sundown. It had taken him three days to reach Virginia City when he fled the trading post, and that included pushing on past sunset on the first night. P. D. seemed intent on cutting the time required to cover the same distance.

"I've gotta go in the bushes for a minute," Cotton announced as they followed the Yellowstone beyond its confluence with another river, one that Cotton couldn't name for them. The disturbance in his bowels made him wonder if the side meat they had packed might have turned rank. No one else seemed to have any complaints.

"We ain't got time to stop," P. D. said. "Get your business done and catch up with us. Bo, you drop back and wait with him."

"Yessum," Bo responded, and immediately reined his horse back.

"I don't reckon I need nobody to watch me," Cotton said.

"I know you don't, Bill, darlin'," P. D. said, a smile of amusement playing faintly upon her lips. "But there may be Injuns around that we don't even know about, and Bo can keep watch for you."

Cotton made no reply, simply giving the grinning Bo a glance before guiding his horse toward a clump of berry bushes near the river. *It ain't much different than taking a shit with a dog or a horse watching you*, he thought as he shucked his gun belt and fumbled to get his britches untied, feeling a sudden need for haste. As his troubled bowel rushed to divorce itself from the tainted meat, Cotton gave thought to another thing that puzzled him. He didn't believe for one second that Bo had been left behind to watch for Indians. It was a thought that had occurred to him the day before. Some one of the Wildmoon family was always watching him. It was almost like he was a prisoner. Why, he wondered, would they suspect he might desert them? The promise of five hundred dollars was incentive aplenty for an outlaw mind like Cotton's. *Maybe they're worried I might go after that wad of money P. D. carries*, he thought, smiling to himself between grunts. *I wonder how much that ol' bitch has got on her.* The more he thought about it, the more he was convinced that it was the reason he was being watched all the time.

He had speculated a great deal about the party he

had joined during the first two days on the trail. The more he thought about it, the more he was convinced that he was being played for a fool. P. D. needed him to take her to that Crow village. Once she found Slaughter, Cotton would indeed be a fool to think she would pay him the money promised. She would most likely tell him that he had to wait until she received the balance of the bounty from some jasper in Virginia—that, or simply shoot him in the back and be done with it. Of the two possibilities, he figured the second most likely. *The joke's on her,* he thought. *Bill Cotton ain't that easy to skunk. I don't exactly know where that Crow camp is, and I sure as hell ain't got no idea where Slaughter is.* He issued a final grunt of relief, and pulled some leaves from the berry bushes. *I expect I'll get my chance to catch Miss Wildmoon and her boys sleeping long before we start looking for that Indian camp.*

It was late afternoon when they reached the point where the Boulder River joined the Yellowstone. A few hundred yards east of that, they came upon the ruins of the Frenchman's trading post. The stockade was still intact, untouched by the flames that had left the store a pile of charred timbers. The gate faced the east, so they could not appreciate the degree of destruction until they rode around to the far side of the compound. Approaching the gate, they were met by Bordeaux's mongrel dog, the only other survivor of Slaughter's vengeance. With fangs bared, the snarling beast challenged the strangers. In a motion that was quick but casual, P. D. drew her pistol and shot the surly cur. "I ain't got much use for dogs," she said.

"That dog never got along with nobody but Luther Rainey," Cotton commented. "We always figured it was because Rainey wasn't much smarter than the dog, hisself." He pulled up to gaze at the two bodies close by the door of the store. "Funny thing, ain't it? I figured that dog would be long gone by now."

"Hell," Arlo replied, pointing toward a charred lump inside the burned-out back wall. "He warn't about to run off and leave his food supply. From the looks of this'un, that ol' hound liked his meat cooked." He laughed at the thought. "I reckon he'da started on them fellers out in the yard next."

Cotton dismounted and stepped closer to view the ragged remains that had once been Luther Rainey. Blackened and baked to a turn, Rainey's half-eaten carcass triggered an amused grunt from his former partner. Cotton found it ironic that the dog had chosen the only person he liked to start in on.

P. D. walked her horse around the ruins, looking the situation over. "There ain't nothin' left worth takin'," she decided. "He musta cleaned the place out before he burned it down." She turned her horse toward the gate. "Let's get outta here and find a place to camp. Somewhere upwind," she added. "These corpses is startin' to get ripe."

"Reckon we oughta bury 'em, Ma?"

P. D. turned to look at her youngest. Of her three boys, Wiley was by far her favorite. P. D. didn't have many soft spots in her heart, but Wiley came the closest to being one. Maybe it was because, of the three different men who sired her sons, she had a casual fondness for Wiley's father, enough to have taken his name for her own. Possibly she nurtured a germ of compassion for the boy because he was slow-witted. Whatever the reason, he was the only one for whom she exhibited any show of patience. "I reckon not," she finally answered his question. "We'll just let the buzzards and the wolves feed off 'em."

Bo, standing next to his younger brother, rapped Wiley on the back of his head with an open palm, knocking his hat off. "Reckon we oughta bury 'em?" he mocked. "I swear, Wiley, you're dumber'n dirt."

Wiley quickly reached down to snatch his hat from the ashes of the cabin wall. When he came up again, he had his pistol in his hand. "Put it away, Wiley," P. D. commanded, and guided her horse between the two brothers. "Get on your horse, and let's get outta here." She watched him with a stern eye until he holstered the weapon. While he turned to step up in the saddle, she rendered a quick swipe across Bo's face with her quirt.

"Goddamn!" Bo howled, and grabbed his cheek. "I was just funnin' with him," he complained. "The dumb bastard," he added under his breath.

The family squabble dispensed with, P. D. turned to question Cotton. "Which way to that Crow camp?"

"Back yonder," he replied, pointing toward the Boulder River. "Up that river." He had no idea if the Crow village was up that river or not, but whenever Indians from the village had come to the trading post, they had followed the river. He figured he could trust to luck, and maybe they would stumble on it. "'Course, there ain't no guarantee they're still in the same place."

"How far?" P. D. wanted to know.

Now Cotton was really out on a limb, but he didn't want to admit that he had no idea. A confession such as that might convince P. D. that his services were unnecessary. "Why," he allowed, "as near as I remember, no more'n half a day's ride."

"As near as you remember?" P. D. questioned. "Hell, back in Virginia City you said you could lead us right to it."

"Well, I could, but like I said, the damn Injuns mighta moved their camp since then." Cotton decided at that moment that P. D. was starting to question his story, and maybe his best bet was to take the first opportunity to kill the lot of them, and be satisfied with what money the suspicious ol' gal had on her.

P. D. said nothing more on the subject, but continued to give Cotton a cold eye for a few moments longer before announcing, "Sun's gettin' low. We'd best find us a place to camp."

Retracing their trail for a few hundred yards, they started up the Boulder River toward the towering Absarokas, riding no more than a mile before P. D. picked a spot for their camp. "Suit you, Bill?" she remarked pointedly, as if his opinion meant something.

Cotton shrugged. "Suits me fine," he said, and dismounted.

They unsaddled the horses and hobbled them after taking them to drink. P. D. took care of building a fire while Arlo took care of her horse. Cotton laid out his blanket a little apart from the other four, next to a sizable rock that extended a foot or more out into the river. The rock would partially shield his movements should he decide to move about any during the night. From that position, he was also a little above the other four. As he finished arranging his blanket, he felt P. D.'s eyes upon him. When he looked around, she was indeed watching him, and when he met her gaze, she smiled. *Like a cat watching a mouse,* he thought. *Thinking how good I'm gonna taste when she eats me.* He returned her smile. *She's on to me,* he thought. *She's thinking I don't know where that village is, and she doesn't need to share that reward with me.* He had little doubt that P. D. would put a bullet in his back with no more compassion than she had with Bordeaux's dog. *Well, this is one mouse that ol' cat ain't gonna get the chance to taste.*

The eye contact was broken when Arlo and Bo started rummaging through the packs that held the supply of bacon. "What are you boys doin' in them packs?" P. D. demanded.

Bo answered, "Lookin' for a little piece of bacon. Me and Arlo's gonna rig up a line to see if we can catch us a fish for supper."

"More'n likely you're feedin' our supper to the damn fish," P. D. retorted. "I didn't tote that slab of bacon all the way out here for you boys to throw in the river."

"We're just gonna take a little piece," Arlo said while his brother cut off a small corner of the slab.

"Wrap that meat up like you found it," P. D. prompted. Then she looked at Cotton and smiled again, like any mother of a couple of rambunctious cubs.

It struck Cotton how much she looked like a man; even more than before with her newly cropped hair. He thought back to the incident in her hotel room, amazed that he had been able to accommodate her. Her attitude had changed perceptibly since they had stopped to make camp. The gruff exterior had given way to something remotely akin to a mannerism approaching femininity. He considered the possibility that she might be thinking along the same lines as during that tussle in the hotel. He quickly rejected that notion. She was getting friendly for a decidedly different purpose, he thought, to put him at ease so she could put a knife in his gut while he slept. *We'll see about that.*

There was nothing approaching romance in P. D.'s mind as she studied her temporary partner. *You lying bastard,* she thought, *sitting there grinning at me. You don't know where that village is, and you don't have any idea where to look for Slaughter. I'm giving you one more night. That damn camp better be where you said it was. In the meantime, I'm going to watch you like a hawk.* Her thoughts were interrupted when Bo's excited whoops distracted her. Looking toward the river, she saw her son climbing the bank, holding a fish up for her to see.

"What'd I tell you," he blurted proudly. "I caught

a big'un, and Arlo ain't caught shit!" He brought the fish up for her to examine. "What kinda fish is that, Ma?"

"Hell, I don't know, son. Fish is fish. We'll cook him up for supper."

The fish was fairly large, but not enough to feed five people, so P. D. cut it in chunks and mixed it in with the bacon. After they had eaten, they sat around the fire for a while. "There's liable to be Injuns hereabouts," P. D. said. "It's best we keep a lookout while we're sleepin'." This especially caught Bill Cotton's attention. Noticing, P. D. continued. Talking directly to Cotton then, she said, "We'll let these young boys take turns watching. They don't need their sleep like us older folks, like you and me, Bill."

"Hell, I'll take my turn," Cotton quickly volunteered. This looked like the opportunity he was hoping for. "Nobody has to stand in for Bill Cotton."

"No, no need," P. D. retorted just as quickly. "We'll let the boys do it." Then, ending all discussion on the matter, she turned to the three disappointed young men. "Wiley can take the first turn. Arlo, you and Bo can decide who goes when after that."

Later, when Cotton walked up into the trees to empty his bladder, P. D. called Arlo over. "I ain't worried 'bout no Injuns. I want you and your brothers to keep an eye on ol' Bill, there—make sure he don't get to wanderin' around during the night."

Arlo grinned. "Yessum," he replied. "We'll watch him."

The night passed peacefully enough, with nothing

untoward to distract from the serenity of the river valley. P. D. snored in contented slumber, oblivious to the night sounds. Cotton, on the other hand, slept fitfully, not at all comfortable with being watched all night long, and frustrated to know that the opportunity he had hoped for was lost to him. Several times during the long night, he awakened and looked around to see if the "sentry" was alert. Each time, he discovered one of P. D.'s boys up and on the job. It was blatantly obvious to him that they were stationed in a position to watch him rather than to look for anyone approaching the camp. Along toward morning, he gave up and went to sleep.

He was awakened by the toe of P. D.'s boot, prodding him in the back. "Come on, Bill, you've done sawed enough logs," she cajoled. "We've got some ridin' to do if we're gonna reach that Crow camp before noon."

Cotton bolted upright, startled that he had overslept. In the process of scrambling out of his bed, he became tangled in his blanket, causing him to trip and land on the ground again—much to the amusement of his audience. "It's a good thing we ain't Injuns," Wiley said, delighted by the confused man's efforts to disengage himself from his blanket. "We'da done had us a scalp."

Bill Cotton was not possessed of a sense of humor. Bitterly mortified for being the butt of the joke, his face reflected the anger he felt inside. "Maybe, maybe not," he uttered as he finally threw off the blanket to reveal the .44 revolver in his hand.

There followed a protracted moment of dead silence as the Wildmoon family stood staring eye to eye with their new partner. P. D., her hand casually resting on the butt of her pistol, finally broke the silence. "Was you expectin' trouble, Bill?"

"I'm always expectin' trouble," he answered gruffly. Looking around him then at the faces watching him with eager looks of anticipation, he holstered the weapon, ending the confrontation. Realizing the odds were definitely not in his favor, he said, "No harm done. I expect we'd best get movin'."

Cotton wasn't comfortable with P. D. and her sons behind his back, but he had little choice but to ride out in front, since his value to the hunting party was as a guide to take them to the Crow village. He glanced up at the sun, now almost directly overhead, as he followed the trail through another narrow gorge. It was beginning to look like he had made a poor guess when he assured P. D. that the camp was a half day's ride from the trading post. He began to doubt whether the village was even on this river. The farther they rode, the more mountainous canyons they encountered with no suitable places to set up a large Indian camp.

He resigned himself to the fact that the showdown with P. D. and the boys was going to be a lot more difficult than he had hoped. At some point, he was going to have to separate Arlo and Bo from their mother. Wiley was of no major concern. Of the four, P. D. was his primary concern, and by far the most dangerous. The element of surprise was going to be the key. If the timing was right, he could gun down the woman and her youngest before Arlo and Bo knew what was going on. He was running out of time, because it was already noon, and P. D. would be asking questions before much longer. "Wouldn't be a bad idea to stop and rest these horses a little," he called out behind him. "I could use a little coffee, myself."

P. D. pulled up beside him on a path so narrow that their stirrups were rubbing together. "We oughta been comin' to that village by now, if what you said was right," she said. "I ain't seen a spot big enough for a camp in these damn canyons. I believe you mighta been tellin' me a story when you said you knew where that village was."

"It ain't much farther," Cotton assured her. "We'll find us a place to rest the horses before long. After that, it won't be far."

He was beginning to believe that there was no end to the steep river canyon, but eventually they came to a pass where the river made a turn, creating a small grassy meadow inside the crook of the bend. Relieved, Cotton called back, "See, I told you there was a place up here to rest a spell." He rode on ahead, and dismounted in the meadow close to a sizable boulder sitting by the water's edge. While he waited for the others to file in behind him, he made his mental preparations for the task he was getting set to perform. *The ol' bitch will send a couple of the boys to water her horse*, he thought. *While they're watching the horses, it'll be easy to shoot her and Wiley before they know what hit them. Then I can use this rock for cover while I pick off the rest of them.* It was as good a plan as any. He was satisfied that he could take down the four of them, maybe before any of them had time to get off a shot. Hearing her horse walking slowly up behind him, he turned to greet P. D. with a smug smile of anticipation on his face, only to have it freeze when he looked into the barrel of her pistol. There was not even an instant of time to realize what was happening before the revolver discharged in his face, ending Bill Cotton's worries in this life.

"Whup!" Bo whooped, as startled by the gunshot as Cotton. "Godamighty," he exclaimed excitedly.

"He ain't got no more idea where that Crow village is than Wiley has," P. D. casually announced, as Cotton's body fell back against the boulder and slid slowly to a sitting position on the ground. "He was just after my money."

"Ma, I ain't got no idea where that Crow camp is," Wiley said, confused by his mother's remark.

P. D. smiled patiently. "I know you ain't, son."

"Dumber'n a stump," Bo mocked, and reached over and knocked Wiley's hat off his head.

"Leave him be, Bo," P. D. scolded her middle son, then turned to Arlo, who was standing over Bill Cotton's body to see if he was dead. "Get his gun belt and that pistol he was aimin' to shoot us with, and anything else you can find on him. Bo, you can lead his horse. That saddle looks to be in good shape. Leave it on. We might as well take it with us."

"Yessum," Bo replied, leaving young Wiley standing there staring at the corpse.

"How we gonna find that Crow camp now, Mama?"

With patience she had only for her dull-witted son, P. D. explained. "The same way that son of a bitch was hopin' to find it. I'm guessin' he just figured it was up this river somewhere. Go get back on your horse. We'll find it, and when we do, there'll be somebody there that knows where Slaughter's holed up."

She sat there on her horse for a while longer, watching Wiley go back for his. Every once in a while she wondered why she had a soft spot in her heart for her simpleminded son. In a litter of puppies, Wiley would have been the flawed one that got knocked in the head. Knowing her compassion for him was because of his father, Buck Wildmoon, she almost sighed when she thought of Buck. *Damn, he was hell between the sheets,* she thought. *Trouble was, he wasn't particular whose sheets he was working between.* It always brought a smile of satisfaction to her face when she recalled the night she walked into that hotel room in Omaha and put a bullet square in the middle of Buck's naked backside. Dismissing the thought, she aimed a final glance at the corpse slumped against the boulder. *You were good for a ride, too, but not as wild as one with Buck Wildmoon.*

Chapter 8

"You're gettin' pretty good at that," Matt said as he walked up behind her, then apologized when she started. "Sorry," he said. "I didn't mean to scare you."

Recovering her composure, Molly favored him with a mock frown of anger. To compensate for her inability to speak, nature had endowed her with a keen sense of hearing. Still, her husband moved with the soft-footed tread of a cat, and if she was not listening for him, he was always startling her. She had let him know before that he should not suddenly appear behind her after being gone from the cabin to hunt, but he often forgot.

He knelt beside her and felt the softness of the doe hide she was working on. "Who taught you to soften a hide like that?" he asked. She poked him on the shoulder to remind him to look at her while she signed Singing Woman's name. He smiled. "You're turnin' into a full-blooded Crow Injun," he remarked as he looked from the deer hide to the strips of meat drying in the sun.

She placed the adze-shaped dressing tool, made from an antler, on the ground beside the deer hide and put her arms around his chest, nestling her head on his shoulder. Contented, like a puppy needing to be petted, she held him tightly, pressing her slender body so close that he could feel her heartbeat. He kissed her gently on her forehead and reached down to pat her swollen belly. It would be in the coldest part of the winter when the baby came.

Matt was now spending most of his time hunting for food to store for the time when the mountain passes would be filled with snow. There was still need for more firewood before fall arrived, also. Thanks to Singing Woman's teaching, Molly was quite prepared for the coming winter. She had learned to dry meat to store for the times when fresh meat was not available. Singing Woman had taught Molly to make pemmican by pounding the sun-dried meat to a fine consistency, then mixing it with melted fat, marrow, and a paste made by crushing wild cherries, including the pits. It had become one of Matt's favorites. Life was good. They were content in the mountains, away from the stench of civilization. Matt knew that he could not avoid contact with the outside world from time to time. There were things that they had to have that could only be obtained in the white man's world. Rifle cartridges would eventually run out, although he had a generous supply, courtesy of the Frenchman's. There were other things: coffee, flour, salt, sugar, things that made life a little more pleasant. But for now there was no need to journey up the Yellowstone to old Fort Manuel and the trading post there. The thought brought to mind the last time he had gone to a trading post and the hell that had resulted from the trip.

"I expect I oughta ride down to see how Zeb's doin'," Matt said, his thoughts turning to his partner and the way he looked the last time he had seen him. The old scout was definitely standing in death's door when he left him in Singing Woman's care. The Crow woman had insisted that she would make him strong again, but, in Matt's opinion, Zeb just might be too old to recover fully from the wounds he had suffered. "If he stays in that Crow camp much longer, he might turn Injun sure enough," he remarked to Molly and laughed. It had been a week since he had brought Zeb to Broken Hand's village, and he felt a little guilty for not having been back to check on the old man's condition. There had been much to do to prepare for the coming winter, and he and Molly had both been busy. "I saw sign of elk on the far side of the ridge." He hesitated as he thought about adding one of the huge beasts to their food supply. "I reckon we'll go get Zeb first, though. I expect he's champin' at the bit to get home." Molly pulled her head away from his chest and smiled up at him. She was always happy to visit Singing Woman.

Zeb was seated on a bearskin robe outside Singing Woman's tipi, taking advantage of the warm sunshine, when Matt and Molly arrived at the Crow camp. Beside him, a pair of crudely carved crutches lay, fashioned from a couple of stout limbs. Already, there was a bit of a chill in the afternoon air, the mountains' promise that cold weather would not be long in coming. Singing Woman, like the other women of the village, was busy drying meat for the cold months ahead. She paused in her work to greet Zeb's visitors.

"I reckon you're about ready to get rid of that old man," Matt teased.

"I think he wants to go home," Singing Woman replied, laughing. "I told him he should stay here till he gets strong again, but he says no."

Matt turned his attention to his old partner. "How 'bout it, Zeb? You ready to go? Think you can stay on a horse?" His tone was light and cheerful, but he was thinking that Zeb still looked fragile and unsteady. He had lost considerable weight during his recovery, leaving his face thin and haggard and looking a little long in the tooth. It was difficult to remember the ruddy, robust scout he had been so recently. Matt dropped his reins and walked over to sit down beside his friend while Molly went off to visit with Singing Woman.

Zeb gave a little shake of his head and sighed. Answering Matt's questions, he said, "I don't know, partner, but I'm gonna damn-sure try. I'm 'bout to go crazy settin' around this camp."

Matt nodded. "I reckon," he allowed. After a few moments' silence, he said, "I thought you might decide to take up with Singing Woman and sit around with a wife to wait on you."

Zeb grinned at the thought. "You know, she would, but I'm damned if I wanna end up my life as a loafer Injun."

"All right, then, if you're ready, we'll head back up in the mountains. I've got plenty of meat packed away, but I'm set on killin' a good-sized elk before I'm done. It would be good if you were there to keep Molly company while I'm gone."

"That's about all I'm good for, right now," Zeb complained, "but maybe, before long, I'll be able to help you hunt."

"Don't worry about it," Matt replied. "Like I said, I've already got meat enough. I just like to be sure."

The two friends were joined by Broken Hand, and the three of them talked about the coming winter. Matt was already thinking about heading back to his camp, but Broken Hand insisted they should wait until morning. Not wishing to reject the old chief's invitation, Matt accepted. It would give Zeb one more night of rest before the hard ride up into the mountains. It would also please Molly to have a longer visit with her friend, Singing Woman.

Morning brought a cloudy sky over the valley. The cool night air caused a mist to rise from the river to mingle with the smoke from the cook fires already rekindled. The result was a thin gray canopy over the Crow village. Matt rolled out of the bearskin robe he used as a bedroll, being careful not to awaken Molly, who had left Singing Woman's tipi sometime during the night to snuggle in beside him by the river. He tucked the robe back around the sleeping girl and paused to gaze at her for a moment before seeking the privacy of the willows to answer nature's call.

It feels like snow, he thought as he walked back to his bed. Peering up at the cloud layer above him, he decided that they looked like snow clouds. Zeb had always maintained that he could smell snow in the air. Matt smiled at the thought. Zeb made a lot of claims that some might challenge. Matt could not be convinced that snow had any detectable odor. He was not even sure that certain clouds *looked* like snow clouds; it was just a feeling. At any rate, he felt an urgency to return to his cabin. His camp was much higher up in a mountain valley, and he had already seen scattered flurries of snow near the peaks. There was a good possibility that he would see snow at his cabin when they returned.

Molly was sitting up with the robe wrapped around her slender shoulders when he walked back up from the river. "Morning," he said. She answered with a sleepy smile and made the sign for *cold*. He smiled and replied, "It is a little chilly. Let's go get some breakfast. Then we'll start back home." She nodded, then got up to seek the privacy of the willows herself. He rolled up his bed and went to saddle the horses.

Though he never complained, it was obvious to Matt and Molly that the ride up into the mountains was extremely painful for Zeb. To reach their little valley, which was little more than a crotch between two of the higher peaks, they followed a game trail that wound up through the spruce and pine. There were many steep places where they almost lay flat on their horses' necks while the animals toiled to make the climb. During some of these stretches, Matt wondered if it might not have been wise to let Zeb remain with Singing Woman a while longer.

When they finally reached the little meadow and the cabin, Matt helped Zeb dismount. As he did, he noticed a spreading spot of fresh blood on his partner's shirt. "Damn, Zeb," he remarked. "You're bleedin' again. I was afraid the ride up might be too rough for you." He couldn't help but think of the worried look in Singing Woman's eyes as she had stood watching them depart.

"Don't pay it no mind," Zeb replied, his attempt to disguise his discomfort not quite convincing. "Hell, it's been bleedin' off and on, anyway, even when I was just layin' around Singing Woman's tipi."

Matt exchanged a quick glance with Molly. She acknowledged his feelings with a frown. Zeb didn't look good. The ride up the mountain had exhausted him. Matt had expected that, but Zeb looked old and worn out, and Matt began to worry that maybe the old man was not going to recover from his wounds.

Zeb must have read the concern in their eyes, for he was quick to assure them, "I'd druther bleed to death comin' up this mountain than lay around that Crow camp for another week. I'll be all right now. The ride up is the only part that mighta done me in, and we've already made that."

Matt just shook his head. "You old buzzard, you ain't ever gonna die, anyway. One of these days, you'll just turn into a pile of dust and blow away."

"I expect so," Zeb replied with a weak chuckle.

The first order of business was to get Zeb settled comfortably. After that, Matt took care of the horses while Molly began making some soup with a bundle of roots that Singing Woman had given her. The Crow woman claimed they would help speed up Zeb's recovery. Molly decided they couldn't hurt, so she cut up some strips of venison and threw them in the pot, thinking she and Matt could eat the soup as well. At suppertime, Zeb did appear to be feeling better, so Matt decided to go after his elk the next morning if his friend was still showing signs of improvement.

Just before dark, Matt heard the horses snorting. He knew the paint's various sounds, and this sounded like a warning snort, so he walked outside to investigate. Something had disturbed them. The paint was tossing his head nervously, and Zeb's sorrel was pawing the ground repeatedly. Matt stepped back inside the cabin door and picked up his rifle. Back outside, he walked around the back of the small corral he and Zeb had built, his eyes constantly sweeping the slope behind the cabin.

He was about to decide there was nothing there. Maybe the horses were spooked by the wind shaking a light snowfall from the branches of the fir trees on the ridge. Then he saw the cause of their concern. *Igmutaka*, he thought, the Lakota word for mountain lion, and the name the Sioux had given him. The tawny predator had watched the man come from the cabin, and now moved silently inside the tree line on the ridge, pausing once as if taking one last look at the cabin. Matt slowly raised his rifle and sighted on the big cat's right shoulder. The lion did not move. After a few long seconds, Matt lowered the rifle, reluctant to shoot the animal. There was really nothing to fear from the mountain lion. There were no chickens or dogs to be concerned for, and the big cat was not likely to approach the horses and risk getting kicked. After another moment, the mountain lion suddenly disappeared into the trees. If Matt believed in such things, he might have felt the lion's visit to his cabin to be an omen, meant to warn his namesake of the four ominous figures approaching the Crow village in the river valley below.

"Well, I'll be damned," P. D. exclaimed when she rode free of the narrow rock walls that formed the steep canyon and found herself staring at some fifty or seventy-five tipis clustered in a small meadow near the river. "Look at that! You suppose ol' Bill was tellin' the truth when he claimed this camp was just ahead?" For, in fact, they had ridden for only an hour since leaving Bill Cotton's body for the vultures. She threw her head back and laughed. "The joke's on me, boys."

"It sure is, Mama," Arlo responded, joining in the laughter.

Though finding it amusing, P. D. remarked that it

really made little difference. "Ol' Bill woulda kilt us if he got the chance, and no doubt about that."

While P. D. and Arlo were entertaining themselves with the irony of finding the village close to where Cotton had said, Bo had an eye on the Crow camp. They had already been spotted by someone in the camp, as evidenced by the gathering of several people at the edge of the river. "We'd best watch ourselves," Bo warned. "Them Injuns has already spotted us."

"Don't get jumpy," P. D. cautioned. "They're Crows—supposed to be friendly." She cast a quick glance in the direction of Arlo and Wiley. "Just keep your rifles handy where them Injuns can see 'em. They ain't likely to try nothin' with the four of us." She grinned then. "Anyway, we're just friendly folks, lookin' for one of our kin from back east."

Broken Hand got to his feet and went outside to stand in front of his lodge when he heard shouts that strangers were approaching. He squinted in the afternoon sunlight, trying to recognize what appeared to be four white men crossing the river and heading toward the village. He continued to stare until they passed the outermost tipis before deciding he had never seen them before. Each man was armed with a rifle, but they appeared to come in peace, judging by the polite exchange of greetings between them and the people who had gathered by the bank.

Judging Broken Hand to be one in authority, since the men and women at the river parted to clear a path for him when he came down to join them, P. D. directed her greeting to him. "P. D. Wildmoon's the name. These here is my boys. We've come lookin' for my cousin." She did her best to display a smile that would convince her audience that she was honest and friendly. It was difficult for P. D. because she had no use for Indians of any tribe. When Broken Hand did not reply at once, but continued to gaze at the strangers in curiosity, she asked, "You speak white man's talk?"

Broken Hand nodded, then said, "Yes."

"Good," P. D. said. "Like I said, we're lookin' for my cousin. We got an important message for him from the family back east. Some folks told me he might be stayin' around here someplace. His name's Slaughter."

Broken Hand's reaction was little more than a raised eyebrow, but the mention of Slaughter's name brought a murmur from the others gathered around the strangers. Their reaction was enough to tell P. D. that she was on the right track. "It's important that we find him," she went on. "We've got some news from his family."

Singing Woman edged up closer to her brother. Like him, she felt a sense of suspicion for the white visitors. From Zeb, they had both learned that Slaughter had enemies in the white world who sought to hunt him down. And the four sitting their horses before them now bore a decided look of deceit. She glanced at Broken Hand and frowned. It was unnecessary, for Broken Hand had already speculated that, if the four had a cousin, it would more likely be a coyote.

"If he ain't hereabouts," P. D. asked impatiently, "maybe you can tell me where I can find him?"

Broken Hand slowly shook his head. "I don't know this man Slaughter."

"Young feller—had a woman ridin' with him?" P. D. pressed. "And an old man?" Broken Hand continued to shake his head. P. D. grinned. Although Broken Hand denied knowing him, several others standing around them had automatically looked toward the eastern ridge in answer to her question. Following their gaze, she stole a quick look at the ridge. Thick with pines, the slope was cut by many game trails, leading in many directions. She then cast a sharp glance in Singing Woman's direction. The Indian woman's frown had not escaped P. D.'s notice. "Well, then," she said. "Looks like we was told wrong. I guess we'll just have to look for Cousin Slaughter somewhere else." She wheeled her horse around. "Come on, boys, let's not bother these nice folks no more."

With a polite nod to Broken Hand, she kicked her horse with her heels and started back the way they had come. Her sons followed along behind her, casting insolent sneers at the faces looking up at them, except for Wiley. He merely looked confused, unable to understand why they were leaving so soon after having traveled days just to find the village.

"Keep an eye on that camp, Arlo," P. D. said when they started to cross the river. "Let me know if you

see anybody ridin' out right away." She had a strong
hunch she was planning to follow up. She was willing to bet the bankroll she carried in her pocket that
Slaughter's camp was somewhere up the ridge now
on her right, but she continued to ride back north
along the river. Once they had rounded the bend
and were hidden from sight of the Crow village, she
turned her horse's head back to the east, spurring
the animal up the steep slope. "Well, come on," she
prompted when Arlo and Bo hesitated, not sure
where she was going.

Finding a ravine that cut between the ridge and the
tall mountain beyond it, P. D. led her sons through a
dense forest of lodgepole pines, making her way back
to a point across the river from the Crow village.
"Leave the horses here," she ordered, and climbed up
to the top of the ridge on foot, to a point where there
was a clear view of the camp.

"What are we doin' up here, Ma?" Bo asked.

"We're just gonna set a spell and watch that
camp," P. D. replied.

"I'll build us a fire," Wiley volunteered.

"No, honey, don't build no fire. They could see the
smoke across the river, and I don't want them to
know we're watchin' 'em."

Bo reached over and knocked Wiley's hat from his
head. "I'll build us a fire," Bo mocked. "Wiley, you're
dumber'n a sack of turds."

With no warning, P. D. burned a welt on Bo's back
with her rawhide whip, causing a yelp of pain from

the injured man. "I told you to quit pickin' on that boy. Now, keep your eyes on that Injun camp."

"What are we watchin' for?" Arlo asked. "You think they'll get a war party after us?"

"No. They ain't interested in us. If my hunch is right, they might lead us right to Slaughter." So they waited for about a quarter of an hour before P. D. saw what she was looking for. "I thought so, by God," she exclaimed with a chuckle. Arlo followed her gaze down toward the bank where a single rider was forging the river. It was difficult to tell at that distance, but P. D. was fairly confident that it was the Indian woman who had sidled up to Broken Hand. "Wiley, go get the horses," she calmly ordered while she got to her feet and stared after the rider.

Unaware that she was being watched, Singing Woman passed a half dozen game trails leading down from the mountain before she picked one and urged her pony to follow it. In a second, she disappeared from view, but P. D. marked the trail she had chosen, and as soon as Wiley was back with the horses, they rode down across the ridge to intercept the same trail.

It was not an easy path to follow, an old game trail leading through a forest of lodgepole pines at the base of the slope, with a thick carpet of pine needles underneath. In fact, the trail might have been impossible to follow had not Singing Woman's pony just disturbed the needles. The trail led up the mountain until it emerged from the pine forest and abruptly turned to lead almost straight up through a maze of boulders and fir trees until reaching a ledge of solid rock with trails branching off in three different directions. With no evidence of tracks on the rock, P. D. had to make a decision. She picked the one that was widest and appeared to continue in the same direction they had been climbing.

They followed the rocky trail, climbing higher up the mountain until it leveled off and descended once more, seeming to double back. After more than a half hour's ride, they arrived back at the same rock ledge. "Dammit!" P. D. exclaimed. "We just rode around in a circle. Bo, get down and find that pony's tracks." Of her three sons, Bo was by far the best tracker. He dismounted and began examining the ground around the other two trails.

"Here's where a horse kicked up some rocks!" Wiley panted excitedly.

P. D., irritated at this point for having wasted over half an hour riding in a circle, had lost her usual patience with her youngest. "Wiley, dammit, them's our tracks. We just rode around that trail." She jerked her head around at once to cast a menacing eye on Bo, who was already grinning at his brother. "You keep your mouth shut and find me the right trail."

Bo, still smirking at his slow-witted brother, dismounted and started out along one of the other trails, walking in a half crouch, his head down, eyes searching the rocky path. P. D. motioned to Arlo. "You might as well start lookin' up that other trail."

Bo followed the trail until he finally left the solid rock floor and came to an area of loose shale. He stopped and looked up the trail ahead, shaking his head in resignation. Then he called back to his mother, "I reckon it's the other trail—ain't no horse or nothin' else crossed over this shale without leavin' tracks."

At almost the same time, Arlo sang out, "I got her! Here's the trail!" He waited for the others to catch up to him. "There's more'n one set of tracks that are pretty fresh."

P. D. didn't bother to dismount to examine them. "Well, let's get goin' then. We've already wasted enough time runnin' around in circles."

Chapter 9

A light tap on his shoulder brought Zeb abruptly back from a dream of chasing antelope across a wide prairie. Still drowsy, he jerked his head up to see what had disturbed such a pleasant vision. Molly was standing before him, signaling for him to listen. His hearing not being as sharp as hers, he was puzzled at first. "What is it?" he asked. "Whaddaya hear?" She signed that someone was coming. He was immediately alert then.

He struggled to get up from the side of the cabin where he had been snoozing in the sunshine. Molly extended her hand to help him up. On his feet, his makeshift crutches under his arms, he stood listening for a few moments before he heard the sound of a horse making the last steep climb up to the stream. "Better fetch me my rifle, honey," he said to Molly. She went at once to get it. They were not accustomed to having visitors. Once in a great while, someone from the Crow village might visit, but not very often, so it paid to be cautious.

Still moving with a great deal of discomfort, Zeb moved over to the corner of the little cabin and waited, his gaze locked on the fir trees where the trail crossed the stream. Molly retreated to stand in the cabin door to watch. In a few minutes, a horse topped the rise, carrying a familiar figure.

"Well, lookee here, Molly," Zeb exclaimed when he recognized Singing Woman. "Looks like we got company." Taking a few unsteady steps away from the cabin, he moved to meet the Indian woman. "So you started missin' me already," he started to say, but his voice trailed off when he saw the serious expression on Singing Woman's face. He took hold of the bridle while she slid off her pony's back.

"Some white men came to our village looking for Slaughter," Singing Woman said, her voice reflecting the concern Zeb had read in her face.

Zeb glanced briefly at Molly, who was now at his elbow, then back to the Indian woman. "White men?" he asked. "Were they soldiers?"

"No, not soldiers," Singing Woman answered excitedly. "Four white men, bad-looking white men. The one older man said he was Slaughter's cousin."

Instinctively, Zeb glanced quickly over her shoulder to make sure there was no one behind her. "Did you tell 'em how to get here?"

"No. Broken Hand told them he did not know the man they looked for. They went back up the river, the way they had come. I waited until they had gone before I rode up here."

"Good," Zeb said. "Matt ain't here. He's gone

huntin'. I don't know if he's got any cousins he wants to see or not, but I kinda doubt it." It entered his mind that the four might be bounty hunters. "Four of 'em, you say? What'd they look like?"

"Bad—they looked like bad men—one older man, three younger men."

Zeb scratched his beard while he thought about it. He didn't know what to make of it, four men looking for Matt, but he could fairly well assume that it meant trouble. Maybe they were friends of the Frenchman. "You say they went back up toward the Yellow-stone?" Singing Woman nodded. "Well," he decided, "maybe they're gone to look somewhere else. We'll keep a sharp eye for a spell. We 'preciate you ridin' up here to tell us."

Molly listened to the exchange between Zeb and the Crow woman, her face etched with a concerned frown. She wished that Matt was there, but he had said he would probably not be back for a couple of days, depending on his luck in finding an elk. Singing Woman had said that the men had gone back the way they had come, so maybe she was worrying need-lessly. She decided that was the case. Tapping Singing Woman lightly on the arm to get her attention, she asked in sign if her Crow friend was hungry.

Singing Woman started to answer in sign, then re-membered that Molly was not deaf. "No. Thank you, but I better not stay. I want to get back before dark."

"You'd best rest that horse for a little spell," Zeb said. "Looks like you rode him pretty hard comin' up this mountain."

Singing Woman smiled at him fondly. The old trapper had wormed his way into her heart since he and Slaughter had built their cabin in the mountains above her village. She turned to Molly. "Did you make him soup from the roots I gave you?" Molly nodded with a smile. Back to Zeb, she said, "It will make you strong again." She favored him with an impish smile. "Then you can come to visit me again."

Singing Woman started back down the mountain after a short visit with Zeb and Molly. It was getting on in the afternoon, and she didn't want to delay her return to the village. The trail could be treacherous in the dark, with many steep stretches and sharp turns through trees and boulders.

Reining back on her pony to prevent the horse from sliding on a steep patch of loose shale, she carefully guided him around a cabin-sized boulder where the trail almost doubled back on itself. Rounding the side of the huge rock, she found herself face-to-face with P. D. Wildmoon. The swarthy female bounty hunter sat on her horse, effectively blocking the narrow path, her rifle lying across her thighs, a bemused grin displayed upon her broad face. "Well, hello there, honey. I reckon you've been up to tell Slaughter we're lookin' for him, ain'tcha?"

Singing Woman tried to back her pony away, but Arlo appeared from the back side of the boulder and rode his horse up to block hers. Seeing that she was trapped, she said, "Slaughter is not there. I could not warn him. Now, let me pass."

Her comments caused P. D. to chuckle. "He ain't there, huh? I don't know why I don't believe you. Earlier this mornin', you said you didn't even know him. Whaddaya think, boys? Think we oughta just turn around? The little Injun woman says he ain't there."

"Reckon we oughta," Bo replied, enjoying the game. He stood up from where he had been lying in wait on top of the boulder. "She sure has got pretty black hair," he commented, thinking of the string of scalps he carried in his saddlebags.

"Let me pass," Singing Woman repeated, realizing she was in grave danger, but trying her best to conceal her fear.

"Now, honey, you know I can't do that and let you go down there and tell all your Injun friends," P. D. replied. She winked at Bo then, and with a mischievous twinkle in her eye said, " 'Course maybe you'd promise you wouldn't tell nobody we're up here."

Desperate for any chance to escape, Singing Woman said, "I won't tell." There was no possible way to get back to warn Zeb and Molly. All she could hope for was to save herself. With no response from P. D., other than a scornful sneer for her agreement not to tell, she had no choice left to her. With a sudden kick with her heels, she attempted to force her pony past P. D.'s. Ready for such a move, P. D. braced herself and held firm. Bellowing like an excited bull, Bo leaped from the top of the boulder, catching Singing Woman by her shoulders, and the two of them landed on the ground almost under her pony's hooves.

Grabbing her by her wrists, Bo dragged the dazed woman out of the way of her frightened pony's feet. Brief seconds later, he was joined by his two brothers, each one anxious to help hold the struggling Indian woman down. Spotting the skinning knife Singing Woman wore on a deerskin belt, Bo drew the weapon with his free hand and examined the blade. "You keep a keen edge on this here knife," he taunted. "I bet it would be just the thing to take that pretty black hair."

"Hold on a minute," P. D. ordered. "I wanna talk to her." She cast a stern eye toward her youngest son, who was taking advantage of the opportunity to grope the helpless woman. "Wiley!" she scolded. "She ain't nothin' but a damn Injun." Wiley grinned sheepishly, but did not remove his hand from the helpless woman's breast. Thrusting her face down almost in Singing Woman's, P. D. said, "Is he up ahead somewhere? How many's with him?" she asked, smiling, then whispered, "If you was to tell me, I might let you go."

Knowing that to be a lie, Singing Woman's reply was to spit in her face.

"Damn you!" P. D. exploded. "Kill her, Bo."

Bo gleefully responded by shoving the knife to the hilt under Singing Woman's ribs. The Crow woman grunted heavily, arching her back as she strained against her captors, and then exhaled noisily. Bo withdrew the knife and thrust it deep into her abdomen again, grinning as she trembled violently before collapsing limply on the rocky path, no longer straining against her captors.

"I don't reckon you'll be goin' to get no war party." P. D. smirked as she wiped Singing Woman's spittle from her face.

Bo wasted little time in scalping the dying Crow woman. Wylie remained wide-eyed, gaping at his brother as he performed the grisly mutilation. Arlo, a less fascinated observer, asked, "What the hell are you gonna do with all them scalps you've been carryin' around?"

"I ain't decided," Bo replied, and held his trophy up to admire. "Maybe I'll braid me a rope out of 'em. That'ud be somethin', wouldn't it? Wouldn't take many more and I'd have enough."

"Quit that jawin' and let's get goin'," P. D. scolded. "We got work to do." She had little patience with Bo's fondness for his macabre trophies, but she supposed there was little harm in it—no more than collecting animal pelts.

"She ain't dead yet," Wiley said. While Bo had been busy with his knife, Wiley had taken advantage of the opportunity to fondle the fatally wounded woman's breast again. "I felt her move a little bit." He pulled out his pistol. "I'll finish her off."

Before he could bring the weapon up to aim it, P. D. struck him hard across his face with her whip. "Dammit, Wiley!" she blurted. "Ain't you got no sense a'tall? You shoot that pistol, and ever'body miles around would hear it."

Bo started to slap his younger brother on the back of the head, but seeing the look in his mother's eye he thought better of it, and decided to settle for a verbal insult. "I swear, Wiley, if dumb was water, you'da done drowned in it."

"Well, she's still alive," Wiley pouted.

"She won't be long," P. D. said. "Drag her outta the way, and get mounted. I'd like to find this Slaughter jasper before Christmas. Arlo, take hold of that horse and bring him along."

Bo took Singing Woman by her wrists and dragged her body over to the side of the narrow trail. Then he stood aside while his mother passed, followed by Arlo leading Singing Woman's horse. After they had started up the trail, he turned to Wiley. "Come on, dummy," he said, and went to retrieve his horse from behind the boulder.

After following the steep trail for another fifteen minutes, they came upon a waterfall, created by a small stream that flowed over a cliff above them. P. D. held up her hand to halt the boys while she studied the trail before them. Looking above the waterfall, she could see blue sky. On either side there were mountain peaks that blocked her view of the sky, so it appeared that the stream probably ran through a clearing, possibly a crotch between the two mountains. "We'd best take 'er slow from here on," she cautioned. "Arlo, go on up ahead and see what's on top of that rise."

"Yessum," Arlo replied, handing the Indian pony's reins to Wiley and pushing on past P. D. He followed the winding trail as it wove its way through the scrubby pines and firs, stopping to dismount before cresting the slope. Going the rest of the way up the cliff on foot, he stopped just short of level ground, and inched up to take a look beyond on his belly. After a long look, he scrambled back down to his horse and returned to make his report.

"It's his place, all right," Arlo said upon reaching P. D. and his brothers, waiting on the trail below. "He's got a cabin up there in a little valley."

"Did you see him?" P. D. asked anxiously. The thought of the balance of the reward money finally moving within reach was enough to stir a little excitement in her mind.

"No," Arlo answered. "I didn't see nobody outside the cabin. There's a fire goin' inside, though. There's some horses in a little corral beside the cabin."

P. D. gave Arlo's report a few minutes' thought. It sounded like there was somebody home in the cabin, but she hesitated to attack it without first knowing just who was inside. According to what the lawyer, Jonathan Mathis, had told her, Slaughter was traveling with a young woman and an older man. It wouldn't do to go into that clearing with guns blazing, only to find that Slaughter wasn't there, possibly scaring him off for good. She squinted up at the sky. The sun was already past the peak of the mountain to the west of the valley. There would not be much time before dark. "We'd best circle around and get up on that mountain above the cabin, where we can watch 'em for a while till we see what's what."

*   *   *

Molly picked up her bucket, and walked down to the stream to fill it with fresh water. Zeb was inside by the fire. The old man was not healing very rapidly from his wounds. She would have to boil some more of the roots Singing Woman had brought. Zeb had eaten the soup she had first made with the roots, but he had balked at sipping some tea Molly had brewed with them. *The old buzzard,* she thought fondly. *I'm gonna cure him in spite of himself.*

Feeling a breeze freshen down the valley, she paused to breathe in the cool fall air. As the wayward breeze combed the needles of the fir trees behind the cabin, causing the horses to nicker, she looked toward the far end of the tiny valley. Their little valley was already draped in shadows. Soon it would be dark. She sighed, knowing it was unlikely Matt would be back that night.

Her bucket full, she started back to the cabin, feeling the chilly breeze upon her back. It made her shiver, thinking of the cold weather that would soon be coming. The horses were moving about in their small corral. Zeb's horse snorted as she approached the cabin door. Molly paused before entering. She was suddenly struck by a feeling that there was something out there. She stood still for a few minutes and listened. She heard nothing but the wind. *Maybe that mountain lion Matt saw last night is prowling around again,* she thought, and dismissed her concern.

Inside, Zeb looked up and gave her a smile when she came in. "It's startin' to get a mite chilly outside, ain't it?" She nodded in response. "I expect we're gonna see some snow pretty soon."

She placed her bucket of water on the stone hearth and picked up the plate of stew she had given him for supper. He still had very little appetite. Only half of the stew had been eaten before he pushed the plate aside, and he had moved his chair over by the fireplace. She shook her head and signed, *Eat—make strong.*

"I just ain't hungry," he replied.

She sighed, as if dealing with a difficult child. Then she picked up his cup. Finding it still filled to the top with Singing Woman's herbal brew, she stomped her foot in mock anger, barely making a sound on the earthen floor of the cabin. He pretended not to notice, looking away from her—a game he liked to play when she tried to scold him. She punched him on the shoulder, but he still refused to look at her, pretending to doze. Fully aware of the little charade he was playing, she picked up the dipper and scooped up a cup of water from the bucket.

"Hold on!" he quickly protested. "I'm hearin' you." He couldn't help but chuckle, knowing how close he had come to getting a bath. He looked directly at her then, taking the scolding she intended. Her sign vocabulary was extensive, but he always made it difficult for her whenever she was trying to scold him. Feigning confusion, he would shake his head and constantly interrupt with "Who? What?" until she would stamp her foot in anger. In the end, he would concede to her determination, and take a few sips of the bitter liquid. Then she would stand over him until he drank it down.

"I can't drink no more of that stuff," he stated vehemently and banged the tin cup down firmly on the table. Satisfied that she had forced him to drink more than half of the dose, she relented and left him to sit by the fire in peace. After a few minutes, however, he got up from the bench, grumbling with the pain the movement caused. "I swear, that stuff runs right through you. I don't see how in hell it can do you any good. It don't stay with you long enough to, just runs right on through." He hobbled slowly to the door on his crutches and went out, leaving her to look after him, shaking her head in exasperation.

Outside, Zeb paused by the door to let his eyes adjust to the deepening darkness. Then, using only one crutch, and one hand on the log wall to steady himself, he made his way around the corner to the side of the cabin where he performed his toilet. Normally, he relieved himself in the cover of the forest, but he found it painful to walk that far with a broken leg, and it was already getting dark anyway. Leaning with one hand on the cabin wall for support, he managed to get his business done, and was in the process of tying up his trousers again when struck.

Zeb knew in that moment that he had erred fatally. The dirty hand that clamped down tightly over his mouth stifled his attempt to cry out a warning to Molly at almost the same instant that his body tensed in response to the cold steel blade that plunged into his side. Already weak from his slowly healing gunshot wounds, he nevertheless retained the will to fight his assailant even as the long skinning knife was withdrawn and thrust deep into his side again. His efforts were useless in the face of Arlo Wildmoon's strength, and within minutes the determination to resist faded with the draining of his soul from his body. Zeb slumped to the ground at Arlo's feet.

"I thought for a minute there I was gonna have to help you," Bo whispered.

"Shit," Arlo scoffed indignantly.

"Quiet!" P. D. whispered.

Inside the cabin, Molly paused to listen. She wasn't certain, but she thought that she might have heard a muffled voice. Maybe she had just imagined it. On the other hand, possibly Zeb was calling for her. In his weakened condition, he could have stumbled and caused his wounds to bleed again. Any other time, she would have immediately gone to see if he was all right. But since she knew the purpose of his trip outside, she was reluctant to rush out and embarrass him. *I'll wait a bit*, she decided, and went back to the meat she was tending over the fire.

A few minutes passed and she heard him at the door. Whatever the sound she thought she had heard before, he was evidently all right. She didn't bother turning to look at him as the door creaked open. When he did not speak, she turned to ask him if he was hungry. Astonished at first to discover a short, barrel-shaped man standing in the open doorway, she was frozen for an instant. When she recovered partially from the shock of a stranger standing in her

cabin, she glanced beyond P. D. to see if Zeb was behind. Instead, two more strange men followed the
short, stocky figure. These two were obviously
younger and considerably more formidable. They
filed into the room, standing on either side of the
older one, a wide grin spread across each face.

No one spoke as the three just stood, glaring at her
with their insipid smiles in place. Confused and
frightened, she looked toward the open door, waiting
for Zeb to come in to explain. After a long moment,
and no sign of Zeb, cold terror began to creep into her
veins. She glanced nervously at Zeb's rifle propped in
the corner. P. D. followed her gaze, and finally broke
the silence. "I don't hardly think so, honey." She
jabbed Wiley in the shoulder and motioned toward
the rifle. He immediately went to retrieve it. Molly's
attention was drawn back to the door again when
Arlo entered the cabin, wiping a bloody knife on a
piece of buckskin cut from Zeb's shirt. The full force
of what had just occurred struck her then, turning her
blood to ice and her brain numb with the inability to
accept it. Her knees threatened to buckle under her as
she stood helplessly before the intruders. There was
no place to run, even if her legs would support her
flight, for the four stood blocking the only way out.

"Where's Slaughter?" P. D. demanded calmly.

Still in a partial state of shock, Molly could not respond at once. P. D. walked over to the frightened girl
to stand face-to-face. "Where's Slaughter?" she repeated, this time in a voice not so patient. When
Molly made no response, P. D. slapped her hard

across the face, hard enough that Molly had to take a step backward to keep from falling.

"She can't say, Ma," Arlo reminded his mother. "That lawyer feller said she can't talk."

P. D. chuckled then, as if she had been the victim of a clever joke. "Damn, that's right. I plum forgot about that." Looking back at Molly again, she said, "You shoulda said somethin', honey." Then she laughed again, this time at her own joke.

Her sons joined in the laughter, all except Wiley, who started to remind his mother again. "She *can't*, Ma . . ." Bo promptly reached over and popped Wiley on the back of the head, leaving the confused young man clueless as to the reason for his brother's abuse.

"Leave him be, Bo," P. D. lectured sternly. Then, turning her attention back to focus squarely upon the frightened woman, she said, "Deef and dumb, that sure-nuff makes it hard to get any answers outta you, don't it, honey?"

Molly gave no indication that she understood, simply staring with eyes glazed with fear and held captive by the cold gaze of P. D. Her mind, numb up to that moment, began to function once more. *They referred to her as Ma,* she thought, realizing that P. D. was, in fact, a woman. The discovery gave her a flicker of hope that she might not be about to face her death after all. Moments later, she found that mercy and compassion were traits that took no root in P. D. Wildmoon's soul.

P. D. took a closer look at the frightened young woman, noticing for the first time the slight bulge in the otherwise loose-fitting deerskin shirt. "I swear, looks to me like you done got yourself pregnant. Look at that, boys, the little lady is gonna have pups. "Well, little lady," P. D. concluded, "I reckon you ain't no use to us if you can't talk."

"Whaddaya gonna do, Ma?" The question came from Bo.

P. D. answered calmly, "Well, I reckon I'm gonna shoot her. Then we won't hafta worry about the dummy sneakin' up on one of us with a knife." The fearful reaction in Molly's gaze caught P. D.'s attention. "Wait a minute," she said. "You understood that, didn't you? Boys, I believe little yeller-hair here knows what we're sayin'. Don't you, honey?" she demanded. When Molly still made no response, she pulled her pistol and pointed it at Molly's forehead. Terrified, Molly nodded. "I thought so," P. D. snorted. "Is Slaughter comin' back tonight?" Molly shook her head. "Is he comin' back tomorrow?" Not sure when Matt would return, Molly could not say yes or no. She tried to convey that with sign language. "I can't understand that Injun talk," P. D. responded. Then she guessed, "You ain't sure when he'll be back. Is that right?" Molly nodded.

P. D. thought about it for a moment. She still didn't know if Slaughter was gone for a long time, or just a short hunting trip. Most likely, she decided, he would be back by morning or later in the afternoon. At any rate, she saw no further use for the girl. "Well, I reckon we'll just make ourselves comfortable, and wait for Slaughter to show up. Most likely he'll turn up pretty soon." She raised her pistol again and pointed it at Molly. "But I reckon we don't need you anymore, darlin'," she said as she cocked the weapon. "Ain't nothin' personal. I just don't fancy havin' you sneakin' up behind me with a knife."

"Wait a minute, Ma!" Bo interrupted. "I want her." His outburst was only seconds ahead of one about to come from Arlo. "Hell, ain't no use to shoot her yet."

"That's right," Arlo chimed in. "Only Bo ain't got no claim on her. I'm the oldest. I oughta get first claim."

P. D. released the hammer slowly while she paused to consider her sons' reaction. She was still of the opinion that a dead girl posed the fewest problems, but she understood the desire that prompted the boys' reaction. After all, she had desires herself about once a year, and her sons had precious few opportunities to consort with women who didn't do it for money. Maybe it wouldn't hurt to have somebody to do the cooking and chores while they waited for her husband to return—if they were married—which she doubted. The decision made, she returned the pistol to her holster.

"All right," P. D. said. "You can keep her, but I don't want no fightin' over the little bitch, or I'll shoot her in a minute. Arlo's right; he's the oldest. He oughta have her first." Arlo glanced toward Bo and smirked.

"Dammit, Ma," Bo complained, "that ain't fair. I spoke up first."

"I'll say what's fair and what ain't," P. D. responded,

watching Molly's reaction closely while the two brothers argued over her fate. "You're both gonna be responsible for watchin' her every minute. She might look frail, but she's liable to slip a knife between your ribs if you give her half a chance. First off, she's gonna finish cookin' that meat for our supper." Molly backed away fearfully when P. D. stuck a finger in her face to emphasize her words. "Before you eat, though, Bo, you and Wiley drag that old man somewhere outta sight, then take them horses off somewhere away from the cabin where nobody can see 'em. I don't want Mr. Slaughter to see he's got company."

"What about Arlo?" Bo wanted to know. "What's he gonna be doin' while me and Wiley are doing all the chores?"

"Well, he ain't gonna be humpin' on no little gal," P. D. snorted. "Not in front of his mama. Now, get."

"Come on, Wiley," Bo said, still irritated by having to concede to his older brother, and stomped out the door.

Wiley, in a state of confusion, a state in which he often resided, paused before following his brother. Unlike his two older brothers, Wiley sometimes had difficulty sorting things out in his mind. He was confused now by his mother's casual decision to kill the girl. He understood the murder of Bill Cotton. Like P. D. had said, Cotton was figuring on killing all of them. As for the hapless Crow woman, she was nothing more than an Indian. He was undecided about the killing of the old man. Maybe it was necessary.

But the fair young white woman had done nothing wrong, although when he thought about it, P. D. had warned that Molly would try to kill one of them if she got the chance. P. D. was always right, so he supposed it was disrespectful on his part to question her. That settled in his simple brain, he turned his thoughts again toward the young pregnant woman. He had never had an opportunity to know a woman in the most intimate sense, and his head was filled with curiosity over the pleasures of the flesh. Why should Arlo and Bo be allowed those pleasures, and not himself? "What about me, Ma?" he asked, glancing toward the terrified girl backed against the wall.

P. D. followed his gaze, and replied, "You've still got plenty of time before you need to worry about rollin' in the hay with some floozy." Seeing the disappointment in his eyes, she said, "We'll see. Now go on and tend the horses." She almost succeeded in constructing a motherly expression as she watched her favorite exit the cabin. It was replaced in an instant when she returned her gaze to fall upon the hapless girl cowering near the fireplace. "Tend to that meat! I'm hungry."

Chapter 10

With constantly trembling hands, and the feeling of ice water flowing through her veins, Molly served her four unholy guests while at least three sets of eyes watched her every move. Feeling almost paralyzed by desperation and the hopelessness of her situation, her thoughts bounded back and forth between her fear for Matt and the dread of what awaited her. Who these people were, she had no idea. That they came for Matt was the one thing she knew for certain. Whether they came to kill or capture, she could only speculate what was in the minds of this treacherous woman who looked like a man and her loathsome sons. They might kill him on sight, just as they had murdered Zeb. Then they would kill her, too, as soon as they were finished with her. She felt she must find some way to warn Matt, but she was helpless to do so at this point.

The meal quickly devoured by the men, Arlo was the first to stand up and announce, "I'm ready to turn in." His eyes locked on Molly.

"I'll just bet you are," Bo responded at once. "I reckon I am, too." He got up to stand beside his brother.

"What the hell do you think you're doin'?" Arlo demanded. "You ain't invited."

P. D., still taking her time to stuff herself with the last of the venison from the spit, interrupted. "Before you young studs get yourselves in a lather, I'm gonna tell you what you're gonna do. We're gonna have to stand guard tonight in case Slaughter comes back before mornin'. Bo, you take the first watch. After a couple of hours, Arlo can take over, and you can take your turn with the woman," she added impatiently. "Wiley can spell you and I'll finish her up."

Filled with terror and a loathing for what the night promised, Molly tried to think of anything to delay the inevitable. She made motions that she should clean the tin plates they had eaten on. "To hell with the dishes," P. D. scoffed. "Go on outta here with her," she said to Arlo. "I don't wanna hear your gruntin' and groanin'."

"Come on, sweetheart," Arlo said, taking Molly by the arm while giving Bo a snide smile. To his brother, he said, "You'd best get your ass out there and watch for Slaughter."

Molly tried to draw back, defying Arlo, but he was a strong brute of a man, and barely noticed her resistance. Desperate then, she tried to make frantic motions with her hands, which only served to confuse Arlo. "What the hell's the matter with her?" he blurted.

P. D. laughed, amused now by her son's awkward impatience to satisfy his lust. "She has to pee." Then, warning him, she said, "You make sure you keep an eye on her."

Arlo pulled Molly out the door. He was followed by his two brothers. P. D. remained seated at the rough plank table. She shook her head and chuckled when she heard Arlo say, "Where the hell do you two think you're goin'?"

"I'm gonna keep an eye on her, too," Bo replied.

"Me, too," Wiley said. "I can watch her pee, same as you."

Inside the cabin, P. D. chuckled again as their voices faded away. They were sons any mother would be proud of, she thought.

Before being dragged out of the cabin, Molly had actually felt the need to relieve herself. But outside, even in the dark, she found it impossible to accomplish this with the three lecherous brothers watching intently. After a long wait, Arlo became impatient. "All right, dammit, that's long enough." He grabbed for her, but she dodged his hand and tried to run.

Bo was upon her before she had run five yards. "Hod-a-mighty!" he yelled as he tackled her, pawing and groping her all over as she struggled against him. Trying to stop her flailing arms with one hand while he pulled her skirt up with the other, he exclaimed gleefully, "Look at that! She's wearin' them long leggin's like a damn Injun." He didn't have time to say more before Arlo grabbed him by one ankle and dragged him off of Molly.

"You can get your ass over by the corner of that corral and keep an eye out for Slaughter like Ma told you!" Arlo scolded. Bo struggled and kicked at his brother with his free foot, but to no avail. He was forcefully hauled several yards before Arlo released him.

"Ma said to hide the horses first," Wiley, an interested spectator to that point, reminded his brothers.

"Yeah, Wiley," Bo replied. "Why don't you do that? Me and Arlo has got to take care of the little lady."

"The hell you say," Arlo responded. "There ain't no me and you about it. You get your turn after I'm done with her. You heard Ma. Now help Wiley with them horses before I have to kick your butt."

"That might be a little more than you can handle," Bo shot back defiantly. The response was nothing more than an empty boast, however. Bo knew Arlo was stronger than he when it came to a fistfight or a wrestling match. He glared at his older brother for an extended moment before getting to his feet. "Come on, Wiley. We'd best do what Ma said."

Arlo pulled Molly to her feet and held her by the arm while he watched Bo and Wiley collect the horses. Once they had disappeared into the stand of pine trees above the cabin, he pushed her toward the back of the corral. With an ever-growing sense of panic, she stumbled along, knowing she could not resist the brute's physical dominance. In her mind was the terrifying thought that she was going to die no matter what happened in the next few hours. She made up her mind then that she was not going to make it easy for them. That determination served to give her failing nervous system new life. When he started to pull her to the ground, she balked, shaking her head. He drew back his hand, preparing to strike her, but she quickly held up her hand, then pointed toward the trees behind the cabin.

Puzzled, he hesitated. "You wanna go over there?" he asked. She nodded. Thinking that she had decided to accept her fate, he said, "Maybe that would be a better place. Easier on my knees in the pine needles."

He led her just inside the trees, and immediately started unbuckling his belt. She started to slowly back away. "Oh, no, you don't," he said. Taking her arm again, he forced her down upon the pine needles. She tried to get up, but she was held down by his massive body. She fought him with all the strength she could muster, but he was gradually overcoming her resistance, finally succeeding in forcing her legs apart. In desperation, her fingers clawed at the pine needles until she felt the rocky soil beneath. Clutching a handful of the gritty soil, she threw it in his face when he leaned close in an effort to kiss her.

"Damn you!" he roared when the grit struck him in his eyes. "I oughta kill you right now!" He rocked back on his heels, and tried to wipe the offending soil from his eyes.

"You sure have got a way with the ladies." The voice came from right behind him as Bo suddenly appeared from the darkness. "You ain't doin' no good. Get offa her and lemme show you how to treat a woman."

Enraged, his eyes still stinging from the grit, Arlo was in no mood to suffer Bo's taunts. "Get the hell away from here before I break your back for you," he threatened gruffly.

"Aw, now, brother, you ought'n let your mouth make no promises your ass can't keep." He reached down to place a hand on Molly's breast. "Hop off her, and I'll get a little before I go on guard duty."

Already at the breaking point in his rage, Bo's taunts were the spark that lit the big man's fuse. Without further warning, he suddenly hurled himself into Bo, knocking him backward, the two of them crashing over and over in the thick brush. Rolling almost out in the open at the edge of the trees, they grappled, each one seeking the advantage. It quickly went to the stronger man, however, and soon Arlo was on top of Bo, hammering him with lefts and rights.

A witness to all this, Wiley stood watching, following the two combatants as they rolled down toward the back of the cabin. When it was obvious that the fight was effectively over, and with the prospect that Arlo was going to bludgeon Bo to death, Wiley tried to intervene. "Arlo!" he cried. "Stop! You're gonna kill him!" He grabbed the back of Arlo's shirt, and tried to pull him away.

Still in a fit of rage, Arlo finally heard Wiley's pleas, and paused. Then, giving Bo one more fist in the mouth, he relented. Getting to his feet, he said, "Get him on away from here, or I'll damn-sure kill him." Brushing his trousers off briefly, he returned to the pine thicket. Molly was gone.

"Damn you and your lustful ways!" P. D. screeched and laid into the backs of her two eldest sons with her rawhide whip. "Find that bitch! She'll be runnin' straight to warn Slaughter, and you damn-sure better find her before she does." The whip snapped like a rifle shot as it kissed Bo's behind, causing him to yelp in pain. Both men hunkered down subserviently, cowering before their mother's rage until she tired of the lashing.

When the beating was over and P. D. had calmed down, Arlo got painfully to his feet. Bo was considerably slower in accomplishing the same, having suffered not only his mother's rage, but still feeling the effects of the sound beating he had just absorbed at the hands of his brother. "I ain't sure we can track her in the dark, Mama," Arlo said.

"You damn-sure better," P. D. fired back. "Get up that mountain and look for her. She can't get far."

There was no hesitation as all three jumped to obey her command. At the pine thicket where Arlo had laid Molly down, he paused to look back at his mother. "What if Slaughter comes back while we're gone?" he asked.

"Then I'll damn-sure shoot his ass," P. D. replied. Then, after a moment's pause, she said, "I'll keep Wiley here with me just in case."

"I'll get the horses," Bo volunteered, but P. D. held up a hand to stop him.

"You don't need no horse," she said. "She ain't got no horse. Get up through them trees and root her out." Without further delay, both men scrambled up through the trees, vanishing in the darkness.

"They'd break their necks tryin' to ride a horse up that mountain in the dark," Wiley said as he and P. D. returned to the cabin.

"Why, that's a fact," she said, surprised by the sensible remark from her youngest. "You seen that right off, didn't you, son?" She reached over and patted Wiley on the back. "Let that be a lesson to you. See what happens when you let your britches get in the way of your business." She glanced back toward the darkened mountainside, her voice stern again. "If their foolishness causes me to lose that Slaughter feller, I'll take the hide off both of 'em."

Huddled in the crevice of a large boulder above the tree line, Molly strained to control her heavy breathing, her heart still pumping solidly after her rapid climb up the steep slope. At least one hundred feet below her, she could hear the thrashing around in a thicket as Arlo and Bo stumbled in the dark, cursing and panting when they blundered into unseen limbs and underbrush.

When the two brothers had been distracted by their lust for her, she had slipped away into the forest. Climbing for all she was worth, ignoring the slaps and scratches encountered in the dark thicket, she pushed onward until she had what she judged to be a safe distance between herself and her pursuers.

Now, upon hearing the confusion below her, she decided it was safer to stay put, right where she was, for to keep going she would have to cross over some very rugged ledges and gullies in the dark. The pause also gave her time to think about her situation.

She had no idea which direction Matt might be coming from. Chances of finding him were slim at best. She had had no choice of escape routes, anyway, even had there been time to think about it. Alone, with no weapon, not even a knife, the only thing she had was a flint and steel in the pocket of her deerskin shirt. With no notion as to how long she had hidden in the crevice, she suddenly realized that it had been some time since she had heard her pursuers. Alarmed at first, thinking that they might be sneaking silently along the rock ledge that led to the boulder she was hiding in, her heart began to beat rapidly once again. Holding very still, afraid to even breathe, she listened, straining to hear even a faint sound that would tell her they were near.

Afraid to leave her hiding place, while fearful that she might be trapped in the fissure, she waited, listening. Moments passed, then minutes, with no sound. A single beam of light suddenly danced across the rocky ledge before the crevice as a full moon began its climb up over the mountain. Her heart skipped a beat then, fearful that the mountaintop would soon be bathed in moonlight. At that moment, she heard a distant voice, as one of the brothers called to the other, and she realized that they had gone in the opposite direction and were heading away from her, toward the far side of the mountain.

This, she realized, was her chance to escape. Now the moonlight was welcome, for it would light her way across the ledges and down the side of the mountain. With luck, she might be able to make her way down to Broken Hand's village when morning came.

He had been fortunate to get close enough to the elk cow to take the shot with his bow. Leaving the paint and his packhorse in a small pocket halfway up the slope, he had climbed up through the rocks before daylight, barely able to see two feet ahead of him. The moon had settled behind the neighboring mountain by the time he reached the high meadow and settled beside a small boulder to await the dawn. He scanned the area around him, trying to get a clear picture in the predawn darkness. The open meadow was a feeding place for elk. He had seen sign there the day before. Off to his right there had appeared to be several large bushes. It had been hard to make them out in the darkness, but he didn't recall noticing them before, when he was up there in the daylight.

He had to laugh when he thought about it. With his rifle as backup, in case he didn't get close enough for the bow, he had sat with his back against the rock awaiting the first rays of the sun. Just as objects around him began to take definitive shape in the gray light, the large bushes on his right began to move. He had realized only then that he had crawled up in the middle of a herd of elk. Unaware of the man's presence, the huge animals had begun to wander out into the meadow. Matt had simply waited behind his rock until a large cow passed close to him.

Zeb would get a good chuckle out of it—the supposedly skilled tracker sitting dumbly in the middle of a herd of elk without even knowing it. *Maybe I won't even tell him how I got the elk,* he thought, smiling to himself as he tied a rope around a hoof. That done, he threw the other end over a tree limb and hauled on the rope, lifting the cow's leg up in the air. With the rope tied off around the tree trunk, he could more easily begin the butchering.

Satisfied that he had plenty of meat to put back in case of a hard winter, he started back toward home. Leading the packhorse, he guided the paint down through a forest of young spruce trees interspersed with larger, burned-out trunks, the result of a lightning strike five years or so before. As he rocked along, his body as one with the easy gait of the paint pony, he thought about the young woman waiting back at the cabin. He had never set out to get married, never wanted to have a woman to worry about. And as he thought back over the past couple of years, he couldn't remember a particular time when he had changed his mind. In all honesty, he had to confess, he *never had* changed his mind. Molly had changed it for him, and he freely admitted to himself that he was happy as hell that she had. The thought made him anxious to get back to his little family. Zeb had become like family. The old man was almost as excited about the arrival of Molly's baby as she was, and had taken to referring to himself as "Uncle Zeb." The thought made him smile. "Uncle Zeb," he murmured under his breath, and the image of the old scout sitting in front of the cabin dandling a baby on his knee suddenly struck another thought. He was now a family man, like his brother Owen, and it occurred to him that he was ready for the transition. Having known so much violence in his young years, he felt he was now at a place in his life where he could live peacefully. With the war against the Sioux to occupy them, surely the army was no longer concerned with searching for him. He had a loving wife, a good friend, and good neighbors in the Crow village. Game was plentiful, as well as good grass and water for his horses. He paused a moment to look around him when he emerged from the burned-out forest and struck the game trail he had followed up the mountain. As far as he could see in any direction there were endless mountain peaks piercing the brilliant, blue sky. The sight never failed to stir deep emotion in his soul. He was where he wanted to be. "Let's go home, boy," he said, and gently nudged his horse with his heels.

"You two can get your lazy asses outta them blankets and go find that girl," P. D. scolded. For emphasis, she gave each of the two a sharp kick with the toe of her boot. "It's already daylight, and you're still layin' around this cabin."

Reluctant to stir from his blanket, Arlo nevertheless

roused himself, knowing that the next kick would be even sharper. Bo remained unmoving, the desire for sleep stronger than his mother's badgering at that early moment. He and Arlo had stumbled around the slopes above the cabin in the darkness for almost the entire night before giving up just hours before dawn. There had been no sign of the woman. Even if there had been, Arlo was convinced that it would have been impossible to see. After the moon came up over the mountaintop, they had followed what they thought might be Molly's trail. It turned out to be a trail left by a deer, or possibly a bear, and it led to a stone ledge and disappeared.

After a few moments, with Bo still unmoving, P. D. turned to Wiley, who was standing by the fireplace. "Hand me a dipper of water from that bucket."

Bo bolted upright when the dipperful of water drenched his head. "Dammit, Ma! I'm up!" he growled.

"Don't you raise your voice to me," P. D. warned. "I'll take the hide offen you with my whip. You two studs let that girl slip away, and I want her back. You ain't the only ones didn't get no sleep. Because of you and Arlo, me and Wiley had to take turns keepin' a lookout for Slaughter."

Bo, his face swollen and bruised from the beating Arlo had administered the night before, crawled out of his blanket and followed his brother out the door to empty his bladder. P. D. was waiting for them when they came back. "Get you some coffee and somethin' to eat," she said. "Then I expect you'd better saddle up and head back down the mountain. That little gal's on the run, and I expect she might try to circle around and head down to that Crow camp by the river. Maybe you can be waitin' for her if she does. We don't want no damn Injun war party comin' after us." She stood over them while they gulped down their breakfast. "And Arlo," she added, "don't do nothin' foolish. Kill her and be done with it."

"Yessum," Arlo answered respectfully. "Don't you want me and Bo to stay here in case he shows up this mornin'?"

"I expect I'm more concerned about havin' a Crow war party on my neck than I am about takin' care of one man. Me and Wiley'll set up a little welcome party for him."

It was the middle of the morning when Matt reined the paint to a halt, and paused to look down at his little homestead in the valley below him. A matter of habit, he always took a few minutes to look over the cabin when he had been away for a day or two. There was no sign of anyone about. He was mildly surprised that Zeb was not already sitting outside, soaking in the sunshine, an almost daily ritual since being wounded. There was smoke coming from the chimney, so he figured Molly to be inside doing some chore.

He started to nudge his horse to descend the slope, but paused again. Something was not right. It was a feeling that just came to him. And then it occurred to him—the horses were still in the corral. Zeb had not turned them out to graze in the meadow below the cabin. Maybe Zeb was feeling poorly, he thought, which could explain why he wasn't taking his customary sunbath. *But Molly certainly knew to turn the horses out to water and graze.* His natural instincts warned him to be cautious. He sat there for a while longer, watching to see if Zeb or Molly appeared. When they did not, he began to become concerned. "Easy now," he counseled himself. "She's all right. Don't go gettin' spooked."

Impatient, but still cautious, he decided it wouldn't hurt to traverse the mountain face, and come up to the cabin from below and behind, just to satisfy the feeling of suspicion that had descended upon him. There was a deep gully that cut a trough from the back of the cabin down a hundred feet or so until fanning out to form an apron on the western side of the valley. Created by the normal runoff of melted snow in the early summer, Matt had almost decided to locate the cabin more toward the edge of the meadow because of it. Zeb had insisted that it was unnecessary, so Matt left the cabin where it was. Zeb had been right. When the snow melted in the spring, the gully was a rushing torrent, but the water never reached the top, and by midsummer it was bone-dry. On this morning, it would serve as Matt's approach to the cabin. He couldn't help thinking that Zeb would no doubt find humor in his secretive return home if, in fact, his gut feeling was wrong.

Riding along a narrow cliff, Matt made his way carefully over the apron of shale to the entrance to the rugged defile. Leaving the horses at the bottom, he started climbing up the gully on foot. Halfway up, he suddenly dropped to one knee and quickly brought his rifle up, ready to fire. He had caught a glimpse of someone lying in wait, partially hidden by a sizable rock resting in the middle of the gully. He was trapped, caught in the bottom of the deep defile. He had no cover, and no chance to run. There was no choice but to prepare to exchange shots with whomever was lying in wait behind the rock.

Several tense moments passed in deathly silence, with no sound save that of a lonely crow somewhere in the pines above the cabin. *Well, come on, then,* he thought, anxious to get it done. A few more moments passed. Tense and impatient, he aimed his rifle at the rock, waiting. Then it occurred to him that the arm and shoulder he could see had not moved. *He was at a standoff with a corpse.* He was immediately overcome by a feeling of dread.

He scrambled up to the rock, knowing inside that it was Zeb, but praying that he was wrong. He was not, and the sight of the old scout lying in an awkward sprawl across the rock was enough to tear away at Matt's very soul. This was the second time he had found his friend battered and discarded, thrown away like so much rubbish. As he gazed at the body that seemed so small and fragile in death, his vision began to blur, his eyes threatening to fill with tears. *Molly!* His inner voice cried out then, and he immediately hurried past the rock and charged up the gully.

The wave of sorrow that had overwhelmed him upon finding Zeb's body had ebbed, replaced by the storm of anger that now took control of his mind. One thought dominated his thinking—to go to Molly. All concerns for his own safety were lost in the desperate need to find her as he climbed recklessly up the rugged defile. As soon as he reached the top, his warrior instincts automatically caused him to pause to look things over before charging into an ambush. The moment's hesitation served to restore a calmer sense of what he was faced with.

Scanning the area around his cabin, he could see no signs of activity. There were no strange horses in the corral or tied in front of the cabin. However, there was smoke coming from the chimney. Were Zeb's killers gone? Or were they inside, and their horses hidden somewhere? And what of Molly? His anger started to rise again with the thought of her, and he cautioned himself to keep his emotions out of his thinking and try not to imagine what might be happening to her. He decided that he had better assume the killers were inside and act accordingly.

There were no windows in the back of the little cabin he and Zeb had built, so he scrambled up over the edge of the gully, and quickly moved to the back wall. He waited a few moments, listening to see if he could hear anyone talking inside the cabin. Hearing nothing, he moved along the log wall, turned the corner, and eased up to the side window. There was no sound coming from inside. He tried to peer in at the bottom of the window, but it was blocked by a deerskin hung over it to keep out the cold. Moving to the front corner of the cabin, he knelt on one knee while he scanned the open area between the corral and the stream once again. Seeing no one, and still hearing no sound of voices, he stood up and went directly to the door.

Dreading that he might find Molly's body inside, he raised his foot and kicked the door open. His rifle ready, he burst into the cabin poised to fire. It was empty—no one, and to his relief, no corpse. He glanced at the fire. New logs had been recently added to the flames. The thought struck him too late as he realized he had walked into a trap.

The solid smack of lead against the cabin wall reached his ears only a fraction of an instant before he heard the sharp report of rifles. He dropped to his knees and crawled to the front window. Like the side window, it was blocked by a deerskin. As soon as he pulled the corner of the hide away to try to locate his assailants, a volley of rifle shots ripped through the pelt. *Why*, he wondered, *had they permitted him to enter the cabin, and refrained from simply shooting him outside when he was defenseless?* He paused to consider his options. They were few and not very promising. They could keep him pinned down for as long as they wanted, or until they decided to burn the cabin down around him. *Maybe the side window*, he thought. Apparently they had been unable to see him when he had paused there before. To refute that possibility, the window was suddenly splintered by a volley of rifle shots that ripped holes in the deer hide. He knew then that there were at least two assailants, for they had the front and side of the cabin covered.

Lying behind the trunk of a pine tree, P. D. was momentarily stunned. The man she had allowed to enter the cabin was the same man who had come to her rescue when they had been attacked by the Sioux war party. Though properly astonished, she could nevertheless appreciate the irony of it. All the trouble she had gone to, all the way to Virginia City and back here, and he had been standing right before her at point-blank range. It was him all right. There was no mistaking the tall, buckskin-clad rifleman. She wondered if Wiley had recognized him as well. *What was it he said his name was? Johnson?* It was almost enough to cause her to chuckle.

P. D. looked across toward the corner of the corral, and gave Wiley a sign of approval. As she had instructed, he had held his fire until Slaughter had entered the cabin. P. D. wanted Slaughter trapped with no way out but the door. It made him easier to deal with. If Wiley had fired too soon, and missed, Slaughter might have dived back in the gully and scrambled away. It would have been the easiest thing to simply put a bullet in Slaughter's back while he was standing outside the cabin door. P. D. would have preferred to do it that way, but Mathis had offered an extra two hundred and fifty dollars if Slaughter was brought back to stand trial.

"Slaughter!" P. D. called out. "If you leave that rifle in there and come out peaceful-like, we won't kill you."

"You mean like you didn't kill Zeb?" Matt called back.

"Were that his name?" P. D. returned sarcastically. "Hell, he looked like he was half dead, anyway. Nah, I ain't gonna shoot you if you come outta there peaceable. You're worth extra money to me if I deliver you alive. That wore-out old man weren't worth nothing." She paused a moment, waiting for his response, then added, "I could use the extra money, but if I have to burn that cabin down around you, I'll sure as hell do it."

"Where's Molly?"

"That little deef and dumb gal?" P. D. answered with a slight chuckle. "Why, she's all right. I got her safe and sound, waitin' for you."

"Who the hell are you?" Matt demanded, listening closely to P. D.'s responses in an effort to try to pinpoint her location. As well as he could guess, the person doing the talking was somewhere near the twin pines by the head of the path. The other, the one who had shot the side window full of holes, had to be positioned at the far corner of the corral.

"Never you mind that," P. D. responded to his question. "I'm the one come to take you back to Virginia, where you murdered that feller, so you might as well make up your mind to that. I always get who I go after. The only choice you have to make is whether you go back settin' in the saddle or belly-down across it. So why don't you lay your rifle down and come on outta there, and we can do this thing without a whole lotta fuss."

Matt did not doubt that P. D. was truthful in saying she would not shoot if he surrendered, for he definitely had presented an easy target when he had been standing before the cabin door. He knew by now that he was dealing with a bounty hunter, and he was obviously worth more alive than dead, just as his assailant had claimed. He also knew that Zeb was lying dead halfway down the gully behind the cabin. Someone was going to have to pay for that, and he had nothing more than the word of a bounty hunter that Molly was alive. "Where's Molly?" Matt demanded once more. "I wanna see her."

"I got her somewhere safe," P. D. lied. "You throw down that rifle and come on out, and I'll take you to see her."

"Yeah, I reckon," Matt mumbled cynically under his breath, and crawled to the other side of the window in an effort to spot the partner of the person doing all the talking. Though it gave him a bit more of an angle, he still could not see all of the corral from there. Calling out to P. D. again, he said, "If you show me the girl, I'll come out."

"Dammit, I told you she ain't here," P. D. replied heatedly. "I've got her somewhere safe." It was beginning to dawn upon her that it had not been a good idea to permit Slaughter to get inside the cabin. *I shoulda just shot him in the leg while I had the chance,* she thought. "I ain't got all day. You come on outta there now, or I'm gonna hafta burn you out."

"I reckon you're gonna have to come and get me," Matt yelled back. He was pretty confident now that his assailants numbered only two, and it was going to be damn difficult for them to set fire to his cabin—at least without giving him a shot at one of them, maybe both.

Seething with frustration over what she realized too late had been a poor decision in an effort to collect a two-hundred-and-fifty-dollar bonus, P. D. paused to ponder her next move. Over by the back corner of the corral, lying flat on his belly, Wiley was still trying to reconcile his mother's order to let Slaughter get inside the cabin. In the past, the policy had always been to shoot whenever the opportunity presented itself, and he had had his sights on Slaughter from the moment he moved along the cabin wall. It had occurred to him that he had seen the man before, but he couldn't recall where. Then another thought occurred to him—while P. D. kept Slaughter talking, he could hustle to the side window, and get the drop on him. Maybe, he thought, that was what his mama hoped he would do, and that was the reason she kept talking. Smiling with satisfaction that he had figured it out for himself, he got up on one knee and prepared to make a run for the cabin wall.

"Wiley! No!" P. D. screamed when she saw what her youngest son had in mind. But it was too late. Inside, at the corner of the front window, Matt caught the movement by the corral. It was an opportunity he had not expected, but his reactions were swift enough to respond before Wiley could take two steps toward the cabin. The Henry rifle spoke twice in rapid succession, each shot finding its mark, slamming Wiley in the chest, knocking him to the ground. He swept the rifle quickly back toward the twin pines by the path, seeking a target. He could not spot anyone, but he was sure that's where the voice had come from. Unconcerned with attack from another quarter, for he was confident now that he was left facing one man, he kept the rifle trained on the pines. While he waited, it occurred to him that when the person screamed out to stop Wiley, the voice had sounded almost feminine in its high pitch.

From her position behind a small boulder just a few feet from the pines, P. D. Wildmoon was stunned by the sight of her youngest, her favorite, when he was dropped awkwardly by the lead slugs, his arms flailing mindlessly, his legs wobbling drunkenly and collapsing beneath his body. *Wiley! My baby!* She screamed silently, the outcry exploding in her brain. Somehow, it had never entered her mind that she could lose one of her sons, and especially not Wiley, her pet. He was the son she had imagined would take care of his mama in her old age. "Wiley!" she screamed again, her brain boiling with the fury of a mama grizzly over the loss of a cub. Unable to control her rage, she rose to one knee and peppered the front window of the cabin with lead, firing until her rifle's magazine was empty.

The barrage caused Matt to pull away from the window while splinters of pine from the window frame went flying all about him. Sensing the situation as it now stood, he moved immediately to the side window and climbed out, landing on the ground beside the cabin. The advantage was now his. There followed a brief silence that lasted for the time it would take to reload a rifle, and then the barrage was resumed as shot after shot tore into the front of the cabin. It was a senseless waste of ammunition, for the bullets would not penetrate the heavy log wall, and Matt paused to consider what manner of maniac he was dealing with.

Edging up to the front of the cabin, he took a cautious peek around the corner. As he had surmised, the assault was coming from the rocks next to the twin pines, but all he could see of his assailant was a rifle barrel continuing to spit lead at the cabin wall. Matt raised his rifle to rest in a notch of the log corner and fired at the only target he could see. His shots were immediately answered, with lead ripping into the wall above his head. He pulled back away from the corner as chunks of pine logs were chipped away and sent flying. Then, after a few moments, the shooting stopped. Matt quickly crawled back to peer around the corner, thinking his adversary was moving to a better position.

Behind the cover of the rocks, P. D. searched her gun belt anxiously, having just realized that she had exhausted her ammunition in her manic reaction to her son's death. The sobering discovery was enough to cool her overheated passion for revenge, and spawn thoughts of self-preservation. *Damn*, she thought as she cocked the rifle, exposing an empty chamber. Suddenly the roles were reversed. It would only be a matter of time before Slaughter would guess her predicament, and she would be the hunted. She could not help remembering how the man calling himself Johnson had effectively routed an entire Sioux war party.

Her pistol was fully loaded, but she could only rely on that if Slaughter was close enough, and she didn't fancy letting him get that close. There were more cartridges in her saddlebags, but the horses were hobbled some fifty yards or more down the mountain in a stand of spruce. With no other option, she hurriedly withdrew from the rocks and made her way quickly down the slope toward the spruce pocket where the horses were hidden. All thoughts of her slain son were effectively crowded out of her brain by a stronger sense of survival. She did not fear for her life. P. D. had never met the man she was afraid of. Her sense of survival was triggered strictly by her determination to win the game. To her, Slaughter was no longer just one more in a long list of desperadoes she had tracked down and collected on. He had killed her baby.

As she descended the slope, moving quickly through the spruce trees that grew thick on the western side of the mountain, she wondered about the whereabouts of Arlo and Bo. If they were anywhere close by, they should have heard the shooting and come to see what it was all about. Since they had not, she assumed that they must have found sign of the girl, and were following her. "Dammit," she swore. "I shoulda kept 'em with me, and said to hell with the girl." She realized all too well that, had she done so, they would have been able to surround the cabin and Slaughter would not be chasing her down the mountain. *And Wiley wouldn't be lying back there dead*, she thought, adding fuel to her anger once again. *That son of a bitch is a dead man*, she thought. *I don't give a damn about the bonus.*

Panting noisily from transporting her stocky body down through the trees, she arrived at the horses. Rushing straight to her saddlebags, she pulled a rolled-up ammunition belt from one of the pockets and hurriedly jammed cartridges into the rifle's magazine. With a fully loaded rifle and the belt across her shoulder like a bandolier, P. D. was ready to rejoin the battle. "Now, by God," she uttered confidently. Leaving her horse again, she started the climb back up the slope to meet her pursuer, determined that one of them would not walk down the mountain again.

Unaware that his assailant had retreated down the mountainside, Matt decided to work his way around the other side of the cabin and attempt to approach his antagonist from the far side of the creek. Pausing at the rear corner of his cabin, he listened for sounds of movement from the twin pines. The frantic rifle fire had stopped, causing him to consider the possibility that his adversary might be moving to a new position. Without further hesitation, he moved quickly across the open area beside the cabin to the cover of the trees beside the stream. Still there were no shots fired. Thinking something strange was afoot, he continued to circle around the rocks near the two pines. His senses sharpened, he prepared to react to whatever he encountered. Just below the rocks now, he paused again to listen. There was nothing but the whisper of the wind through the pine needles. *What the hell?* he thought, and charged up into the rocks, his rifle ready. There was no one there. He looked down at his feet to discover a multitude of spent cartridges. This was definitely the spot. He looked all around him, expecting a barrage of shots from any direction. After a few more moments, he had to conclude that his assailant had fled the scene. Kneeling then to examine the ground, he discovered boot prints indicating the man had retreated down the slope.

Matt's first inclination was to follow his adversary down the slope and finish the job. But with the intruders driven from his homestead, his thoughts shifted immediately to finding Molly. There were only two bounty hunters, and even though the one who did all the talking claimed to have Molly in a "safe place," she might be close by, bound hand and foot. Or she might have somehow escaped, and be hiding somewhere on the mountain. On impulse, he called out, "Molly!" again and again. "It's all right now. If you can hear me, it's all right to come out now." He waited, but there was no response. He had to figure that, if indeed she had managed to escape, she would most likely try to make her way down to Broken Hand's village. He would look for her there. If she was not there, he would comb every inch of the mountains to find her. He thought then of the man he had sent fleeing down the mountain. If the bounty hunter had hunted him down all this way from Virginia, he was not likely to give up after one confrontation. Even though finding Molly was foremost in his mind, he realized that the bounty hunter had to be dealt with.

He paused a moment to go and look at the man he had killed. The body lay sprawled with arms outstretched awkwardly. A young man, it appeared, his shirt red with the blood that had seeped from two bullet holes neatly placed near his heart. A thought flashed through his mind that he might have seen the man somewhere before, but he could not be sure. He wondered if he could possibly be the one that escaped him when he cleaned out the Frenchman's trading post. In the heat of that confrontation, there had been little time to get a good look at him.

Matt felt no remorse for killing the young man. He had chosen a deadly business, and he had paid the price for failure. It mattered not to Matt if Zeb died at the hand of this man, or from that of his partner. They were both guilty, and should be held equally accountable for the murder. He turned away from the body and stared for a moment at the rocks by the twin pines. There was a job to be finished. The sooner he finished it, the sooner he could go in search of Molly.

Grunting with the effort required to climb back up the rocky slope she had just hurriedly descended, P. D. made her way toward the clearing where the cabin stood. Her breath coming in short, labored gasps, she murmured bitter threats to herself as she recalled the picture of Wiley crashing to the ground. Approximately fifty feet below the clearing, she came to a steep rise that required her to use her free hand to help pull her bulky body up. When fleeing Slaughter before, she had slid down the incline, never giving thought to the difficulty in climbing back up. Determined, and seething with anger, she pushed upward, steadying herself by grasping handholds on the rocks and the occasional scrub pine. Approaching the top of the rise, she looked up just as Matt appeared at the rim.

Both rifles went off almost simultaneously. Due to P. D.'s lack of steady footing, her feet slid in the loose shale, causing her aim to err, her shot snapping harmlessly by Matt's ear. Matt did not miss. However, P. D.'s slippery footing resulted in his bullet striking her in the shoulder, spinning her around to go crashing down the slope, rolling over and over all the way down to the edge of a cliff several hundred feet below the clearing. In the split second before they both fired, Matt realized he had seen the man before. There had not been time for more than a glimpse of his face, but he knew he had seen the short, stocky man, and it came to him then. It had been south of the Big Horns.

Certain now that it was the same man, he followed P. D. down the mountain, making his way as quickly as possible while trying his best not to lose his footing and join his adversary. He arrived at the bottom of the slope just in time to see P. D.'s body drop over the edge of the cliff. For one brief moment, he could see one hand grasping desperately for a small rock at the rim of the cliff. Then the rock dislodged, and both rock and hand were gone.

On hands and knees, Matt crawled to the cliff's edge and peered over into several hundred feet of clear space. There was no sign of a body in the tops of the tall pines thrusting up from a shelf far below. There was no way a man could survive that fall. When he had prevented Iron Claw's Sioux warriors from killing the white men before, there had been four of them. He could only account for two. Where were the other two? It was possible they had split up after reaching Virginia City. It was troubling, but his concentration shifted to finding Molly now.

Sidling along the face of the slope, in search of a more forgiving climb back to his cabin, he found P. D. and Wiley's horses tethered in the trees. He took the reins of one of the horses and started leading it back up the narrow game trail Wiley had followed down when he hid them. He figured the other horse would probably follow. Back at the cabin, he turned the horses in with the other two in the corral, and then went to get the paint and packhorse at the bottom of the gully behind the cabin.

Making his way down the gully, he paused when he came to Zeb's body. "I'm sorry, partner," he said softly, suddenly feeling the burden of responsibility for the death of another friend and partner. It seemed that every man who had befriended him had met with a violent death. Not all of them were his fault, but Zeb was definitely dead because of him. He reached down and patted the old scout on the shoulder.

"I'll be back for you. I ain't gonna leave you here like this."

When he reached the horses, he dumped the load of elk meat over the edge of the cliff. With no time to dry it, it would only spoil. Then he led the horses back up the gully to pick up Zeb's body. Upon reaching the cabin again, he paused to decide what to do. His first thought was to put Zeb in the cabin where his body would be safe from predators until he returned. But he was not sure when that would be. He was anxious to find Molly, but he was sure she would make her way down to Broken Hand's camp. He told himself that, with both of the bounty hunters dead, she should be all right, and he could at least take a little time to lay Zeb in the ground. He picked a spot on the north edge of the clearing for the old scout's final resting place.

The grave was dug with a little more haste than he would have preferred, but he promised his old friend that he would return to improve upon it after he had gone after Molly. There was one more thing to do before going after her. He decided to turn the other horses out of the corral. He could not be sure how long he would be gone, and he wanted them to be able to get to water and grass. He figured they wouldn't wander far from home.

With one foot in the stirrup, he paused before climbing up in the saddle. Something had caught his eye. Withdrawing his foot, he took a few steps toward the pine trees behind the cabin before kneeling to examine the ground. Someone unaccustomed to reading sign would probably have missed the faint marks and disturbed pine needles, but he saw at once that someone had been led toward the trees. The sign told him that person had not gone willingly, for the needles had been scuffed and dragged, much more so than prints left by the mere act of walking. He felt his heart go icy cold, for he knew the tracks could only have belonged to Molly. He feared that they also answered the question as to the whereabouts of the other two of the four ambushed by Iron Claw.

He glanced up, and peered at the stand of pine trees behind the cabin. A feeling of dread descended upon him as he stared at the dark pines. He tried to convince himself that Molly had fled the killers, and was probably on her way to Broken Hand's village. Afraid now of what he might find, he nevertheless hurried to follow the faint trail into the forest. Just inside the tree line, he discovered unmistakable signs of a struggle. His first thoughts almost caused him to cry out in anguish, for he interpreted the disturbed patch in the forest floor as evidence of Molly's attempts to resist an assault upon her body. Trying to force the mental image of her struggle from his mind, he studied the signs more closely. He could not help but question the apparent battle that the slight girl had managed. It looked more like a fight of some consequence had occurred. Maybe the two men had fought over Molly. The thought caused him to quickly begin a wider search around the thicket. Soon he found sign that gave him hope once again, for there was one small print in the dirt where the needles had been scraped away.

He stood up and took a few steps back, as if taking a look at the overall picture. He decided that the two men had fought over Molly and, while they fought, she had escaped. That had to be it. She had fled up the mountain. She was alive.

Chapter II

"Ma said to find the woman," Arlo said. "Maybe we'd best get back up on that mountain and look for her."

"Ma said," Bo mocked. "I swear, Arlo, sometimes I think you're as dumb as Wiley." He leaned back against the tree that served as his backrest, and began to gnaw on a strip of deer jerky he had found in the cabin. "We could climb all over them mountains for a week of Sundays and still not find her." When his remark was met with a frown from his brother, he said, "The only reason Ma wants us to find the woman is so she don't get down to that Injun camp. Ain't that right?"

"I reckon," Arlo replied reluctantly. Unlike his younger brother, Arlo never questioned P. D.'s orders.

"Well, then," Bo went on, "as long as we're settin' here at the bottom of the mountain, watchin' the trail, we're gonna catch her when she tries to come down to the river. Ain't *that* right?"

"What if she don't take this trail? What if she takes

some other trail, and we're settin' here when a Crow war party shows up?"

"Damn, brother," Bo exclaimed. "There ain't no other trail up to that cabin. When we were up there, did you see any other trails that led down the mountain?" Anticipating Arlo's next question, he added, "And if she don't take the trail, she'll have to show up on this ridge somewhere before she can cross the river to that camp. You just keep your eye on the ridge. If she shows up, we'll see her as soon as she comes outta the trees."

"Maybe so," Arlo conceded, still thinking that, if P. D. said to search the mountain for the woman, they should be searching the mountain.

Bo watched his brother's obvious consternation over the issue. He shook his head contemptuously. "I swear, Arlo, if Ma told you to change the color of your shit, you'd crap a rainbow. Sometimes I think you're *dumber'n* Wiley."

"How'd you like another whuppin'?" Arlo threatened, beginning to tire of Bo's verbal abuse.

"I expect last night was the last whuppin' I'll take from you, brother." Bo's frown was deadly serious. "You come at me again, and I'll put a bullet between your eyes."

"Is that a fact?" Arlo responded. "I reckon I'll kick your ass any time I think you need it. And when I'm done, I might put a bullet between *your* eyes. Any time I feel like it," he repeated for emphasis.

"You mean, like right now?" Bo replied, sitting up straight, his hand resting on the butt of his revolver.

Arlo's eyes narrowed under a deep frown as he stared his younger brother down. "You pull that damn pistol on me, and I'll beat your head in with it," he threatened.

Sired by different fathers, the two brothers had never held any fondness for each other. Bo had always resented the fact that nature had seen fit to endow Arlo with superiority in size and strength, resulting in many beatings over the years. Consequently, the threat that Bo had just issued was no idle boast. He was determined to put an end to Arlo's dominance. Even now, as the bigger, more powerful Arlo stood menacingly over him, Bo considered his chances of drawing his revolver before his brother had time to react. It was clear that Arlo gave little thought to the possibility that Bo would actually shoot him. Bo, on the other hand, was mulling over the consequences that might result. P. D. would have only his word for how Arlo happened to get shot. The longer Arlo stood glaring at him, the more Bo thought about it. Finally, he made up his mind and snatched the revolver from the holster.

Bo was quick, but Arlo was just as quick to react. Before Bo could level his weapon and pull the trigger, Arlo was on top of him, one hand clamped on Bo's wrist. The two brothers rolled over and over in the pine thicket, each straining against the other in a desperate effort to control the weapon. Suddenly the gun went off, firing one shot up through the trees. The unexpected report of the pistol momentarily stunned both men, and the struggle ceased.

Arlo, seated upon Bo's chest, wrenched the pistol from his brother's grasp. "I oughta whup you good for pullin' this damn gun on me," he said, "but right now we'd better get the hell outta here. Them damn Injuns across the river will hear that shot and might take a notion to come see what it's about." He got off Bo's chest and hurried to the edge of the trees to peer out across the river. Bo got to his feet and moved up beside him. The fight between them was temporarily forgotten. Arlo handed Bo's pistol back to him. "Let's get the hell outta here," he said.

Bo didn't move right away, continuing to stare at the distant tipis on the far side of the river. "I don't see nobody gettin' stirred up over there," he said. "I don't think nobody heard that shot, or if they did, they didn't pay it no mind." Like Arlo, Bo was not anxious to incite a reaction from the Crow camp, but he still retained thoughts of the fair-haired young woman and his intentions regarding her. This was a good spot to lie in wait for her. He didn't want to chance missing her if she tried to make her way down to her Crow friends. He had heard P. D.'s instructions to Arlo to kill the girl immediately, but he had other plans. "Hell, we might as well stay right here until we see some sign from them Injuns. If we spot a war party ridin' out, we've already got a good head start on 'em."

"Maybe so," Arlo conceded, thoughts of the slender mother-to-be lingering in his mind as well. "I don't fancy goin' back to tell Ma we give up on lookin' for the woman." Another concern entered his thoughts then. "What about that Injun woman we killed back up the trail? They might decide to come lookin' for her when she don't come back. I don't care much for just settin' here till a whole bunch of Injuns come down on our necks."

That was a concern that had left Bo's mind as well. "Damn, that is somethin' to think about, ain't it?" He changed his mind, thinking that, for once, Arlo was right. "Let's get the hell back up there."

Some thirty or forty yards above them, a terrified young girl crouched beside the trail, stunned moments before by the sudden gunshot that had whistled up through the thick pines just below her. Thinking at first that the shot had been meant for her, Molly had immediately dived for cover in a thicket beside the trail where she lay waiting, shivering like a startled rabbit. After a few moments had passed with no further shots, she crawled back closer to the trail and listened. Over the heavy pounding of her heart, she heard bits of conversation rising from the lodgepole pines at the edge of the ridge overlooking the river. They had anticipated her intention to seek the safety of Broken Hand's village, and she had almost blundered into their trap. Had it not been for that single gunshot, she would have. A few yards farther down, the narrow trail took a sharp turn around a huge boulder. She moved quickly down to take cover behind it. There she waited, listening, trying to control the rapid beating of her heart.

Weary from a night on the mountain, frightened for

her safety, and near devastation from uncertainty for Matt's welfare, she must now decide whether to make her way around the two brothers and gain the safety of the village, or stay where she was until they tired of waiting. She was almost sick with worry, thinking about what could have happened back up the mountain when Matt returned. She tried not to think about the possibility that he might have blundered blindly into an ambush, and could even now be lying dead back at the cabin. *Please, God,* she prayed, *I can't face life without him.*

Forcing herself to control her panic, she thought again about her options. After thinking it through, she decided the best thing for her and Matt was to get to Broken Hand. He would send a party out to look for Matt. Her decision made, she rose from her hiding place and started to cross over the trail, only to dive back behind the boulder when she heard the sound of horses coming up from below. Lying flat upon the pine needles, afraid to breathe, she watched in terror as Arlo and Bo filed past her on their way back up the trail. Afraid to move until the horses were well past her and she could no longer hear them on the path above her, she left the cover of the rock. Hurrying down the trail once more, her glance was captured for an instant by a dark smear on the pine needles beside the path. In her haste to escape the mountain, she almost dismissed it as insignificant, but something made her pause to identify it. She realized at once that it was blood. A sizable stain of dried blood coated the needles next to her foot. Upon a moment's investigation, she could readily see where something had disturbed the bed of pine needles, as if it had been dragged from the trail. Following the stains with her eyes, she gazed farther into the thicket and suddenly her breath caught in her throat, causing her to gasp. There, a few yards off the trail, lying in a tangle of vines and brush, was the unmistakable form of a body. Horrifying moments later, she recognized the corpse of Singing Woman, her doeskin shirt crusted with blood and her scalp brutally severed.

Stunned by the grisly discovery of her friend, Molly dropped to her knees, suddenly weakened by her grief. Through tears blurring her eyes, she looked around her as if searching in the quiet forest for the reason for such purposeless slaughter. *Why would these monsters kill Singing Woman?* The killers had obviously come for Matt, and even though he had no control over their actions, she felt the blame for Singing Woman's death. Now she must bring this dreadful news to Broken Hand and the rest of the Crow village. Helpless to do anything for Singing Woman at this point, she looked around her frantically in search of something to cover the body. There was nothing. *I'm sorry,* she thought, and reluctantly left her friend to lie among the brambles.

Her arm on fire from the strain of bearing most of her body weight as she dangled precariously from a single scrub pine, P. D. Wildmoon struggled to catch a toehold on the rock ledge just below her feet. Blood from the wound in her other shoulder soaked her sleeve, but, in desperation, she was forced to try to hold on with that arm as well. The pain was excruciating, but she knew she could not hold onto the skinny pine with one hand for very long.

It had been pure luck that her arms had caught on the pine when she lost her grip on the edge of the cliff some ten feet above her now. Below her boots, there was nothing but thin mountain air for another two hundred feet to the tops of the trees beneath the cliff. Her rifle lay somewhere among those trees. The test for her now was whether or not she had the strength and determination to save her life. Already, the shallow roots of the pine were giving way under the strain of her weight. Her shoulders were progressing from a state of pain toward one of numbness, as if they were being pulled from their sockets.

The narrow ledge of rock was only inches from the toe of her boot but, straining as much as possible, she still could not gain purchase. The desperation of her situation was rapidly pushing her toward outright panic. When a root suddenly pulled free, causing the pine to drop almost a foot, she thought she was about to fall to her death. She knew that she was not done just yet, however, when she felt her foot settle on the solid rock of the ledge and realized that the tree had swung her in closer to the face of the cliff.

As soon as she took a firm grasp on the rocky face, and decided that she could now release her hold on the pine, her confidence returned, along with a burning determination for revenge. She was not out of danger quite yet. There were perhaps fifty feet of steep cliff face to cross before reaching the safety of a gentler slope, but she had enough space on the narrow ledge to place one foot before the other and ample handholds to keep from falling.

Moving slowly and carefully, she inched her way across the cliff face, testing each handhold before releasing the one before it, her blood-soaked shirt leaving smudges of red on the rock wall. She dared not look down, but kept sliding one foot after the other until she neared the safety of the trees and underbrush that beckoned. Six feet, four feet, two feet, until finally she reached out to grab a handful of thick brush, and pulled herself off the face of the cliff.

On a more forgiving slope at last, she sat down and leaned against a sizable pine tree, feeling totally exhausted, her shoulders still aching from the strain. "It'll take a helluva lot more than that to kill P. D. Wildmoon," she boasted as she felt her old sense of confidence restored. Taking a look at the bullet wound in her shoulder, she determined it not to be too serious. Her initial reaction to it was one of anger, for she had never before even considered the possibility of getting shot. As she fumed over the bloody hole in her shirt, she was once again reminded of the loss of her youngest son. Thoughts of Wiley had left her during the perilous minutes on the cliff face, pushed from her mind by the fight for her own life. They returned now to remind her of the vengeance she must have for Wiley's death.

She took time to consider her present situation. Sitting on the side of a mountain with nothing but a pis-

tol for a weapon—The thought caused her to automatically reach for the weapon, only to discover an
empty holster. The pistol was at the bottom of the cliff
with her rifle. "Dammit!" she uttered in disgust.
There was no decision to be made; she must make her
way down the mountainside and search for her
weapons. But first, she had to climb back up a short
way to see if the horses were still where she had left
them. Finding them gone, she hesitated for only a
moment while she thought things out. There was still
the question to be answered as to where Slaughter
was now—back at his cabin, or gone in search of his
woman? The game had taken on a new meaning now.
No longer was money the driving force that would
keep her on Slaughter's trail. She longed for his
blood, and she swore she would have it. And where
were Arlo and Bo? Her lack of control over the situation was rapidly fueling her anger, and she was
determined to regain her dominance. Thinking of
Slaughter, she vowed, "I'll hunt that son of a bitch
down if it takes the rest of my life."

It was slow and painful, but driven by the rage of
a mama grizzly that has lost a cub, she descended the
slope and searched among the tall pines below the
cliff until she found her rifle. Looking it over to assess
any damage that might have occurred as a result of
the fall, she cocked the lever several times, ejecting
the cartridges. The action was smooth, and there
were no signs of damage other than a few small
scratches on the stock. It was one of the new Winchester 66 rifles, and with it back in her hands, she felt

whole again, in spite of the wound in her shoulder. She picked up the ejected cartridges and started back up the mountain, not willing to spend additional time to search for her pistol. If luck and the devil were with her, she might catch Slaughter at the cabin.

The climb was long and difficult, made more so by the loss of blood from her shoulder. Driven onward by her lust for revenge, she chose to ignore her wound when it started bleeding again. The image of her youngest son, her favorite, lying sprawled on the ground, his arms reaching grotesquely in death, was the one burning vision that filled her brain. Making her way up past the cliff, she barely glanced at the treacherous ledge that had almost sent her to her death. Striking the game trail where the horses had been tied, she followed it up to the clearing where the cabin stood.

On one knee, her breath coming in short gasps from the climb, she looked the cabin over carefully. There was no sign of Slaughter. Wiley's body lay where he had fallen, between the corral and the cabin. The sight of it almost made her charge into the clearing, but she forced herself to remain calm. In the meadow beyond the corral she saw the horses grazing, hers and Wiley's among them, their saddles on the ground by the corral. The other horses were the same ones she had seen in the corral before, which told her that the man she hunted was not there.

She stood up and walked toward the cabin, confident that it was empty, but with the Winchester ready just in case. As she expected, there was no one inside.

She then turned and went directly to her son's body. Standing over the corpse, she could not help thinking how pitiful he appeared in death. He had been slow-witted and clumsy, but he was her baby, and she felt a sudden gut-wrenching sob forming in her abdomen as she peered banefully down at him. "I ain't got time to bury you, honey," she muttered, "but I ain't gonna leave you to the wolves."

Taking him by his shoulders, she tried dragging the body toward the cabin door. She did not move him more than twenty feet before she was forced to stop and rest, already feeling light-headed and dizzy. For better leverage, she dropped his shoulders and grabbed his ankles. This proved to work much better, and she was able to drag him inside the cabin, although the strain caused her wound to bleed again. Once inside, the grieving mother tried to lift her son's body up on the bed. It was too heavy for her, so she propped his legs up on the bed, and then managed to lift his shoulders up high enough to get her back under him and shove him over to settle on the blanket. Feeling a little faint after such a minimal exertion, she knew that she must be weakened by the loss of too much blood. Unwilling to rest, however, she pushed herself to continue.

Wrapping the blanket around Wiley, she looked around her, searching for coal oil or kerosene. There was none, but there were live coals in the stone fireplace. A bed of these on the straw tick should prove to be ample to start a fire, she decided. The dry straw in the homemade mattress caught almost immedi-

ately. She stacked kindling she found near the fireplace on top of the coals, and soon she had a healthy
flame going. Remembering the half-burned corpse
that the cur dog had dined upon in the Frenchman's
trading post, she piled everything flammable she
could find on top of Wiley's corpse. She was determined to give her son a complete cremation—there
would be no wolves or coyotes feasting on Wiley's
body.

The tiny cabin soon filled with smoke, making it
impossible for P. D. to remain any longer to watch
over her son. She backed toward the open door as the
flames burst into a raging fire that began to lick hun-
grily at the cabin walls. Satisfied that there would be
no grisly remains for the scavengers, as well as nothing left of Slaughter's home, she backed away from
the burning cabin. In her hatred for this man, she
wanted to destroy everything he owned and everyone he held dear. If she had not been so weakened by
the loss of blood, she would have pulled the pine rails
from the corral and piled them on the funeral pyre as
well.

When the flames began to climb higher, and the
smoke rose high over the treetops, she finally decided
it best to vacate the clearing. Weak and wounded, she
realized she was in no condition to face Slaughter
should he happen to see the smoke and return to investigate before she was ready for him. Even with
limbs heavy with an almost numbing fatigue, she
looked about her, searching for the best spot to lie in
ambush for the man who had killed her son. She had

no sooner settled herself behind the same corner where Wiley had hidden earlier, than it occurred to her that it would be wise to catch her horse and saddle it.

Functioning on nothing more than pure, vengeful hatred, the weary woman willed herself to her feet once more, and moved painfully toward the meadow where the horses stood fascinated by the burning log cabin. Feeling a sudden spell of dizziness, she hesitated, uncertain for a moment as to which horse was hers. The animal, a blue roan stallion, recognized his mistress, and came to meet her. "Good boy," she mumbled, steadying herself with a hand grasping the horse's mane. Suddenly the afternoon sky became dark, as dark as night, and objects around her lost definition and faded into the darkness. With all consciousness gone, she dropped to her knees and fell facedown in the grass at the stallion's feet. This was where her sons found her.

"Look!" Arlo blurted out. "Yonder!" He reined his horse back and pointed toward the body lying still in the grass. "It's Ma!" He kicked his horse hard and charged into the meadow at a gallop.

"She looks like she's dead," Bo remarked, in effect talking to himself, because Arlo was already out of earshot. The sight of his mother's body did not overly excite him. Unlike his brothers, Bo had never possessed any particular fondness for P. D., having never been one of her favorites. It occurred to him then that Wiley was nowhere around. He prodded his horse and followed Arlo into the meadow. "Where's Wiley?" he asked when he dismounted.

"She's been shot!" Arlo said, ignoring Bo's question, "but she's still breathin'." He turned his full attention back to his mother. "Ma," he pleaded. "Ma, it's me, Arlo. Can you hear me?"

After a few moments, P. D.'s eyelids fluttered a few times, then opened wide. "I hear you," she muttered weakly. "I took a dizzy spell. Saddle my horse. We've got to catch that son of a bitch."

"You've been shot," Arlo protested.

"I reckon she knows that," Bo remarked, then asked, "Where's the turnip-head?"

It had not registered with Arlo until then that his younger brother was missing. "Yeah, Ma, where's Wiley? How come he ain't here?"

"He's dead," P. D. replied solemnly. "Shot through the heart by that damn devil we're after. Now I'll tell you somethin' else that'll sour your gizzard. Slaughter's the same feller that told us his name was Johnson when we had that run-in with them Injuns."

"Well, I'll be . . ." Bo remarked. Looking back at the burning cabin then, he guessed why there was no sign of Wiley's body. "He got both of you . . ." He didn't finish the thought as a feeling of concern for his own neck suddenly occurred to him.

"Damn," Arlo sighed, knowing the grief his mother must be feeling, although, like Bo, he felt no deep emotion over the loss. For P. D.'s sake, he tried to think of some words of comfort. "Brother Wiley's gone on to a better . . ."

P. D. cut him off. "We're wastin' time," she said, feeling the return of a small measure of strength now that her two sons were with her. "Bo, saddle my horse." Turning her attention back to Arlo, she asked, "Where's the woman?"

"Uh . . ." Arlo hesitated. "I don't know. We couldn't find her." He hastened to excuse their lack of success. "We seen the smoke risin' up on the mountain, and come a'runnin' 'cause we feared you was in trouble. Ain't that right, Bo?"

P. D. glanced at Bo, who acknowledged with a nod of his head as he looked around him for any sign of Slaughter's return. Feeling some of the previous fire in her veins again, P. D. admonished them both. "You let that damn girl get away?" she shrieked. "She'll have every damn Injun in that camp up here!"

Seeing no point in both he and Arlo taking the tongue-lashing, Bo led P. D.'s horse back toward the corral to fetch her saddle, as he had been told to do. While doing so, he gave some serious thought toward the situation they now found themselves in. It seemed to him that the advantage had shifted over to the other side. There they were, the three of them, and one of them wounded, on top of a mountain they were unfamiliar with. The girl would most likely make her way back to the Crow camp. And even if she didn't, the fire would most likely cause some curiosity among the Indians. Then there was the matter of Slaughter out there somewhere. He might have decided to run, but if he was the same man that said his name was Johnson, he sure as hell didn't seem like the running kind. The situation didn't look healthy for the Wildmoon family. He decided the best thing for the only member of the family he gave a damn about was to put this mountain behind him. He made up his mind that, if his mama intended to stay, he was leaving on his own.

"Help me up on my horse," P. D. commanded. With Arlo's help, she managed to get up in the saddle, but almost fell off again when he released his hold upon her arm. Arlo quickly caught the arm again, and held on until she managed to settle herself.

An interested observer, Bo said nothing while Arlo tried to get his mother firmly situated in the saddle. When Arlo cautiously withdrew his hand, and stepped away from the horse, P. D. held onto the saddle horn with both hands, causing Bo to remark, "Hell, she can't ride. She'll be off that horse before we get ten feet." Addressing his mother directly, he said, "Ma, you're hurt too bad to ride."

"The hell I am. I want that son of a bitch!" P. D. protested.

As reluctant as he was to go against his mother's orders, Arlo had to agree with his brother. "Ma, Bo's right. One of us is gonna have to climb up behind you to keep you from fallin' outta the saddle. You're lookin' weak as hell, and it's a rough ride down this mountain. You've been shot," he needlessly reminded her.

Already starting to reel in the saddle, P. D.'s eyes flashed with anger. "I want that son of a bitch!" she repeated. "If you two was worth a shit, you'da found that one, pitiful, little gal, and we'da hemmed Slaughter up in that cabin."

Bo took a cautious look around him as he spoke. "I expect we'd better think about our own asses right now, and I don't cotton much to standin' around here while that feller is loose. He might be drawin' a bead on one of us right now while we're standin' around jawin'." He couldn't resist throwing a barb at his brother then. "Most likely you, Arlo. You're the biggest target."

"You'd best hope he ain't aimin' at the biggest mouth," Arlo retorted.

"That's enough!" P. D. blurted. "We've got work to do. Let's get at it."

Releasing the saddle horn with one hand, she grabbed the reins and, with a kick of her heels, started toward the trail down the mountain. Almost immediately, she began to list to one side, and before her horse had taken a dozen paces, she keeled over and landed on the ground. Horrified, Arlo hurried to help her. Bo shook his head, chagrined by his mother's stubbornness, a little half smile on his face. "Well, I was wrong," he chortled. "She made it about twenty feet before she fell off."

"We've got to get the hell off of this mountain and get her to a doctor," Arlo insisted. "She's lost way too much blood."

"Where the hell are we gonna find a doctor out here?" Bo responded. "The closest doctor around is in Virginia City, and that's a helluva long ride from this damn mountaintop. Besides, I expect by now there's a passel of Injuns standin' between us and that river canyon we come up from the Yellowstone."

"Well, what are we gonna do?" Arlo pleaded, realizing the truth in Bo's remarks.

"I don't know about you, but I'm fixin' to get my ass to hell away from this mountain. To hell with Slaughter. There's gotta be another way outta these mountains besides goin' back down that same trail."

Arlo cocked his head to one side, giving his brother a questioning look. "I don't know," he said. "Ma's pretty set on gettin' that Slaughter feller now, especially since he killed Wiley."

Disgusted with Arlo's apparent inability to realize the seriousness of their situation, Bo spat back, "Look at her! Does she look like she can go after anybody?"

"What about Wiley? Are we gonna let that son of a bitch get away with killin' him?"

Bo had little sympathy for his younger brother. "That dummy was bound to get hisself killed one way or another. He probably made it easy for Slaughter. Besides, Ma was the only one gave a damn about him, anyway." When Arlo still showed signs of hesitation, Bo tried to set the situation for him. "You wanna save Ma, don'tcha? Well, like you said, we gotta get her outta here. We can't fight a whole damn tribe of Injuns, and maybe Slaughter, too. And the longer we stand here jawin' about it, the worse our chances are. We've got to head around the other side of this mountain, and find another way back to that river." He watched Arlo for a few moments while the big man thought about it. "We don't know that

Slaughter took off runnin', anyway. He might be comin' to look for us. He might be more to worry about than the damn Injuns."

Arlo finally conceded to his brother's logic. Although P. D. regained consciousness, she was still too weak to protest the planned retreat. Confronted with the fact that the mountainside was too steep and rugged to permit carrying her on a travois, they concluded that one of them would have to ride double with her. If not that, they would have to tie her on her own horse. They decided it best to try the latter choice, so between the two of them, they managed to lift her up on her horse. Once she was seated in the saddle, Bo held her while Arlo tied her feet in the stirrups, then looped the rope around her waist and tied it off on the saddle horn. "Ma, just lay forward on the horse's neck and hold on," Arlo told her. "Me and Bo'll get you outta here. After we get some distance between us and them Injuns, we'll see what we can do to help ease that shoulder."

Too weak to protest, P. D. did as her son instructed, mumbling only one faint objection. "I want that son of a bitch."

Chapter 12

Broken Hand's village was alive with urgent preparation for war, as a party of Crow warriors hurriedly caught up their favorite war ponies and readied their weapons. Some took brief moments to apply war paint to themselves and their ponies. Within a few minutes of Molly's arrival, the war party was ready to ride. Singing Woman was not only Broken Hand's sister, she was generally beloved by everyone in the Crow camp. Even the young boys begged to accompany the war party. Broken Hand restricted the search party to thirty experienced warriors, knowing a larger number to be a hindrance on the steep mountain trails. His plan was to leave some of the camp's warriors to guard the trails that ended on the ridge above the village in case the bounty hunters came back the same way they went up. The Crow chief asked Molly about Slaughter, but she could only tell him that Matt was somewhere in the mountains—alive, she hoped, but she was uncertain about that.

"Look!" one of the warriors cried, and pointed toward the mountaintop.

Following his gaze, Molly looked up to see a thin trail of smoke rising up from between two mountain peaks until caught and sheared by a lofty wind current that flattened it, drawing it out across the mountaintop. She knew at once that it had to come from the high valley between the two peaks, and could only mean a fire at the cabin. Frantic, she looked at once toward Broken Hand. He acknowledged her concern with a slight nod, turned his pony's head toward the river, and led the war party out. Feeling helpless, Molly watched until the warriors were out of sight, then she turned and went to Singing Woman's tipi to wait.

Still thinking there had been four bounty hunters, and confident that two of them were dead, Matt was startled to see smoke rising from the opposite side of the mountain. Judging by the trail of smoke, he felt reasonably sure the fire had to be from his little valley. He had happened upon a faint trail that he felt certain was left by Molly. It was not easy to follow up through the forest of pines, but it had eventually led him to a rock shelf and a boulder with a deep crevice. He studied the crevice for a few moments, thinking it a likely place for her to hide, but he could find no sign on the rocky shelf. With no trail to follow from that point, he had decided to go down to the Crow village, certain that Molly would try to go there.

Now, having seen the column of smoke rising above the mountains, his plans were changed. He headed back to the cabin as quickly as he could. As he guided the paint back down through the pines, his mind was busy conjuring any number of explanations, all of which were based upon the possibility that the two bounty hunters were not alone.

By the time he reached the clearing where his cabin had stood, his worst fears were confirmed. It was too late to save his cabin. Entering the clearing cautiously, he could see no sign of anyone, even though whomever set the fire could not be long departed, for the cabin was still in full blaze. Thinking then of the livestock, he looked beyond the burning structure to spot the horses scattered in the meadow—Zeb's sorrel, Molly's horse, the packhorse, but no others. Then he noticed that the body that had been lying between the corral and the cabin was gone.

Seeing there was nothing he could do to save his homestead, he immediately set to work scouting the clearing, searching for some sign that might talk to him. Whoever had taken the body and set fire to his home could not have gotten far. A careful examination of the trail down to the Crow village produced no evidence of shod horses leaving the clearing. After almost half an hour of meticulous study, he found what he was looking for—a fresh trail of shod hoofprints leading from the south edge of the clearing. He knelt to examine them closely, his fingers lightly tracing the outline of one as if feeling for something the print might tell him. They were recent tracks, and not some left before by the two bounty hunters he had killed. He was sure he would have seen them earlier if that had been the case.

Getting to his feet again, he followed the direction of the hoofprints with his eyes, looking beyond the edge of the clearing, past the thick belt of lodgepole pines, toward the steep rocky slopes above. Had they determined the game was too costly and decided to let him be? They had lost two of their party. These thoughts raced across his mind as he tried to decide what he must do. It was only a moment's hesitation, however, for the one person who dominated his thoughts was Molly. He knew that he could do nothing until he found her. He turned back toward the clearing. In the saddle again, he guided the paint past the twin pines and the rocks where P. D. had lain in ambush, and started down the trail toward Broken Hand's camp.

Halfway down the mountain, at the huge boulder where the trail made a hard turn to the right, he met the war party from the Crow village. Matt called out to identify himself before emerging from the trees above. Broken Hand waved for him to approach, pulling his pony aside to give Matt room on the narrow trail. Surprised to see the Crow warriors, Matt started to proceed, then stopped when he saw several of Broken Hand's warriors carrying a body from the bushes beside the trail. Matt's breath suddenly caught in his throat when he realized it was a woman's body. *It could be no one but Molly*, he thought. *She had escaped, and this was where they had caught her.* Devastated, he hurried down to meet Broken Hand.

The Crow chief read the distress in Matt's face as he urged the paint pony closer. "It is my sorrow, and not yours, my friend," Broken Hand called out. "It is Singing Woman."

Matt's entire nervous system was immediately flooded with relief. Seconds later, he felt guilty for his resulting sense of reprieve upon hearing the body was Singing Woman instead of Molly. Then he shared the chief's feeling of grief over the loss of his sister. Singing Woman had been his friend, and almost like a doting aunt to Molly. The anger returned to take dominance in his thoughts. First it was Zeb, and now Singing Woman. The evil that had followed him to these mountains must be eliminated. He sought to console the Crow chief, but could not find the proper words.

Broken Hand nodded, understanding Matt's inability to express his empathy for his loss. "Bird With No Song is safe in my village," he said, referring to Molly by the name the Indians had given her. "She waits for you there."

Matt expressed a silent prayer of thanks, free then from long moments of worrisome thoughts. *She was safe in the Crow camp. There could not be a better place for her.* His mind turned at once toward the obligation owed his two friends.

"We saw the smoke from our village," Broken Hand said. "Was it from your cabin?"

"Yes," Matt replied. "The men who killed Zeb and Singing Woman burned it down. I killed two of the men, but there are two more. I found tracks where they left my cabin, and now that I know Molly is safe in your camp, I'm going after them."

"They are the four white men I saw before," Broken Hand said. "They came to our village looking for you. I told them we did not know of anyone named Slaughter. They left, and Singing Woman went to warn you." He shook his head sadly as he turned to look at the body now wrapped in a blanket. "They must have followed her to your cabin. Bird With No Song said they killed Zeb Benson." Seeing a look of distress appear in Matt's face, he quickly assured him. "The men did not harm her. She was able to escape and come to us. My warriors and I were going to look for you after we found Singing Woman. Now that I know you are safe, I will take Singing Woman back to prepare her body for her journey. Take my warriors with you to hunt these men."

Matt was grateful for the offer, although he was at first inclined to reject Broken Hand's assistance, preferring to scout on his own. A large war party might be too easily seen. On second thought, however, he decided to take two of the warriors to help him read sign. Now knowing he would be trailing only two men, he figured a greater number of warriors would not be necessary, anyway. But he wanted to take no chances on losing these two murderers. The Crow scouts would be along simply to make sure he missed no sign. Having hunted with several of the warriors in the past, Matt already knew who he would pick to go after the killers with him: Wounded Horse and Looks Ahead. Both men were more than willing to go. After a brief farewell to Broken Hand, Matt and his two Crow scouts set out for his cabin, where they would follow the trail Matt had discovered earlier.

Upon reaching the cabin, they found the walls still smoldering. The lusty flames that had fed upon the interior of the structure had evidently been partially extinguished when the roof collapsed, leaving a blackened shell of what had once been his home. In spite of the sense of urgency to track the killers, Matt took a moment to survey the ruins of his cabin. The fallen timbers in the roof had formed a shelter over Wiley's funeral pyre, leaving the badly scorched body to remain a grisly feast for the vultures. Matt took a brief look around the clearing where he and Zeb had toiled to make a home for the three of them, knowing that it would be his last glance. The little valley was now haunted by too many bad memories.

His momentary wandering was interrupted then by a call from Wounded Horse. "Here," the Crow scout called out, having found the tracks leading away from the clearing to the south that Matt had discovered earlier. Matt and Looks Ahead joined him.

"Two horses?" Matt asked.

"Hard to say," Wounded Horse replied after

studying the prints partially exposed in the pine needles. As Matt had done before, the scout stood up and followed the direction the tracks indicated.

Looks Ahead knelt beside Wounded Horse to examine the tracks for himself. After a few moments he shrugged his shoulders, unable to determine any more than Wounded Horse had. Getting to his feet, he followed Wounded Horse's gaze toward the rugged mountain above them. "They ride to the higher slopes, maybe hoping to lead us into an ambush," he said.

"Maybe," Matt said, hesitating. "And maybe they're just lookin' for another way outta these mountains, figurin' we'd be waitin' for them if they came down the trail." Either way, he knew he had to find them. With two of the four dead, it was possible they had decided the mission was too costly, but he doubted they would give up at this point. It was more likely that they had just withdrawn to decide upon a new plan to capture him. He had no intention to wait around for them to make their next move.

Already, shadows were lengthening, threatening to cloak the little valley where Matt had built his cabin. It would soon be too dark to follow a trail as difficult as the one the bounty hunters had left. Reluctantly, Matt decided to camp there next to the smoldering cabin, and start out early the next morning. They decided it wise to take turns keeping watch during the night in the unlikely event the men they hunted might return. The night passed peacefully, however, with no unusual sounds other than the occasional popping and hissing from the live coals still eating away at the charred timbers that framed Wiley Wildmoon's grisly cremation. At daylight the following morning the three hunters were in the saddle, making their way up the steep slope behind the corral.

Chapter 13

"Gawdammit!" Arlo swore upon returning to the rocky shelf where Bo and P. D. waited. "There ain't no way to get across to that next mountain the way we're goin'. About fifty yards up ahead, I come to a damn cliff—must be a two or three hundred foot drop."

"I told you we was climbing too high up this damn mountain," Bo said. "We shoulda dropped down back there and followed that game trail back down through the trees." He shook his head in contempt. "But, hell, you knew better," he said sarcastically.

"Well," Arlo offered in defense, "it looked like we was never gonna find a way outta them trees." Half the morning had been spent following the narrow game trail through a forest of lodgepole pines that seemed as thick as hairs on a dog. They had plodded endlessly over ground covered with pine needles, ground that never saw the sun due to the towering height of the closely packed trees. When they had reached an opening that offered a way up out of the maze of pines, Arlo insisted upon climbing up to where they could at least see the way before them. Now, after sidling across fields of loose gravel and shell rock, they had reached a dead end.

"If you'da listened to me," Bo complained, "we wouldn't a'been walkin' the last hour. We'da been ridin' these horses instead of leadin' 'em halfway across the Rockies."

"All right, dammit," Arlo shot back angrily. "I was wrong, so we'll just have to turn around and go back the way we come." Anxious to change the subject, he asked, "How's Ma?"

"I'm all right," P. D. answered for herself. Leaning forward in the saddle, lying across her horse's neck, she opened her eyes briefly. "You two stop arguing, and let's get goin'. I ain't gettin' no better layin' across this damn horse." She had had plenty of time to think about her situation during the morning while her horse was being led across the treacherous mountainside. With her face pressed tightly against the warm neck of the dark stallion, she fought to remain conscious. With all sense of time lost, she felt that she had been led helplessly for days, through dark pine forests, across rocky stretches of soft shale, through scattered patches of snow. All the while, a burning hatred for the man called Slaughter continued to intensify, and she wanted to scream out her rage for her body's weakness. Time and again, she tried to will her body to sit upright in the saddle. Each time she failed.

She finally decided to curb her immediate passion for revenge, reluctantly accepting the fact that she had lost too much blood. She would have her revenge for the death of her youngest son, but it would have to wait until she was recovered enough to take on the task. Slaughter had proven to be no easy prey, and one who might be too much for Arlo and Bo to handle without her help. There was also the underlying craving to take Slaughter's blood with her own hand. She would have her revenge, this she vowed upon her soul.

Upon backtracking to pick up the game trail, it turned out that Bo had been right. After winding almost halfway around the mountain's midsection, the trail led to a narrow hogback that joined the neighboring slope. Feeling vindicated, Bo assumed additional authority. "When we get on the north side of this here mountain, we oughta be able to risk a shot without them Injuns hearin' it. I can find us somethin' to eat. Ma needs fresh meat to build her blood back up."

"That's a fact," P. D. softly agreed, resigned now to what had to be done. *I'll find him again. I found him this time, and I'll find him again.*

"Three horses," Wounded Horse announced as Matt and Looks Ahead caught up to him. There was no need for Matt to step down from the saddle to examine the hoofprints crossing the little patch of snow. They clearly revealed three distinct sets of tracks. Up to this point, they had assumed they were following two men on two horses.

"Maybe three men," Wounded Horse speculated.

"Maybe two men, one packhorse." Judging by the depth of the imprints, it was obvious to them that all three horses were carrying loads—whether riders or packs, it was difficult to say. The fact that the men they chased had not taken the precaution of riding around the small patch of snow told Matt that they were no longer concerned with being followed. It struck him as kind of careless on their part—either that, or perhaps they were smarter than he gave them credit for. Perhaps they purposely left tracks, planning to draw them into an ambush.

The trail had not been difficult to follow, but there had been occasions when a little extra time was required to make sure they were still on it, especially in the dark forest of lodgepole pines where the pine straw was hardly disturbed. At one point the bounty hunters had left the game trail and climbed up out of the trees, only to return once again to follow the trail. Matt was familiar with the mountains around his cabin, so it was not difficult to guess what had caused them to return. He had hoped that the wasted time on the bounty hunters' part would allow him to make up a great portion of the distance, but there was still no evidence that would suggest he was getting close to them. They were making good time, and that worried him. He had hoped to overtake them before they were able to find their way out of the mountains. It had not happened, and the trail was no warmer than it had been two days before when it emerged from the trees and ended in the steep bluffs beside the river.

Following the tracks down close to the river's edge, they came upon the half-butchered remains of a six-point buck. Their arrival disturbed a feast under way as a half-dozen buzzards worked on the carcass. It was not difficult to re-create the scene that had taken place here. The deer had evidently been shot almost exactly where he now lay. The butchering had been hasty and wasteful, taking only a haunch—only enough for a couple of meals, and the rest left behind.

"Cook meat here," Looks Ahead called to Matt. The ashes of a small fire bore evidence that the bounty hunters had camped in a willow stand only a few yards away from the carcass. Looks Ahead dug his fingers into the ashes to feel their warmth. "Not long," he said. "Maybe half a day."

Matt knelt down beside him to feel the ashes himself. He had to agree with Looks Ahead's estimate. At last they were gaining on them. The quantity of ashes told him that the men had camped overnight. The warmth suggested they had left the camp no more than four hours before. Horse droppings close to the campfire confirmed the time factor as well. There was renewed excitement stirring Matt's emotions as he climbed up in the saddle and nudged the paint up into the bluffs. There were tracks, but he did not bother to study them, for he was confident now that the bounty hunters were heading for the Yellowstone, with no evident intention of returning.

Following the trail along the Boulder River as it flowed north to its confluence with the Yellowstone, Matt was intent on making the best time possible. Behind him, Looks Ahead and Wounded Horse pushed their ponies to keep up. His eyes constantly searching the trail ahead of him, he counseled himself to be alert lest he ride headlong into an ambush.

At last he could see the waters of the Yellowstone ahead. Under a gray, overcast sky, the mighty river's waters seemed milky and dull as they consumed the Boulder's body. Following the trail he had last used when making his vengeful visit to rid the world of Bordeaux and his cutthroats, he continued toward the sandy ford where he had crossed before. Some three or four hundred yards to the east, and on the opposite shore, he could see the blackened walls of the former trading post. Thoughts of Zeb lying broken and bleeding at the bottom of a narrow ravine returned to his mind as he paused to look for any sign of the men he followed. Wounded Horse pulled up beside him.

"White men long gone," he stated simply.

Matt had already noticed a growing decline in enthusiasm for the hunt on the part of his two Crow scouts as the afternoon hours passed. It had been two days since leaving his burned-out cabin, and he now detected a reluctance to continue past the confluence with the Yellowstone. Wounded Horse and Looks Ahead obviously thought the chase should be terminated, the bounty hunters had been chased away, apparently for good. But, having volunteered to come along, it was also obvious that they felt obligated to continue. Seeing this to be the case, Matt knew it was his responsibility to release them. He knew that his skills as a tracker, while better than most, were not equal to those of either of the Crow scouts. But he had a feeling that the men he hunted had decided to leave this part of the mountains, possibly to enlist others to help them claim the reward money. He could only speculate on their reasons, but after picking up their trail on the opposite shore of the Yellowstone, it appeared they might be heading toward Virginia City. Tracking them should be fairly easy.

"I thank you both for your help," he began after the trail west along the river was confirmed by both Crows. "It is better for me to go on alone now. Give my thanks to Broken Hand when you get back."

In spite of an effort to hide it, Matt detected a look of relief in the eyes of both scouts. They offered a polite protest, insisting that they would stay with him until the men were run to ground. When Matt again declined, they wished him good hunting, and wasted little time heading back home. He was alone again, a state that caused him no concern. Turning west, heading once again toward the mountains, he set out along the Yellowstone. The men he chased could not be far ahead of him.

Bo Wildmoon pulled his horse to a sliding stop and dismounted. "Looks like we run up on a piece of good luck," he announced excitedly.

"What is it?" Arlo asked. When they had heard a single rifle shot beyond the hills ahead of them, they had immediately ridden down the riverbank to seek cover. While Arlo stayed with P. D., Bo had ridden ahead to scout the river beyond.

"Injuns," Bo reported. "Three of 'em." He grinned at Arlo's look of concern. "They're butcherin' an antelope. That was the shot we heard. They're on the other side of that hill yonder, down near the water."

"Maybe we'd best set tight right here till they're gone," Arlo said.

P. D., resting against the trunk of a small tree, spoke then. "We could use the meat. Three of 'em, you say?"

Bo's grin widened mischievously. "Yessum, three of 'em, but ain't but one of 'em got a rifle."

"We need the meat more'n them damn Injuns," P. D. said. She had felt a slight improvement in her weakened state after a good meal of venison the night before. She was no longer feeling faint and light-headed, and was once again able to take charge of her sons. The prospect of readily available fresh meat was especially appealing to her at this point. She had been in a daze when they left their last camp that morning. Otherwise, she would not have let her two unthinking sons leave the major part of that deer behind. "I ain't gonna be much help with one arm in a damn sling," she said, "but you two boys oughta be able to handle three Injuns that ain't got but one rifle between 'em."

"Damn right," Bo exclaimed, immediately thinking about the opportunity to add to his string of scalps.

"Help me up on my horse," P. D. said, "and we'll go fetch our supper."

Bo led the way, holding close to the riverbank until

approaching the hill rising up from the river. Halfway up the hill, he reined his horse back and waited for P. D. and Arlo to catch up to him. "We'd best leave the horses here and go the rest of the way on foot," he whispered.

Arlo nodded, then asked, "What about Ma?"

P. D. answered, "I'll stay here with the horses. And Bo, you boys oughta wait till they've finished all the butcherin'. Might as well let them do all the work."

"Might as well," Bo echoed, eagerly anticipating the fun ahead.

"You gonna be all right?" Arlo asked.

"I'm all right," P. D. answered. "A helluva lot better than I was last night. You just be sure you take care of them Injuns. We don't want any of 'em to get back to their village and bring the whole damn band after us."

After making their way up to the top of the hill on foot, Arlo and Bo lay low on the ground to watch. Below, at the base of the hill where it sloped down to the riverbank, the three unsuspecting Blackfoot hunters worked away at the antelope carcass. They estimated the range to be close to two hundred yards. Knowing their instructions were to make sure none of the three Indians escaped, Arlo declared, "I'd like to get a little closer if we could."

Bo, the better shot of the two, was of the same opinion although he was fairly confident he could make the shot from where they were. "Wouldn't hurt to get a little closer," he said. They both studied the descending slope for a few moments before he suggested, "I suspect we could crawl down to that gully below us." Arlo agreed, and the two brothers made their way halfway down the slope, most of the way on their hands and knees.

"This is better," Arlo commented when they had settled in the gully. They both crawled up to the edge and laid their rifles down in the grass, sighting in on the three Indians busily carving up the carcass. "Which'un you aimin' at?"

"The little one on the left," Bo replied, his finger resting lightly on the trigger, his target a Blackfoot boy of perhaps thirteen or fourteen.

"All right, then, I'll take the one in the middle. Let 'er rip." They fired almost in unison. Both targets staggered backward before dropping to the ground. The third hunter seemed paralyzed for a moment as his two companions fell away from him. But then he scrambled to his feet and started running toward the trees on the riverbank. In no particular hurry, Bo got to his feet and braced for the final shot. Taking dead aim, he squeezed the trigger. The running Indian tumbled, rolling over several times before lying still, a bullet squarely planted between his shoulder blades.

"Hoo-wee!" Bo yelled excitedly, and started running down the slope to claim the scalps.

Arlo got to his feet, stood there a moment watching his brother charge down the hill, then went back over the crest to get his mother. When he and P. D. arrived at the site of the slaughter, Bo was busily engaged in the taking of his grisly trophies. "Boys will be boys," P. D. snorted, not really caring. "Arlo, start packin' that meat on one of them Injun ponies. I expect we'd best not linger here in case they got friends come lookin' for 'em." She cocked her head to glance at Bo again. "And, Bo, mind you clean that knife before you go carvin' up any of that antelope." Bo, happily sawing off the last of the three scalps, merely grinned in reply.

Matt pulled the paint to a sudden stop and paused to listen. Two shots carried to him on the gentle wind, followed shortly after by a single shot. They seemed to have come from the hills he could see rising before him, and probably had been fired by the men he chased. They told him that he was rapidly closing the distance between himself and the bounty hunters. He nudged his horse gently, and the paint immediately sprang into a lope.

He had covered no more than a quarter mile, however, when the trail he had followed since leaving the Boulder suddenly veered off to his left. Exercising caution again, he followed the tracks down the riverbank with a sharp eye for any sign of ambush. Below the bank, near the water's edge, he found tracks that told him his prey had stopped here for a short period, and then had gone on. He could see no explanation for the sudden veering off their line of travel. Perhaps, he thought, they might have sighted an Indian war party, and hid there until the hostiles had passed. Whatever their reason, they had resumed their original trail, but only until reaching the first of a line of hills. At that point, the tracks led up the slope of the hill. Matt had a feeling that if he followed the tracks to the top of the slope, he would discover what had prompted the shots he had heard. His hunch proved to be right.

There, at the base of the hill, lay two bodies—Indians from their appearance. Thirty yards or so toward the trees lining the river, another body lay sprawled in the grass. Matt sat motionless for several minutes while he surveyed the scene below him. There was no sign of anyone else around. When he was sure of this, he rode down for a closer look.

Stepping down from the saddle, he knelt beside the body of a boy. Although the skin on his forehead had sagged and wrinkled slightly—a result of having been scalped—Matt could see that he was no more than a boy. There was little doubt who was responsible for the killing. It only intensified his passion to catch up to the murderers. Seeing the remains of an antelope, he was able to guess what had happened. The three Indians had been assassinated without warning, and at a distance, he speculated. Two had been shot in the chest, one in the back. They had not been dead long, so he wasted no more time at the bloody scene. Stepping toward his horse, he grabbed the saddle horn with one hand and placed his foot in the stirrup. Before he could pull himself up, he felt a solid blow on the back of his left shoulder, followed by the sharp crack of a rifle. Dropping immediately, he reached for his rifle as he fell. Everything went black with a blow to his head, and he never heard the shot that grazed his skull, knocking him unconscious.

Chapter 14

Black Fox charged down the slope and leaped from his pony in such haste that he almost stumbled and fell. Taking his war ax in hand, he strode angrily toward the fallen white man, intent upon bludgeoning him to death. He paused for a moment when he saw the mutilated bodies of his friends. Unable to control his anger, he threw his head back and screamed his rage to the heavens—for the young boy was his wife's brother. Then he straddled the helpless white man, and raised his ax for the lethal blow.

"Wait," Little Hawk said, and grabbed Black Fox's wrist. Startled, Black Fox stared at his friend, confused by his action. "He may not have done this evil thing," Little Hawk said. Looking around him then as the rest of the hunting party gathered to watch, he explained. "If he killed our brothers, where is the meat? The antelope is gone. Where are the scalps that were taken?" He waited a moment for a response before concluding. "I think someone else killed them, and he has only found them, the same as us."

Black Fox was still intent upon extracting vengeance. "Maybe that is true," he allowed, "but what does it matter? He is a white man, and probably a friend of those who did this."

"Turn him over," Little Hawk said. Black Fox got off Matt and rolled him over on his back. Matt's eyelids fluttered briefly, then opened wide as he regained consciousness. He immediately tried to spring up, but was held firm by Black Fox and one of the other hunters. Little Hawk gazed into the wounded man's face for a long moment. "This is the white warrior who killed the evil men at the trading post and burned it to the ground. It was he who gave us these rifles and ponies." Black Fox hesitated, not sure now what to do. Little Hawk continued to argue the wounded man's case. "I think he is hunting the men who did this."

Held securely by the Blackfoot warriors, Matt was helpless to resist. There was blood in his right eye from the scalp wound where the second bullet grazed him, and his shoulder felt numb. He did not understand the Blackfoot tongue, so he had no idea what the discussion was, nor why the fierce-looking Indian with the ax had decided not to kill him. He figured he was done for unless by some miracle he was given an opportunity to make a break for his life. His miracle came in the form of broken English, spoken by the Indian who had had the discussion with the fierce one.

"You see me before?" Little Hawk asked. Matt, staring up at the seemingly hostile faces gathered over him, slowly shook his head. Little Hawk raised his rifle in the air. "You give me rifle, burn store." Matt remembered then. At the time, his mind had been so filled with rage that he had taken little note of the faces of the Indians that had been at Bordeaux's. It came to him now; this was the Indian who had hidden behind the counter. He nodded slowly. Little Hawk smiled and pointed to his chest. "Little Hawk," he said, then pointed at Matt.

"Slaughter," Matt replied.

There was a low murmuring of voices behind Little Hawk. The Blackfoot warrior raised an eyebrow and turned to those gathered around. "Igmutaka," he announced softly, pronouncing the Lakota word. He turned back to Matt. "Igmutaka?"

Recognizing his Sioux name, he nodded and answered, "That's what the Sioux call me. My name's Slaughter."

"Release him," Little Hawk said. "He is enemy of the Sioux, not the Blackfoot." Feeling himself free, Matt sat up, still wary of what might come next. He tried to get to his feet, but the effort reminded him of the bullet in his shoulder, and he sat back down. Little Hawk knelt down to examine the wound. "Bad, we shoot," he said, searching for the right words. Matt realized he was trying to apologize for shooting him. Then Little Hawk asked, "Who shoot my people?" He pointed at the bodies.

Still uncertain if he was tracking three men or two men and a packhorse, Matt tried to answer. "Bad men," he said. Using sign language then, he was finally able to tell Little Hawk that he had been tracking the men who had killed the three Blackfoot hunters.

"White men?" Little Hawk asked.

"Yes, white men—maybe two, maybe three."

With the help of sign language, a skill Matt had learned after living with Zeb Benson and the Crows, and a necessary asset in understanding Molly, Little Hawk told Matt that he would take him back to his village to heal his wound. Matt tried to protest that he had to continue after the bounty hunters, but the Blackfoot warrior convinced him that he was in no condition to do so. "Black Fox will go after these men," Little Hawk said. "You must heal."

Matt was in no position to argue. His shoulder, having been numb moments before, was now pain- ing him with every move of his arm. He had been so close to catching up with Zeb's murderers, that the frustration of letting them go was more painful than his wounds.

Reading the white warrior's face, Little Hawk nod- ded and said, "Black Fox will find them."

Knowing it useless to resist, Matt relented. The fierce warrior took six others with him, and followed the trail left by P. D. and her sons. The rest of the Blackfoot hunting party loaded their dead on their ponies and, with Matt on the paint, returned to their village.

"I ain't got time to get to no doctor," P. D. said as she examined the swollen shoulder around the bullet hole. In spite of the pain from the wound, she was feeling stronger than days before. "I need to get this damn bullet outta there *now*," she decided. "Arlo, you've seen me cut enough lead outta wounds to know how to do it. Clean off my knife and let's get it done."

None too enthusiastic about it, Arlo balked. "Ma, I ain't no good at nothin' like that. I'm afraid I might do somethin' wrong."

"What are you worrying about?" she snapped. "I'm the one who's hurtin'. Hell, I'll tell you if you're about to kill me."

"I'll do it," Bo volunteered. Sitting by the fire, he had listened to the exchange between his brother and P. D. with some amusement.

"I expect I shoulda known you'd do it," P. D. said. "All right, then, you cut it outta me, but you use my knife. I don't want you mixin' none of that Injun blood with mine."

Far from squeamish about operating on his mother's shoulder, Bo was more than willing to perform the surgery. He enjoyed anything that required using a knife. Producing a bottle from her saddlebag, P. D. took a couple of stiff drinks, and announced that she was ready. Bo set to work, eagerly cutting into the wound. P. D. remained steely quiet while watching her son probe deep into her shoulder to find the slug. Both sons were astonished by their mother's seeming immunity to the pain as she stared unmoving and unblinking into the bloody hole made by the knife. When Bo finally found the slug and dislodged it, she calmly instructed him to pour some whiskey into the wound. "That always seems to help it heal faster," she calmly commented while the fiery liquid blistered the open wound. "Now you can heat that knife up in the fire." The only indication that she felt any pain was a sudden tensing of her body when Bo cauterized the wound.

"You can tie a rag around her shoulder," Bo said to his brother. "If you ain't too squeamish to do that."

Arlo didn't bother to answer Bo's barb. He knew he wasn't shy when it came to cutting or shooting, and he knew Bo knew that. Bo would never understand that it was different when it came to their mother. Arlo would always find it difficult to do anything that might inflict pain on her. He obediently went to his saddlebags to look for something suitable to use as a bandage. Finding nothing, he looked in Bo's saddlebags, where he discovered Bo's spare shirt. With a trace of a smile upon his lips, he ripped it in two and poked one half back in the saddlebag. The other half he used for his bandage. That done, with Bo none the wiser, they settled in for the night.

"Hey, what the hell . . . ?" Bo exclaimed when he pulled the remains of his good shirt from his saddlebag. Then it struck him. He turned at once to stare at P. D.'s bandage. Next he turned his irate gaze upon his brother, who met his accusing stare with a wide grin. "Why you low-down son of a . . ." Unable to finish the sentence in his fury, he launched his body at his grinning brother. Expecting the attack, Arlo blocked the wild right hand Bo threw, and slung the smaller man aside, rolling him over in the ashes of the fire. Yelping with pain, Bo scrambled away from the fire, frantically brushing the hot coals from his coat. On his feet again, he drew his pistol. "Now, by God, we'll see once and for all who's the big dog around here."

"Put it away, Bo." P. D.'s stern command effectively caused her irate son to pause. A rebel, but not to the extent that he could defy the steely voice of his mother, Bo stood where he was for a long moment, still with the pistol aimed at Arlo. "Put it away, I said," she repeated, this time punctuating it with the metallic sound of her revolver cocking.

Another few frozen moments passed—Bo's pistol pointed at Arlo, P. D.'s pistol pointed at Bo. Then, suddenly, Bo's irate expression softened into a sheepish smile. He released the hammer on his pistol and lowered it. "Damn, Ma, I wasn't really gonna shoot him," he lied, "but you saw what the big jackass did. That was my good shirt." He holstered the weapon. "You wasn't really gonna shoot me, was you?" he asked then.

"Don't you doubt it for a minute," she replied, her voice cold and without emotion.

"You crazy bastard," Arlo said, "I oughta break your neck for pulling that damn gun on me." Moments before, he had been shaken, staring death in the face. Now he wanted restitution, in spite of the fact that his bullying had placed him in that dire situation.

"You oughta try," Bo answered. "One of these days Ma ain't gonna be around to save your ass."

"Hush!" P. D. suddenly commanded, and held up her hand to silence them both. "Listen!"

At first there was no sound other than the soft gurgle of an eddy caused by a large rock near the water's edge. Then the sound that had caught P. D.'s attention was repeated. It was the sound of her big blue roan's inquisitive whinny. It was soon followed by a similar whinny from the other horses. "Somebody's comin'," P. D. warned. "Bo, scramble up that bank and see what you can see." When it came to scouting or tracking, Bo was always the first choice, since he seemed to have a knack for it that was absent in Arlo. Although in a weakened state, P. D. had regained enough strength to handle a rifle, even though it would be with one hand. She reached for it then with her good hand while directing her eldest son. "Arlo, back outta that firelight. Them horses hear somethin'."

Bo was gone for no more than a few minutes before he reappeared out of the darkness that cloaked the riverbank. "Injuns," he whispered. "I counted seven of 'em, and they're comin' this way. I figure they saw our campfire, 'cause they're walkin', leading their horses, like they was fixin' to sneak up on us."

"Must be friends of them three we left back there," P. D. said. "How far away are they?"

"Hundred yards, I reckon," Bo replied. "Maybe a little more."

"Well, we'll just have to set up a little welcome party

for 'em," P. D. said. Wasting no more time, she hurriedly positioned her sons in the willows by the river so they could lay down a cross fire over their camp. With Arlo's help, she settled herself behind a low bluff where she could prop her rifle on the sand. Ready to receive their company, she cautioned Bo and Arlo to hold their fire until the Indians reached the campfire.

P. D. and her sons had barely gotten into position when the first Indian appeared. Moving silently in the darkness, Black Fox paused near the top of the riverbank to study the camp. There was no sign of anyone about the small fire that had now died to form a soft glow in the pitch black of the bluff. Thinking the white men to be asleep, he focused his gaze upon the dark lumps that were three saddles and blankets. In the darkness he could not see with any definition, but judging by the dying campfire, he assumed that the lumps were three sleeping men.

"Move quickly," he whispered when the others caught up to him. "They are all sleeping. If we move all at once, we can kill them with our war axes before they know we're upon them." He looped his pony's reins over a willow limb, and with ax in hand, led his party of warriors toward the fire.

A slow grin formed upon Bo's face as a line of dark shadows suddenly materialized above him on the low bluff. He counted the silhouettes as they filed down toward the fire—five, six, seven, all accounted for. *A real turkey shoot,* he thought. P. D. had said to wait until the Indians reached the fire before shooting, but Bo could see no reason to wait. All seven of the warriors he had spotted before were parading unsuspecting right before him. So he put the front sight of his rifle on the last Blackfoot in line and squeezed off the first shot.

Instant pandemonium erupted on the darkened riverbank as Bo, anxious to kill as many of the warriors as he could, set off the killing rain of rifle fire that came from the willows.

That damn Bo, P. D. thought when the first shot rang out. Working with only one effective arm, she would have preferred to let the Indians get closer before she fired. With little choice left to her, she aimed at the center of the line of warriors and fired. Several yards away, Arlo opened up with his Winchester while she fumbled to crank another round into the chamber. Then, caught up in the resulting massacre, she ignored the wounded shoulder and blazed away using both hands.

Caught in a blistering hail of rifle fire, Black Fox went down with a slug in his left thigh. It no doubt saved his life, for he could hear the snapping sounds of bullets ripping the air overhead where he had been standing. Behind him, he heard the screams of pain as his followers were systematically cut down by the devastating barrage of lead. It was over in a matter of seconds and the war party all lay dead and dying on the riverbank, all save one. Black Fox rolled over into a shallow gully, and began a painful crawl back to his pony. There was nothing he could do for his friends. The only obligation left to him was to try to save himself.

"By God," P. D. exclaimed as she walked up to ex-

amine the bodies, her wounded arm bleeding again
from the exertion. "These godless heathens come in
here thinkin' they can murder innocent folks." Seeing
a slight movement from one of the bodies, she
pumped two more shots into the dying warrior.

"Ma," Arlo said, "your shoulder's bleedin' again."

"Ain't nothin'," she replied, still caught up in the
excitement of the killing. "It ain't painin' me a'tall."

"There ain't but six bodies," Bo observed.
"Where's the other one?"

His question was answered for him by the sudden
sound of a horse's hooves as Black Fox galloped
away in the darkness. Bo immediately spun around
and emptied the remaining bullets from his magazine
in the direction of the sound. "Should I saddle my
horse?" Arlo asked, ready to give chase.

"Naw, let him go," P. D. decided. "I'm pretty sure
he was hit. I saw every one of 'em go down. He'll
most likely run off somewhere and die." She turned
her attention back to the bodies lying sprawled on the
ground. "I reckon them Injuns learned who to mess
with all right. You boys drag 'em away from the fire.
Throw 'em over the bank yonder so's I don't have to
smell 'em. It's a while yet till daylight. We'd best get
some sleep."

"I want them scalps," Bo interjected.

"Well, you're gonna have to climb down there and
get 'em," Arlo said, already dragging a body to the
edge of the bank.

Chapter 15

Even with his shoulder throbbing with pain, Matt had managed to remain upright in the saddle while following Little Hawk along a trail that skirted the bank of a wide stream. Leading north from the Yellowstone, the trail followed the water through a rolling prairie of knee-high grass and treeless hills. The journey took no more than a few hours, though it had seemed much longer to the wounded man. Finally, they had arrived at a fork in the stream and the Blackfoot village, some fifty lodges in a circle between the forks. Met by a small gathering of people down by the stream's edge, the warriors were immediately pressed for news of the scouting party. Thinking Matt a prisoner, they pressed close around his horse, casting insults and threats, until Little Hawk silenced them. After learning of Matt's innocence in the tragic event that claimed three men of their village, they were anxious to help, especially when informed that he was the vengeful warrior who had cleaned out the Frenchman's nest of vipers. The med-

icine man was sent for at once, and Matt was taken to
Little Hawk's tipi.

Word soon spread through the rest of the village
that the fearsome white warrior who had slain the
evil white men and burned the Frenchman's trading
post was lying wounded in Little Hawk's lodge. A
crowd gathered outside the tipi while Two Bears, the
medicine man, administered to Matt's wounds. Little
Hawk watched as Two Bears applied a poultice to
Matt's head before probing his shoulder wound to
make it bleed. The bullet was judged to be too deep
to extract without cutting through too much muscle,
so it was deemed best to leave it. Two Bears explained
to Little Hawk, and Little Hawk translated to Matt,
that it would heal all right as long as it was allowed
to bleed freely long enough to cleanse the wound.
When he was satisfied that it had bled sufficiently, he
applied a poultice and bandage. Matt only hoped that
the medicine man knew what he was doing, for he
couldn't argue with him. He couldn't help thinking
that Two Bears' attitude might be entirely different
had he known of Matt's close relationship with the
Crows. *He'd probably pack that poultice with dog shit*, he
thought.

At Little Hawk's insistence, Matt agreed to rest
there that night, although he still felt an urgency to
ride after the bounty hunters. His common sense told
him that he was in no condition to go after them until
he gave his shoulder a chance to heal. The question
might be irrelevant, anyway, since Black Fox and six
warriors had gone after the white murderers. *I'll just*

cool my heels till I'm well enough to ride, he decided. *This stuff the medicine man put on me will either kill me or heal me.* One night stretched into two before he had rested sufficiently.

Matt awoke to the sound of voices outside the lodge. He soon determined that someone was approaching the village, and the sounds he heard were voices calling out in alarm. Rolling out of his blanket, he discovered he was alone in the tipi. With some discomfort due to the stiffness in his shoulder, he pulled his moccasins on and laced them. Then, with a little grunt of pain, he got to his feet, and stood motionless for a minute until his head stopped spinning. When he was confident he was steady enough, he went outside to see what had caused the commotion.

Near the edge of the stream, a crowd had gathered around a lone rider. Matt recognized the rider as the fearsome warrior, Black Fox. One legging was soaked with blood, and he appeared to be exhausted. Matt knew what had happened without being told.

"Six more warriors killed by these murderers," Little Hawk wailed in his anguish. "Now they have killed nine of my people." He went on to explain to Matt what had happened. After the ambush, Black Fox had escaped into the night. Although he was wounded in his thigh, he had circled back at daylight to see if he could get a shot at the white men. But they had already broken camp and were gone. He picked up their trail, and followed for a while until he became weak and sick. Knowing he was helpless to fight the three white men, he gave up the trail and rode all night to reach his village.

"So there *were* three of them," Matt commented, having been unsure until then.

"We will mount a war party to go after these murderers," Little Hawk exclaimed. "There must be vengeance for my people."

Matt studied the grieving Blackfoot's face for a long moment, knowing the pain and frustration Little Hawk felt. It was the same pain he felt for Zeb's death. He knew that he alone could seek that vengeance. "Listen, my friend," he said. "You can't go after these men. Most likely they're heading for Virginia City. You can't take a war party into Virginia City. It's a white man's town, with too many people. Your warriors would be massacred, and you have already lost nine. It would be foolish to lose even more."

"Waugh!" Little Hawk cried out in frustration, for he knew what Slaughter said was true.

"It's up to me to track these men down. I'm the reason they came to this territory. They came to capture me, or kill me, and your people were just unlucky enough to get caught in the cross fire. As soon as my shoulder is well enough, I'll find them."

"But you are only one man," Little Hawk said, forgetting the scene he had witnessed at the Frenchman's.

"One is enough," Matt replied.

He did not linger in the Blackfoot village any longer than necessary. On the third day, he felt that his left arm was strong enough to support his rifle, so he announced his intention to leave. The following morning he thanked those who had cared for him, and saddled up, ready to ride. Little Hawk and Black Fox, along with a party of a dozen warriors insisted upon accompanying him. "They may not have gone to Virginia City," Little Hawk explained. "White men are pushing farther north, looking for the yellow dirt your people worship. If the men you seek have gone into the mountains, you will need good scouts to help you find them." So, on a chilly, cloudy morning, Matt set out once again to find Zeb Benson's killers, accompanied by fourteen Blackfoot warriors leading extra horses to recover their dead.

Retracing their earlier journey, the scouting party returned to pick up the trail where Black Fox had been ambushed. There they found the bodies of their slain brothers in a pile just under the bank of the river, easily located by the gathering of buzzards that had already discovered them. Yelling and firing their weapons, the warriors scattered the squawking, protesting dinner guests, and loaded the bodies on the extra horses. Sending four of the party back with the dead, Black Fox led the rest of the scouting party after P. D. and her two sons.

The trail was easy enough to follow. There had been no effort to cover their tracks. It held close to the Yellowstone until reaching the point where the Yellowstone took a turn to the south. It was still too early to determine if the three they followed were heading for Virginia City. From that point, Alder Gulch and the mining towns of Virginia City and Nevada City were on the far side of the mountains to the south-east. But the trail they followed continued on west-ward. It was not until reaching the Madison River that their prey turned south on a well-used trail that led to Virginia City. From this point the Blackfoot warriors knew it was unwise for them to continue.

Little Hawk and Black Fox pulled their ponies up on either side of Matt, and sat silently gazing toward the south. They were obviously reluctant to give up the chase, but both knew they could not ride into the white man's town of thousands of people. "We will say good-bye here," Little Hawk finally spoke. "I hope that the Great Spirit will guide your eyes." Matt nodded in reply and nudged the paint forward. The two Blackfoot warriors watched him depart. Then, a long way from home, they wheeled their ponies and loped away.

Passing the outermost buildings of Virginia City, his mind was churning with confusing and often con-flicting thoughts about the men he sought. They had come a long way to capture him, if indeed they had started from Virginia. It had cost them the lives of two of their number—one cut down near his corral, and the one he had seen disappear over the edge of a cliff. And yet the trail he followed was that of three men. Where had the other man come from? Even with two dead, it still didn't make sense to him that they would give up on their mission and turn tail. He thought then of the angry little man who had exchanged shots with him on the mountainside before sliding over the cliff to his death. He wondered if that was the reason the others had given up and headed back to civilization. Maybe the stout little man was the boss, and the others didn't have the stomach to come after him again. There were questions, but Matt did not expect to find the answers, as his intention was to shoot on sight as soon as he was sure of his target.

Walking his horse slowly along Wallace Street, the main street that ran up Daylight Gulch, Matt shifted his gaze from side to side as he passed the shops and houses. His first impression of the town was that it might be a little more difficult to find the men he searched for than he had anticipated. Having never been to Virginia City before this day, he had expected a much smaller town. To his dismay, there were hundreds of houses and stores, located on several streets. There appeared to be no shortage of saloons and bawdy houses with the customary loafers lolling on the board sidewalks out front. There was a lot more bustle than he had a taste for, though many of the town's residents had left the town back in the summer of '64 after hearing news of a gold strike in Last Chance Gulch in Helena. In spite of that, Virginia City was still too crowded by Matt's standards. He decided the first place to start his search was the livery stable.

Clyde Newton looked up from the saddle he was polishing when a shadow fell across the potbellied stove before him. With the lantern hanging on the side of a stall behind his visitor, Clyde was unable to make out the man's features. Seeing that the owner of the stable was squinting hard in an effort to identify him, the stranger stepped away from the lantern. Able to see him clearly now, Clyde was a little surprised. *A real wild-and-woolly one,* he thought as he took a quiet inventory of Matt's buckskin clothes and moccasins, the rifle in his hand, and the bow he carried on his back. He also noticed the tail of a bandage protruding from under his hat. *I ain't seen one of the real wild ones in quite a spell,* he thought. He placed the can of saddle soap on the dirt floor, folded his polishing cloth, and placed it on top of the open can. "Evenin', mister," he said. "What can I do for ya?"

"I'm lookin' for three men that mighta rode in durin' this past week. They rode in from north of here—thought maybe they mighta put their horses up in your stable."

Clyde didn't answer right away, but continued to assess the tall young man. After several moments of silence, during which Matt obviously lost his patience and shifted his Henry rifle from his right hand to cradle it before him, Clyde spoke. "That ain't a helluva lot to go on, young feller. I've seed one or two strangers all week—don't recollect seein' three come in together."

"Is this the only stable in town?"

"No, there's others," Clyde replied. "You can check with them. They're easy enough to find." He continued to study the sober young man standing uneasily in the confines of the crowded stable. "If you don't mind me askin', what do these fellers look like? Are they prospectors? Maybe I've seed somebody new in the saloon or the blacksmith's, or somewhere else."

It was difficult to explain to the stable owner that he didn't really know for certain if he could identify the three men, even if he bumped into them. He was counting on finding the three together. As far as describing them, the only thing he had to go on was the description of the young one he had killed between his cabin and corral, and the short stocky one he saw go over the cliff. He figured the other three would probably be similarly attired. "Well, they ain't hardly prospectors," he answered. "I expect the only tools they'd be carrying are rifles and pistols."

Clyde thought about that for a moment. This didn't strike him as a reunion of family or friends. It might even be worthwhile to alert the deputy marshal that there might be some troublemakers in town. At the moment, however, he deemed it prudent to remain cordial with the steel-eyed young mountain man before him. "Sounds like you might wanna look in the saloon for your friends," he suggested. "Might try the Bale of Hay. That's where a lot of folks go."

"Much obliged," Matt replied, and turned to leave.

"Not a'tall," Clyde returned. He walked to the end of the stable and watched as Matt rode up the muddy street. Then he crossed the street and walked down to the deputy marshal's office. Virginia City had seen its share of outlaws and killers, and Clyde remembered that it was not that long ago when the only defense the town had was an active vigilante committee. At least now there was a deputy marshal, since Virginia City had become the territorial capital. As he walked in the door of the marshal's office, he congratulated himself upon being smart enough to send Matt someplace where the marshal could find him right away.

Matt didn't have much money to spare, but he decided he could spend a little for one drink to kindle a spark of fire in his veins. It had been a chilly ride for most of the afternoon, and a shot of something strong might serve to burn the cobwebs from his heart. "Pour you another?" the bartender asked, holding the bottle to hover over his glass. Like the man who owned the stable, the bartender had looked Matt over with an appraising eye.

"Reckon not," Matt replied, placing his palm over the empty glass. "One'll do." He had turned away to search the faces of the patrons seated around the tables when he heard a voice at his elbow.

"Have another, friend. Ed, put another one on my bill for the stranger."

Matt turned to see who his benefactor might be. The most obvious thing that met his eye was the badge pinned to his black lapel. His initial reaction was a sudden tensing of his muscles, a reaction that was not evident to the marshal. In fact, Matt himself might not have noticed it had it not caused a pain to shoot through his shoulder. It was enough to remind him to find a doctor to take a look at his shoulder. The wound seemed to be healing, but Matt felt it wise to check on the Blackfoot medicine man's work. Looking the lawman straight in the eye, he said, "That's awfully neighborly of you, Sheriff. Does every new face in town get a free drink?"

The marshal grinned. "It's Marshal," he corrected. "Tate's the name. I'm the law around here. And, no, ever'body don't get a free drink—just the ones that come outta the mountains lookin' like an Injun."

Matt returned the marshal's smile. "Well, then, I guess I'd better take it." He slid his glass toward the bartender. When it was filled, he tossed it back and replaced the shot glass solidly on the counter. "Now, Marshal, what is it you really wanna know?"

Tate's smile froze on an otherwise frowning face. "It ain't so much what I wanna know. It's more a matter of what *you* need to know. I don't know what you mighta heard, but Virginia City ain't the lawless town it used to be. We got solid folks livin' and workin' here now, and I aim to keep it peaceful. Now, I don't know who you might be lookin' for, or for what reason, but it damn-sure better be peaceful. Am I makin' myself clear enough?"

"Yeah, I reckon you are," Matt replied. "I shoulda checked to see if it was against the law to be wearin' buckskins."

"Now, it ain't gonna do you no good a'tall to smart off at me, young feller. I know you come into my town lookin' for three fellers, and I expect you'd best tell me what you're aimin' to do when you find 'em."

"I expect that's my business," Matt retorted. His patience was rapidly evaporating with the marshal's manner. He had broken no laws, and he found it

exasperating that he was being subjected to harass-
ment when three wanton murderers were probably
not even noticed when they had hit town.

"Now, you see," Tate shot back, "there's that
smart-mouth attitude I'm talkin' about. I've a good
mind to lock you up for a while till you learn some respect for the law."

Matt was suddenly astonished, finding it incredi-
ble that he was involved in this conversation in the
first place. Marshal Tate had evidently already la-
beled him a troublemaker, and he was in no mood to
continue bantering with him. He thought about
Molly, frail and frightened, running for her life from
the band of bounty hunters that had invaded his valley. He thought about Zeb Benson and Singing
Woman, and the twilight years they might have
shared together, years now that would never be. In
his mind, there could be no greater wrong than per-
mitting these wanton murderers to go free. He made
up his mind that no one was going to prevent him
from ensuring that justice was done. He simply had
no time for posturing lawmen.

He calmly picked his rifle up from where it had
been propped against the bar. Then, with his eyes
locked on Tate's, he reached in his pocket, pulled out
a couple of coins and tossed them on the counter.
"That's for the drink. I haven't broken any laws, and
I haven't threatened any of your citizens. I didn't
come here to cause innocent folks any trouble, but I
aim to do what I came here to do, and that don't in-

clude spendin' any time in your jail." He glared into the marshal's eyes. "Do I make *myself* clear?"

As soon as he said it, those few who stood closest to him and Tate backed away, anticipating an explosion about to occur. Tate's eyes flashed with anger, obviously accustomed to greater respect for his badge. He had been issued a direct challenge to his authority. It had been laid out for him in pure and simple terms by this sandy-haired cougar standing resolutely before him. And now it was up to him to respond. He was at once painfully aware of the eyes upon him from everyone in the room. He dared not show any weakness of backbone before the many witnesses to his actions at this moment. Yet the cold, clear, blue eyes that penetrated his gaze gave evidence of a certain truth. They were the eyes of a hunter, a man who had killed before. And Tate knew in that timeless moment that he would not hesitate to kill again, given no other choice. As if the earth had halted for a moment, the barroom was suspended motionless, as quiet as a tomb. The stillness pounded with a steady heartbeat in the marshal's temples. It was his move. Grimacing his lips tightly against his teeth, he made the decision that saved his life.

"Why, hell, young feller," Tate blurted nervously. "I was just japin' you a little bit. I didn't figure you'd take it to heart." Sensing the silent judgment of the barroom patrons, he made a feeble attempt to exhibit some backbone. "It would be smart to keep in mind that we aim to keep the peace in this town, and it's my job to see that we do."

Relieved, although with no change of expression, Matt realized that the marshal was backing down, and his last remark was a desperate show of bravado for the sake of his reputation. He was willing to allow the marshal that consideration. He had no wish to destroy Tate's standing in his community. "I'll try not to cause you any trouble," he said in a quiet but clear voice. "I'll be on my way now." He walked out the door.

No one moved for a full minute after the tall stranger disappeared through the doorway. Not until the swinging doors returned to their resting position, standing still once again, did anyone speak. And then the room filled with conversation. One, who had been seated at a corner table in the back of the room, rose to his feet. A big man, he, too, was a stranger in town, and the incident just witnessed seemed to have impacted on him more than any of the other patrons. He moved quickly to the door and pushed through to the board sidewalk, looking anxiously up and down the muddy street. In the gathering darkness of the early evening, he just managed to catch sight of a rider as he disappeared into the night. *Slaughter!* the big man thought.

"Arlo! Damn your hide. What's the matter with you, bustin' in here like that? Don't you know enough to knock before you come bustin' in a lady's room?" P. D. quickly pulled her shirt over her to cover her exposed shoulder. Bare from the waist up, she had been in the process of changing the bandage on her wound.

"Slaughter!" Arlo exclaimed, ignoring his mother's nakedness as well as her scolding. "He's here! I seen him!"

"What the hell are you talkin' about? Slaughter? Here? How do you know it was Slaughter?"

"Oh, it was him all right," Arlo gloated confidently. "Tall feller, wearin' animal hides like an Injun, totin' a Henry rifle. It was him. He come into town lookin' for three men. The marshal tried to stand up to him and he backed the marshal down, right down in front of ever'body."

P. D. was momentarily stunned, finding Arlo's report hard to believe. The man she was determined to hunt down had actually come after her? The thought of such a thing quickly triggered her anger. Nobody came after P. D. Wildmoon. She was the hunter, not the hunted. *You were lucky the first time we met*, she thought, thinking things would have been different had her foot not slipped on the loose shale of that mountainside. *Next time you won't be so lucky.*

After giving it a few moments additional thought, it began to dawn on her that this news might be more than she could have hoped for. She slipped into her shirt and slowly buttoned it while she thought about the possibility of such good fortune. Only she and Wiley had come face-to-face with Slaughter, and upon second thought, she had to say that poor, dead Wiley had no more than a glimpse of him when he entered the cabin. Arlo and Bo had only seen the man called Slaughter for a brief few seconds, when he said his name was Johnson, and that was at a fair distance. "Did you hear anybody call his name?" she asked.

"No, but it was him, Ma," Arlo insisted.

"You say he come lookin' for three men? How do you know that?"

"That's what the marshal said."

She felt a gradual tensing of the muscles in her whole body as she began to feel what Arlo said was a real possibility. *Well,* she thought, *he's come to his own funeral.* "Where is he now?"

"I don't know," Arlo admitted. "He rode off toward Nevada City, but it was gettin' dark, so I couldn't see real good. Anyway, I came back to tell you."

P. D. paused to consider that. Nevada City was only about a mile and a half up the gulch. Maybe he was going to look for a place to stay up that way. Her shirt tucked in, she tested her shoulder, picking up her rifle and sighting on the washbasin several times. Satisfied that the wound would no longer hinder her, she put the rifle down. "Where's Bo?"

"I don't know," Arlo said. "He was in the saloon with me for a while, but he left to find him a whore-house a half hour or so before Slaughter came in."

"I told you two to keep an eye on each other," P. D. scolded, but with no real conviction. Her mind was consumed with thoughts of revenge, and the picture of Wiley lying dead on the ground. "Go find Bo. We're gonna take a look around town."

*　　*　　*

A search of every saloon and hotel in Virginia City and Nevada City turned up no trace of the man P. D. so passionately wished to kill. With no choice but to give up the search for the night, she was worried that Slaughter might have moved on. Her common sense told her that it was unlikely, and her instincts told her that he was still near. "He's gotta show up somewhere," she assured her sons, "and when he does, he's a dead man. I ain't aimin' to take nothin' but his head back to Virginia for the reward."

While P. D. and her sons returned to pass the night in their hotel rooms, Matt made his way up into the mountains to find a suitable place to make camp. Having no money to waste on hotels or dining rooms, he was content to bed his horse and himself down by a tiny stream at the bottom of a narrow ravine. His chosen campsite was more than a couple of miles from the busy town. It seemed that every shovelful of dirt in Alder Gulch had been turned over in the relentless search for gold, with claims and abandoned claims rendering the ravine uninhabitable for a man of the mountains.

The ravine offered some protection from a cold wind that had freshened at sundown, and looking up at the slate gray sky, he wondered if he might see snow when he awoke in the morning. With that in mind, he gathered plenty of dead branches for a fire and unrolled the bearskin robe he carried behind his saddle. He couldn't help thinking about his old partner then. Zeb would have *smelled* snow. When morning came, he would search the town for the three men who had come to kill him. Thoughts of the slender blond girl, whose faint smile and innocent eyes formed a picture that often visited his mind before falling asleep, now came to ease him into the night.

More than ninety miles to the east, as the hawk flies, the inspiration for Matt's vision lay awake watching the soft flames that patiently consumed the fir branches in her fire. It had been days since Broken Hand had brought Matt's message that he had gone after the men who had killed Zeb and Singing Woman. The people of Broken Hand's village had been kind, and eager to help her, but she felt helpless and alone without Matt. With her cabin burned to the ground, she had no choice but to accept the Crows' hospitality, and the use of Singing Woman's tipi.

Each day since he was gone, she remained close to the tipi, watching the river for sign of a lone rider on a paint pony. And each day passed with no sign. The nights were the worst. Sleepless until exhaustion overcame her, her mind was filled with the dread that he might never return, leaving her with no notion if he were living or dead. There was nothing left to her but to wait out the long, lonely days and the fitful nights, praying that tomorrow she would see him fording the river, returning to her.

Chapter 16

Malcolm Early paused while a bull train of sixteen horses, pulling three wagons, rolled past, churning up the muddy main street of Virginia City. A former freighter himself, Malcolm touched a finger to his hat. The freighter returned the greeting with a nod of his head. Folks in Virginia City said that Malcolm was properly named, seeing as how he was one of the early settlers in the gulch. A burly man, now in his middle years, Early had been instrumental in the establishment of a vigilante posse that had hung more than a few road agents and murderers in the wild young years of Alder Gulch and its sprawling town, Virginia City. He was still the man to consult when storm clouds gathered to threaten the peace of the town.

The bull train having passed, Early crossed the narrow street, taking pains to avoid the puddles that looked to be more than ankle deep. Reaching the walkway on the other side, he paused to stomp some of the mud from his boots before entering the marshal's office.

Deputy Marshal Alvin Tate looked up from his desk when the door opened. "Mornin', Malcolm," he said. "'Preciate you comin' by." He got up and extended his hand. "Still snowin' outside?"

"Alvin," Early acknowledged, shaking the marshal's hand. "Yeah, a little," he said, answering Tate's question. "It ain't gonna amount to much, just make more mud." Brushing the salutations aside, he got to the point of his visit. "Barney Fletcher said you were in the Best Chance lookin' for me."

"Yeah, I thought I might catch you at breakfast, but you hadn't come in yet. I probably just missed you."

"I reckon." Early shrugged. "I had some things to take care of before breakfast. What's on your mind?" he asked, but he had a suspicion that he already knew. Tate confirmed it.

"I need to talk to you about some trouble that might be just waitin' to happen, and I thought it best to head it off before it gets started." He paused to make sure he had Early's attention. "There's a dangerous feller come into town yesterday, and he's lookin' for trouble."

"I heard you had a little set-to with some stranger at the Bale of Hay," Early said, "but what's that got to do with me?" He refrained from commenting on reports he had heard that the marshal had effectively been backed down by the buckskin-clad stranger. "If he was causing trouble, why didn't you just arrest him?"

"Now, see, that's just it," Tate came back, eager to defend his lack of action. "He ain't really done nothin' yet. I couldn't hardly throw him in jail for doin' nothin'."

Early shook his head, obviously at a loss. "Don't sound to me like you got any problem if he ain't done nothin'. Even if he does, he's just one man. Hell, arrest him."

"Well, now, see, there's more to it than that. Otherwise, I wouldn't have wanted to talk to you about it." He puffed a little as he added, "Hell, one man, I'da just throwed his ass in jail. But, like I said, he hadn't broke no laws, so I didn't arrest him. The thing that I wanted to talk to you about is this. I got word that this feller is lookin' for three other fellers he followed here, and he's got blood in his eye for certain. And John Sawyer said he rented a couple of rooms to three strangers this week, and one of 'em's got a gunshot wound in the shoulder. I'm thinkin' we might have us a shoot-out on our hands if we don't head it off." He cocked his head sideways in a gesture of concern. "Some innocent folks could get hurt."

Early was beginning to see the reason for Tate wanting to see him. "And you're thinkin' it might be wise to call the posse out to make sure these desperadoes take their mischief elsewhere."

"It might be in the best interest of the town," Tate said. Though both men referred to the loosely organized mob that still looked toward Malcolm Early as their leader as the posse, the gang of volunteers was in fact the remnant of the vigilantes who enforced the peace in the years before Tate was hired as deputy marshal.

"Well, maybe that's somethin' to think about, all right," Early replied, stroking his chin whiskers thoughtfully. It had been over two years since he had led a band of vigilantes that strung up five road agents from the ceiling beam of Clyde Newton's new barn. Their activity was generally frowned upon now that Virginia City was the territorial capital and there was an official marshal in place, but Early had to admit he missed the excitement of running the hounds.

"Of course, I could handle this by myself," Tate insisted. "I just thought it might be a good thing to show these gunmen that come to roost in Virginia City that the whole town is gonna stand up to 'em."

Early stood there, slowly nodding his head up and down while he thought it over. "All right," he decided. "I'll get the word out to some of the boys, and we'll go visit these no-accounts."

It was a little past noon when Malcolm Early returned to Tate's office with seven volunteers, all eager to participate in what might prove to be a wild party. "This was all I could get hold of on short notice," Early reported, "but they, by God, oughta be plenty for this job."

Tate looked over the assembly of vigilantes, all armed with pistols, or shotguns, or both. Though there were only seven, he agreed with Early. They were all good men, tempered hard and willing. Jack Porter and his brother-in-law, Will Peterson, both tough as new leather, were the first Early called in. Billy Hyde, a blacksmith, and Johnny Duncan, a freighter, had ridden with Early when the five road agents were strung up a couple of years back. The other three were prospectors who had done pretty well for themselves. Partners in a large claim, they were naturally resentful of all strangers in the gulch. By anyone's assessment, it was a hard bunch that had been assembled.

As he had done with Malcolm Early, the marshal laid out the potential problem as he saw it, summing up with the statement, "We got one wild son of a bitch lookin' for three other fellers to settle up for who knows what, and thinkin' he can do it in our town."

"Three fellers you say?" This from Billy Hyde. "That's mighty interesting. I was talkin' to Bill Dolen, the bartender over at the Lucky Strike, and he was tellin' me about three fellers in there last night. He said they was in the Lucky Strike a couple of weeks ago, too—only there was four of 'em then. He said they looked like the kind that would cut a man's throat just to hear him whistle. Another feller come in; he'd been gunshot. Bill said the other four took up with him, and they left the saloon together. Anyway, now they're back in town. Ain't but three of 'em now, and one of *them's* been shot. Now, I'm thinkin' they just might be the three gents this other feller has come lookin' for."

There was a fair amount of nodding and conversation rumbling among the posse following Billy

Hyde's comments. Early looked at the marshal and nodded slowly.

"There, now, you see," Marshal Tate said. "Where there's stink, there's shit. I think it'd be a good idea to go over and have a talk with these three fellers; see what they're up to."

"We might as well just run 'em outta town right now," Early said, "before they start somethin' on our streets."

Everyone started shuffling toward the door, intent upon taking care of business, when they were halted by Jack Porter, who suddenly stopped in the doorway. "Look what's ridin' down the middle of the street, pretty as you please," he said. "I bet that's your wild mountain man right there, Marshal."

Tate edged past the others to stand beside Porter in the doorway. "That's him all right," he stated. "Told me straight out that he was gonna do what he came to do, and nobody better try to stop him." As soon as he said it, he realized that it again reflected upon his reputation as the town's lawman. He quickly tried to retract. "I mean, of course he didn't out and out say that, but that's what he was thinkin' all right."

"Looks to me like it's plain enough he's out to spill blood. Whaddaya say we lock his ass up till we run them other fellers outta town?" He looked toward Tate, waiting for an answer.

"That's exactly what I was about to say," Tate replied.

* * *

With no better plan in mind, Matt guided his horse along the main street of Virginia City with the intention of visiting every saloon he could find. He figured that, sooner or later, he was sure to run into the men he sought. Men like that just naturally gravitated to the saloons. Walking the paint slowly past the stable, he nodded briefly to Clyde Newton. The owner of the stable returned the nod, and stood watching the buckskin-clad rider as he made his way leisurely up the street.

Just as he was about to pass the marshal's office, the marshal stepped out the door. Signaling Matt with his hand, he walked out in the street to meet him. "I need to have a word with you," Tate called out while striding purposely toward him.

Mildly puzzled, Matt pulled the paint pony to a stop. "Is that a fact?"

"Yessir," Tate replied and caught the paint's bridle in his hand. With his other hand, he leveled his pistol at Matt. "Now, I'm gonna ask you real nice to step down off that horse, and keep your hands on that saddle horn."

Matt hadn't figured the marshal to possess backbone enough to confront him. Still, he had no intention of obeying Tate's demand. Remaining seated in the saddle, he responded, "You've got no call to pull a gun on me, Marshal. I haven't broke any laws."

Tate cocked the pistol. "I warned you we didn't want your kind around here, and I gave you a chance to leave. Now, by God, I reckon you'll have a longer stay with us. Now, get down from there."

Matt remained motionless for a few moments, staring at the .44 Colt Army model revolver aimed at his stomach. Then he glanced at the grim face of the marshal as Tate waited for his response. He considered his options. They were few, but he was not ready to surrender his weapons and go meekly to jail. Then, out of the corner of his eye, he noticed a couple of heavily armed men moving up from behind him to take a stand on his right side. Seconds later, two more appeared on his left. He glanced back at the marshal's face. Now the grim expression had changed to a sly smile, and Matt understood at once that he had been trapped.

"I ain't gonna tell you again," Tate growled. "If you don't get down off that horse, I'll shoot you off."

Seeing no alternative, Matt shrugged and slowly threw a leg over and stepped down. He was immediately relieved of his sidearm by Malcolm Early, and with the muzzle of a double-barreled shotgun prodding him in the back, he was herded into the jail. Turning the key in the cell door, Tate stepped back and fixed Matt with a smug expression. "I reckon you found out what we think of your kind in this town," he said.

"My kind?" Matt snapped. "What the hell is my kind?"

Malcolm Early, standing beside Tate, answered for the marshal. "Your kind is the no-good, trouble-makin' riffraff that we got rid of around here a few years back, and the kind we ain't gonna tolerate no more." He turned to Tate then. "Now let's go get them other three skunks."

The last remark caught Matt's attention immediately. *The other three* had to be referring to the same three he had followed here. He stood helpless while the gang of vigilantes filed out of the marshal's office, his frustration feeding on the hopelessness of the situation. When the door closed behind the posse, he at once began testing the bars and the cell door for any sign of weakness, only to be further frustrated. Finally, he accepted the fact that he was going to remain there until somebody unlocked the door.

P. D. Wildmoon pushed her chair back from the table and stretched her arms out to the side. Her shoulder was still stiff and sore, but she was satisfied that it would no longer be a hindrance to her. Content, she watched her two sons continue to devour the remains of their supper. *Like starving coyotes,* she thought as Arlo snatched the last biscuit from the plate before Bo could claim it. It had been an unsuccessful day. They had cautiously canvassed the entire town, but found no trace of Slaughter. P. D. was beginning to question whether Arlo had actually seen Slaughter in the first place. It was a good-sized town, but it wasn't so big that a man like that could go completely unnoticed. She had finally decided to abandon the search, figuring that, if Slaughter actually had been in Virginia City, he had moved on. With no better plan, she intended to head out again in the morning to Nevada City, hoping that maybe they might pick up his trail.

She focused her gaze upon Arlo for a few moments, as her oversized son slurped noisily at his coffee, then consumed the final biscuit in two bites. She couldn't help but smile, and was about to comment on his ability to put away great quantities of food when activity at the door of the hotel dining room caught her attention.

A group of men, nine altogether, filed in the door. Stern-faced and businesslike, they scanned the tables, apparently searching for something or someone. P. D. was immediately alert, her instincts signaling trouble. She noticed then that one of the men wore a badge. Very slowly, with little show of movement, she slipped her pistol out of its holster and held it under the table. "Arlo, Bo," she hissed, "mind yourselves. I think we got company." Something in their mother's tone told them to get ready for trouble. They each dropped their forks immediately. Arlo followed his mother's gaze toward the group of men at the door. He cocked an eye at Bo, and Bo nodded in reply before pushing his chair back to give himself room. "Just hold still," P. D. cautioned.

Looking over the dining room patrons, it took only a moment to spot the three at the back corner table. Tate nodded to Early and the burly vigilante grinned in reply. With an aside to Jack Porter, he said, "You boys spread out and be ready in case they put up a fight." He then followed the marshal to the table.

"Howdy, boys," Tate said, stopping right before the table. "What are you boys doin' in my town?"

P. D. met the marshal's stare with one of her own. After locking eyes with the lawman for a long moment, she answered. "Minding our own business," she said sarcastically, her gaze shifting to take in the vigilantes lined up across the front of the room.

Tate merely grunted at this, and looked to his left to make sure Early was backing him. Emboldened by his superiority in numbers, he couldn't help but swagger a bit. "Well, mister, I'm the law around here, and my business is to run scum like you outta town. Now, on your feet!" he ordered.

Unmoved, P. D. remained seated. "I'll tell you what, Marshal, if you just turn around and walk your ass outta here, and take your men with you—why, I'll forget about the whole thing. If you knew me, you'd know that nobody runs P. D. Wildmoon outta town."

"Why you cocky son of a bitch . . ." Malcolm Early blurted, unable to remain a spectator. "Get up from there or, by God, we'll drag your ass outta here." He grabbed the edge of the table, preparing to jerk it out of the way.

"Hold steady," P. D. cautioned Bo and Arlo, who were visibly uncomfortable. Back to Early, she warned, "I wouldn't if I was you."

There followed just a short moment of silence that filled the entire dining room as the other patrons realized what was going on. Cutting the silence was a light tapping of metal on wood as P. D. fixed the two confronting her with a benign expression approaching smugness. At that moment, Tate realized that the tapping was that of a gun barrel against the bottom of the table. Suddenly blanching, he immediately took a step backward, but Early failed to understand the warning. He pulled the table over sideways, turning it upside down.

The crash of the table with dishes hitting the floor shattered the silence that had descended upon the room. It was followed a split second later by the crack of P. D.'s pistol—two shots in quick succession. The first doubled Early over with a slug in his gut. The second caught Tate in the upper thigh, causing him to fall over another table, which had not yet been cleared of dirty dishes. Pandemonium followed. Terrified diners scrambled to escape the scene, knocking chairs and tables over in a desperate stampede toward the front door. "Shotgun!" P. D. bellowed at Bo, but Bo was one step ahead of the warning. His pistol already in hand from the moment the table was overturned, he cut down on Billy Hyde, who was the first of the vigilantes to bring a weapon to bear. Bo's shot smashed Billy dead center in his chest, dropping the blacksmith to the floor. His finger tightened on the trigger of the shotgun as he fell, firing a blast that almost decapitated an unfortunate woman who was not fast enough to have reached the door.

Total bedlam was now the rule in the heretofore peaceful dining room. The members of Early's posse, all lined up across the front wall of the room, were caught in a state of total confusion. Those who could react quickly enough to return fire were hampered by the exodus of the frightened patrons. One of the vigilantes, Johnny Duncan, shoved a terrified diner aside and fired at P. D., tearing a chunk of wood from the edge of the table she was now using as a shield. A split second later, Johnny went over backward, dropping his weapon to grasp his forehead with both hands over the hole Arlo's bullet left there.

With all three Wildmoons spraying the room with bullets, randomly striking vigilantes as well as innocent patrons, the rest of Early's posse threw valor to the wind, deeming it more important to save their skins. Out the door they fled, the three prospectors in the lead, never taking the time to look back. Of the survivors of the sudden firestorm set off inside the dining room, only Jack Porter and Will Peterson made an attempt to recover. Diving behind a horse trough, they laid in wait for the three desperadoes to come outside. Cautious now, when surprise was no longer in her favor, P. D. warned her sons to beware of ambush. She went to the front door and, with it cracked just enough to peer out, scanned the street, now almost empty of fleeing citizens. Scanning the street again, she almost passed over the watering trough, but something caught her eye, and she came back to check it. There was something on the ground beyond the trough. A grin slowly formed on her face when she identified the objects. They were two sets of boot heels. "Arlo, Bo," she said, directing them to the two windows that flanked the door. "There's two of them bastards layin' behind the horse trough." No further instruction was needed. When they were in place, P. D. gave the signal, and the three of them released a heavy rain of lead upon the trough. There was no reaction at first. Then, finally, it got too hot behind the trough, and the brothers-in-law decided they'd best get out of there. "Sou-weeee," Bo yelled when the two jumped up and made a run for it. "Pig, pig, sou-wee," he called after them while sighting his rifle on Jack Porter's shoulder blades. Both men almost made it to the opposite side of the street before dropping dead in the mud.

Distracted by the sport of shooting at fleeing vigilantes, P. D. and her sons did not notice a slight movement in the back of the room. Deputy Marshal Alvin Tate had remained hugging the floor amid a scattering of dirty dishes, afraid to make a move during the chaos that consumed the dining room. He was shot in the leg, but he knew it was not fatal. He thought about shooting when the three gunmen were at the front with their backs to him. The thing that kept him from doing so was the fear that, even if he got one of them, the other two might react quickly enough to kill him. So, moving as quietly as he could manage, he started inching his way toward the kitchen door, crawling on hands and knees, his palms sweating in cold fear. Once inside the kitchen, he pulled himself up to his feet, and limped out the back door, only pausing briefly to exchange glances with a terrified Chinese cook who was huddled behind the stove.

Once he found himself safely outside in the alley behind the hotel, he hobbled along the side of the building toward the street. At the corner of the building, he stopped to peer around the front to survey the carnage in the street. The sight was enough to turn him sick with fear. The bodies of Jack Porter and Will Peterson were lying where they had fallen, almost at the board walkway on the opposite side of the street. Tate was almost in shock, hardly able to believe the massacre he had touched off. Malcolm Early was dead, so were Johnny Duncan and Billy Hyde; five of the posse had been gunned down, and not a scratch on the three gunmen he had thought to run out of town. Adding to the horror, there was no telling how many bystanders were murdered. There were two bodies that he could see near the middle of the street, and he had witnessed the death of the woman inside. What to do? What *could* he do? The rest of the posse had taken flight. He couldn't do anything about the three still holed up in the dining room without help. Looking down at his bloody leg then, he decided the best thing to do was to get back to the jail and lock himself safely inside. Maybe the gunmen would ride out of Virginia City.

Locked inside his jail cell, Matt heard the eruption of gunfire down the street—a couple of shots at first, followed almost immediately by a barrage of gunfire. It sounded like a major skirmish had broken forth. With no outside window in his cell, he could only imagine what was going on, but he was prone to assume that the posse that had affected his arrest had proceeded to slaughter the three men he was after. The shooting lasted for no longer than ten or fifteen minutes, but he could hear an occasional excited voice as ordinary townsfolk ran by the jail on their flight to safety. Maybe his mission had been completed for him by the vigilante committee of Virginia City. Ironic, he admitted, but the satisfaction of exacting justice by his own hand was missing.

Near quiet had returned to the street outside the jail, and he was left to once again ponder his fate at the hand of the Virginia City marshal. He wondered what crime the spiteful lawman could concoct to hold him for. Mindful of that, he resumed his careful inspection of the bars in his cell, hoping to find a weakness he might exploit. He was stopped abruptly when the front door suddenly opened, and Deputy Marshal Tate staggered inside.

Matt read at once the state of shock that had descended upon the marshal. Wild-eyed and desperate, Tate slammed the door behind him and threw the bolt. One trouser leg soaked with blood, he hobbled over to his desk and started rummaging through the drawers, looking for something to tend his wound. Without so much as a glance in Matt's direction, he dropped his trousers to his ankles to expose dingy gray underwear with one leg solid red from the thigh down. With trembling fingers, he took a pair of scissors from one of the drawers, and began to gingerly cut away at the leg of his underwear.

"Looks like you need a doctor," Matt said.

Engrossed in his desperation to examine his wound, Tate recoiled in surprise when Matt spoke.

As if just then remembering his prisoner, he turned to glare at him.

"I heard the shootin'," Matt said. "Looks like you came out on the short end of it. Where's the rest of your posse?" When Tate did not answer, but continued to glare accusingly at him, it occurred to Matt that the marshal and his men may have come out on the losing side of the gunfight. He was immediately concerned. "Son of a bitch," he cursed. "You let 'em get away."

Finding his tongue finally, Tate snarled, "You brought this on, damn you. I've a mind to hang you for bringing this trouble to my town."

Matt was rapidly sizing up the situation. Judging by Tate bursting in the door and bolting it behind him, and the fact that none of his appointed vigilantes had come back with him, Matt figured Tate was afraid to go out the door, even to see the doctor. The marshal and his vigilante committee had run into a buzz saw, a little more than they had expected.

"Those three you went after, they're still here, aren't they?" Matt demanded. "You didn't get a one of them."

"None of your damn business," Tate shot back. "I reckon I got you, all right, and you'll still be here after your friends have gone."

"When the hell are you gonna understand? They ain't friends of mine. I followed 'em here to put an end to their devilry." Fighting a feeling of total frustration, Matt went on. "Where's the rest of your posse?" he repeated. "They got run off with their tails between their legs, didn't they? Dammit, Marshal, you're foolin' with three dangerous men. You think they're gonna just ride on outta here now that they've whipped you and your men? Why the hell should they? Hell, they own the town."

Alvin Tate stared back at his prisoner with the eyes of a defeated man. He wanted to strike back at Matt's accusations, but he was all out of courage, and feared deep inside that what Matt said was true. "The citizens of this town will band together to drive the bastards out," he offered without conviction.

"The hell they will," Matt snapped back. "They'll crawl in their holes and lock the door just like you did. I'm the best bet you've got to get rid of those three. That's what I came here to do. Let me outta here, and I'll take care of your problem. And as soon as it's done, I'll be on my way. I can promise you that."

Tate hesitated, unable to immediately reject Slaughter's proposition. He was sorely tempted to take him up on it, by sending a killer to stop a killer. It might be difficult to explain such a move to the town council, none of whom were likely to pick up their guns and take the posse's place. "How do I know, if I let you outta here, you won't just hightail it outta town?" he asked, hedging.

"Because that's what I came here to do. If you had left me alone, maybe you wouldn't be carryin' lead in your leg and there'd be fewer dead people around here."

The idea was working on Tate's mind. It wasn't the

right thing to do, but it might be the only thing to do. He despised himself for admitting it, but he knew that he had no stomach for a second confrontation with P. D. Wildmoon. He stood for a long moment with his hand on the ring of keys that would open the cell door, trying to make up his mind. "You ain't really broke no laws, that's true," he rationalized. His mind made up, he walked to the cell door and inserted the key. Before turning it, he said, "I'm gonna deputize you, so you'll be workin' for law."

"Any way you want it," Matt said, quickly stepping through the open cell door in case Tate had a change of heart. "I need my rifle."

Tate went to a cabinet in the corner of the room to retrieve the Henry rifle. "You ain't goin' back on me, are you?" he asked while maintaining a firm hand on the weapon.

"Reckon not," Matt replied, taking the rifle from him. "Now, where are they?"

"The hotel dining room, Tate answered.

Matt checked the magazine and cranked a cartridge into the chamber. Then, as an afterthought, he asked, "Do you know who they are?"

"No," Tate replied nervously. "I never seen 'em before." Then he remembered. "Wait, the one that does all the talkin' said his name was P. D. Wildmoon."

P. D. Wildmoon: it was the name he had heard when he first crossed paths with the four bounty hunters south of the Big Horns.

Chapter 17

P. D. Wildmoon had not intended to take on the law in Virginia City. The incident in the hotel dining room was not something that she could have foreseen. But, when confronted by the enforcement committee, she had not been given time to think of the possible consequences of an aggressive reaction. Her response was a reflex action that came naturally to her. Luckily, her actions did not result in any harm to herself or her sons. To the contrary, the short but totally one-sided gunfight in the dining room had instilled a sense of invincibility in all three Wildmoons, a feeling that the town was theirs for the taking. They could turn the town upside down now in a search for Slaughter, unhindered by nosey lawmen. And after they had taken care of Slaughter, they could take what they wanted from the town before they left. P. D. had always been confident, but she was now experiencing euphoric feelings with the power she had gained with the routing of the marshal and the vigilantes. Still, she was not naive enough to think there was no threat to her and her boys just because she had destroyed any semblance of law in the town. Virginia City had a history of vigilante activity long before the law arrived in the territory, and she knew it was simply a matter of time before the citizens would organize to take action against her. She fully understood that her time of dominance was short, so she intended to take advantage of it while she could. "We'll find Slaughter," she told Arlo and Bo, "then we'll loot this damn town and head back east before the good citizens know what hit 'em."

The normally busy Wallace Street was now deserted as the three desperadoes left the hotel after picking up their belongings. P. D. wanted the horses saddled and their gear packed in case a quick departure became necessary. With a cautious eye on each door they passed, they walked toward the livery stable at the far end of the muddy thoroughfare, each with their saddlebags over their shoulders and Winchester rifles in hand. Anxious store owners and shopkeepers peeked from behind drawn shades and bolted doors, breathing easily only after the three passed them by.

"Whaddaya say we burn the damn jailhouse down?" Bo suggested, swaggering down the board sidewalk on one side of the street.

"Maybe we will," P. D. replied from the opposite side of the street, "but we'll take care of business first." It was good to see her boys enjoying themselves. Approaching the general store, she called out, "Stop here. We might as well get some ammunition."

Trying the door and finding it locked, P. D. called
Arlo from the middle of the street. "I want in" was all
she said to her son. Arlo grinned. Lowering his shoulder, he threw his oversized body against the door.
The door was stout and failed to break, but the frame
could not resist Arlo's brute force. It splintered and
split away from the jamb, leaving the door free to
swing open.

P. D. walked into the store, holding her Winchester
66 before her. Backed against the rear wall, a frightened clerk cringed behind a stack of feed sacks.
Pleased by the fear she obviously instilled in the man,
she smirked and said, "You need to fix that door. It
don't open too easy." Her remark caused Arlo and Bo
to snicker. The smirk faded away from her face and
then she demanded, "Where's your .44 cartridges?"
The clerk was quick to jump to her demand, pulling
a box of the cartridges from under the counter at the
back of the store. P. D. picked up the box, glanced at
it to make sure it held the right ammunition, then
tossed it to Bo. Giving the clerk a contemptuous grin,
she went around behind the counter and pulled out
several more boxes of cartridges, which Bo and Arlo
quickly scooped up. "How much do we owe you?"
P. D. asked. Then, before the terrified clerk could answer, she added, "Put it on the marshal's account."

Slaughter stepped out on the sidewalk. No sooner
had his feet found the weathered gray boards than he
heard the bolt thrown on the door behind him. Shadows were lengthening, and a thin mist of gun smoke

still lay hovering over the muddy street. Several yards away, two bodies lay next to the sidewalk. Another body lay in the middle of the empty street. Diagonally across from him, on the other side, he saw the hotel dining room, its windows shattered and lifeless. He didn't expect the three he sought to still be in the dining room, but he crossed the street and checked to be sure. It was empty. He walked on.

Like the quiet street, the man was patient as he searched each doorway he came to. It had been a long trail leading him to this town and this street, and there was a calmness in his manner as he anticipated the final showdown. He paused when he came to the smashed-in door of the general store. Nudging the door slowly with the barrel of his rifle, he peered in to discover a disconcerted clerk standing near the door, holding a couple of pieces of the splintered doorjamb in his hand. Frightened, the clerk stepped back when he saw Matt.

"Where'd they go?" Matt asked softly.

Unable to speak, the clerk pointed toward the end of the street. Matt nodded and continued toward the stables.

Clyde Newton paused to lean on his pitchfork as he eyed the three who came in the open end of his stable. Like everyone else within earshot of the shooting, Clyde had run up the street to see what had caused the fuss. And like everyone else, when the killing spilled over into the street, he lit out for safer surroundings. With no time to get any details on what had happened inside the dining room, all he was able to learn was that Alvin Tate and Malcolm Early had gone into the hotel to make an arrest, and that's when the shooting started. He got that bit of information from someone running past him, and the man wasn't inclined to slow down long enough to offer details. Whatever had happened, and whoever was involved, it couldn't have been good. Clyde had seen the bodies in the street. He didn't get close enough to tell, but two of the bodies looked like Jack Porter and Will Peterson.

Now, as P. D. Wildmoon and her two sons ambled toward him, he wasn't sure whether he should be running for his shotgun or not. Since it was too late to do that at this point, he remained where he was, leaning on his pitchfork.

"We'll be needin' our horses," P. D. said.

"You fixin' to leave us?" Clyde asked, trying to sound as casual as possible. "Thought you fellers might be in town for a spell." They had just brought their horses in the night before. The thought struck him then that the stranger he had reported to the marshal had been in only a few hours earlier asking after three riders. If Clyde was a betting man, and he was, he would have bet plenty that these three rough-looking saddle tramps were involved in the shooting. Since all three looked pretty damn healthy, it seemed to confirm his earlier assumption that it hadn't gone well for the marshal. Right then, he knew that his best bet was to play dumb and hope they didn't linger.

"You just bring our horses in the stable, here, so we

can saddle 'em up," P. D. said. Then, to her boys, she said, "We'll leave 'em tied up here by these front stalls, so they'll be ready if we need 'em in a hurry." She turned back to Clyde again. "That's all right with you, ain't it, old man?"

"Anything you say's all right with me," Clyde quickly replied. He hesitated a moment before asking, "If you think you boys might be leavin' in a hurry, you wanna settle up now?"

P. D. cast a cold eye in his direction. "We'll settle up when we leave. We might decide to stay a while longer."

"Fine, fine," Clyde replied at once. "What suits you, suits me just fine." He went straightaway to the corral to fetch the horses. As soon as he had led them all inside the stable, he started walking slowly toward the front. "I expect I'd better see if there's any more feed outside," he mumbled, unable to think of a better excuse. He made an effort to keep his steps leisurely until reaching the open end of the stable. Then, as soon as he was out of their sight, he broke into a sprint, running with abandon to the marshal's office.

"He lit out runnin', Ma," Bo said, having followed behind the frightened stable owner to the open door. He raised his rifle and sighted down on the fleeing man. "Should I shoot him?"

"No, son," P. D. replied patiently. "Let him be." Disappointed, Bo lowered his rifle.

Unaware that he had been held squarely in the sights of a Winchester 66 rifle, Clyde Newton ran as hard as a man his age could. Already gasping for air, he turned to see if anyone followed him. Seeing no one running after him, he started to slow down to catch his breath just a split second before crashing into a solid wall of hard muscle and buckskin. The old man would have gone over backward onto the ground had not Matt grabbed his arm to stop him.

"You!" Clyde forced through panting lungs. Unable to move, he gasped, "I don't want no trouble."

"Where are they?" Matt asked.

"Them three?" Clyde replied, immediately relieved that he was of no interest to the buckskinned mountain man. "They're in my stable." Matt released his arm.

Still watching Clyde's frantic escape from the stable, Bo chuckled when he saw the running man collide with someone on the street. A moment later, when Clyde collected himself and ran on, Bo's laughter caught in his throat, and he took a harder look at the cause of Clyde's stumble. There was something ominous about the imposing figure standing solidly in the middle of the street. With the sun setting below the mountains to the west of the town, there remained a few stranded rays of light that traced the outline of a buckskin shirt and danced off the brass receiver plate of the rifle in his hand. *Slaughter!* Bo knew it to be him even without benefit of a closer look.

Bo's reaction was automatic. He raised his rifle again and fired, but in his excitement, his shot was wide left, barely causing the buckskin fringe on

Matt's shirt to flutter at the bullet's passing. Focusing instantly on the muzzle blast, Matt dropped to one knee and systematically cranked out a deadly pattern of four rounds that walked across the startled Bo's chest.

Stunned by the sudden burst of rifle fire, both P. D. and Arlo stood frozen for a brief few seconds when Bo staggered backward from the doorway. The mortally wounded man turned to look at them, and attempted to speak. He died before the words would come, collapsing in a heap in the open doorway of the stable.

"Bo!" P. D. screamed, and rushed to his side. "Arlo!" she yelled, pointing at the wide door of the stable.

Understanding, Arlo sprang forward to the doorway, his rifle ready to return fire. He scanned the street to left and right. There was no one in sight. "I don't see nobody, Ma."

"Keep lookin', dammit!" she raged. "He's out there somewhere." Frantic now, she cradled Bo's head and shoulders in her arms, rocking gently back and forth. "Bo . . . Bo," she moaned desperately. "Don't leave me, son. You was always my brightest, even if you was the orneriest." She paused long enough to yell, "Arlo!"

"Don't see a thing, Ma," Arlo replied, still squinting to pick up some movement on either side of the street. Bo's killer had vanished into thin air.

"It's him. It's Slaughter," P. D. moaned in gut-wrenching agony. "I know it's him. I can feel him."

Like a mama wolf whose cubs have been slain, she poured out her hatred for this one man who had killed two of her babies. Arlo stood stupefied by the hellish howling coming forth from his mother's throat. She carefully lowered Bo's head, and turned to glare at her eldest. "Don't just stand there, dammit! I want him dead. Find him!"

The normally slow-witted Arlo was at last aware of the urgency of the moment. He had never before seen his mother lose her self-control in such an explosive manner. It was enough to send him charging out of the stable into the fading light, roaring like a bull. He was halfway across the street, searching frantically from side to side, before his momentum slowed to a walk. He stopped, uncertain where to look, when he heard a soft voice behind him.

"His name was Zeb Benson. Hers was Singing Woman."

Arlo spun around, pulling the trigger as he did. His shot was wild, glancing sharply off the roof of the stable. His head was suddenly thrown backward by the force of the .44 slug that slammed under his chin and tore into his brain, extinguishing forever the tiny flame that had flickered in the simple organ. Like a mighty oak felled by the woodsman's ax, Arlo crashed to the ground and lay still. Matt cocked the Henry; there was one to go.

Inside the stable, P. D. heard the exchange of shots. She hesitated. With no shots following the first two, she had to assume that one of them must have hit the target. Frantic to know which one, she called out,

"Arlo!" There was no response to her call. "Arlo, dammit! . . . Answer me!"

"Arlo can't answer," a calm and steady voice came back.

Panic-stricken, P. D. started to run to the back of the stalls. Seeing the horses saddled and ready to ride, she made a quick decision. Unwilling to be trapped inside the stable, she untied Bo's and Arlo's. She slapped one on the rump and discharged her pistol into the dirt floor behind the other one. Her own horse jerked frantically at the reins in an attempt to follow the two stampeding out of the stable. Straining against the frightened stallion, P. D. untied the reins and managed to get a foot in the stirrup before the crazed animal took off after the others.

Outside the open end of the stable, Matt heard the shot and jumped back just in time to avoid the galloping horses in flight. There was no time to get off a shot, but he realized in that instant that both saddles were empty. Immediately alert that another horse followed, he set himself to receive it. In another instant, it was upon him. This one carried a rider, but Matt was forced to dive behind the stable door because P. D. came out with her six-gun blazing away. As soon as her firing pin clicked on an empty cylinder, Matt rose to one knee and took careful aim on the rider galloping away. His bullet slammed into P. D.'s back, knocking her over onto the horse's neck, but she managed to hang on.

The horse came to a stop several yards farther up the street, and P. D. appeared to reseat herself in the saddle. Matt watched, puzzled by the rider's actions. He kept his rifle aimed at P. D. while she seemed to be making a decision. Finally, she prodded the horse back toward the stable while trying to pull her rifle from the saddle sling. Matt continued to hold his fire, fascinated by the rider weaving drunkenly in the saddle as her horse came closer. The rifle was almost free of the sling when it fell from her hand and dropped to the ground. A few steps closer and the rider slumped over to one side and slid off the horse.

With the feeling of a heavy shroud draped across his shoulders, Matt walked slowly over to stand looking down upon the last of the gang of murderers that had brought such sorrow into his life. In the faint twilight, he gazed down at the stocky figure lying in the muddy street. Then, almost stunned, he recognized the dying man as the same man who had gone over the cliff back on the mountain below his cabin. "How many times am I gonna have to kill you?" he said, raising his rifle again to finish it.

P. D.'s eyelids fluttered open, and she looked up at her executioner. "Don't kill me," she pleaded. "I'm a woman. You wouldn't shoot a woman, would you?"

Surprised, he squinted hard in an effort to get a better look. There was nothing feminine about her that he could see. She raised a feeble hand and fumbled with the buttons on her coat in a desperate attempt to prove to him that she was, indeed, female. Knowing the vile murderer he was dealing with, Matt simply assumed she was going for a hidden weapon. He aimed the muzzle of the Henry rifle at her forehead and ended her struggle. "No, I probably wouldn't shoot a woman, but I don't have a problem with a coyote bitch."

Feeling suddenly weary, he remained standing over the body lying sprawled in the muddy street. For several long moments he stared down at the last of those who had hunted him, wondering if, indeed, she were the last—or would there be others? How long would he be hunted for a crime he did not commit? He thought of the many people who had suffered simply because they befriended him—most recently Zeb and Singing Woman. Then he thought of Molly, sweet innocent Molly. Maybe it would be better for her if he simply rode out of her life. Now would be the time, with no long good-byes. The great north country was out there, waiting to be explored.

As darkness descended upon the town, the normal quiet of that far end of the muddy main street of Virginia City returned. Rising over the ridge behind the stables, a pale half moon, the kind Zeb Benson often referred to as a Vengeance Moon, began its journey across Alder Gulch. Up the street, toward the center of town where the saloons were located, the noisy nightlife began, only vaguely aware of the shots fired near the stable. A good portion of the town was not yet aware of the hotel massacre, the undertaker having gathered the bodies as soon as the shooting stopped. Prospectors hitting the town after working their claims all day would scarcely believe that their appointed deputy marshal was locked inside his jail, peeking through the wooden shutters of his window.

Two partners on their way to a night of drinking at the Lucky Strike approached a lone rider at the north end of the gulch. He was a formidable man, outfitted entirely in animal skins and riding a paint pony. "Evenin'," one of the prospectors greeted the rider.

"Evenin'," the stranger replied.

"You're a-headin' the wrong way if you're lookin' fer a drink of likker," the other prospector said in passing.

"Reckon so," Matt replied, without slowing the paint's pace.

"He's a friendly cuss, ain't he?" the first prospector said when the stranger was out of earshot.

"He's one of them wild ones from the look of 'em. Most likely laid around outside a saloon till the marshal run 'im outta town."

Broken Hand stood near the edge of his village watching the slight young white girl working with a bone awl on a deer hide. She was down near the water's edge, and every once in a while she would pause to look down the river for a few minutes before returning her attention to the deer hide. After a short period Broken Hand walked down to the river's edge to speak to her.

"How are you getting along in Singing Woman's tipi?" Broken Hand asked.

Molly looked up and smiled, then made the sign for *good*. The Crow chief noted that, even though she smiled a lot, they always seemed to be sad smiles. All traces of happiness had left her face. He thought this was not a good thing for one so young. Slaughter had been gone a long time. He might never return. Who could say? "I have been thinking," he said. "I think it would be good if you take Singing Woman's tipi for your own. I think Singing Woman would like that." She smiled again, pleased by his generosity. Broken Hand went on, "I think maybe you should know that Slaughter might not come back."

She shook her head at once and signed, *He will come back.*

Broken Hand nodded slowly. "I know he will try to come back, but you must realize that he may not be able to. Just know that you will always have a place in our village."

I thank you, she signed. He nodded and, having said his piece, turned to retrace his steps. She thought about what he had said as a tear threatened to start. Turning her gaze once again to focus on the pines on the far side of the river, where the trail led from the north, she could almost imagine an image of her tall rider. On so many late afternoons she had imagined a misty image approaching the water's edge. As on those many occasions, her tearful eyes created that familiar image, just now appearing from the pine trees. She closed her eyes for a second, heartbroken by the vision that seemed to want to torment her. When she opened her eyes again, the vision was still there, as he cleared the pines and started across the river. Afraid she was losing her mind, she dared not move lest she drive it away. He spotted her then, and raised his arm. Her heart fairly exploded with joy, and on legs suddenly feeling incapable of supporting her, she ran to meet him, pushing through the crystal-clear water up to her breast. He reached down and, with one powerful arm, swept her from the water and up behind him on the paint pony. She clung to him so tightly he could barely breathe.

Once across the river, he dismounted and then lifted her off the horse. Holding her close in his arms, he scolded her softly, "Look at you—you're soakin' wet." She looked up at him and smiled, a happy smile, as the rest of the village hurried down to greet him.

Ready to find
your next great read?

Let us help.

Visit prh.com/nextread

Penguin
Random
House